Lovely Dirty Business - 1
Angel Eyes

LOVELY DIRTY BUSINESS - 1

Angel Eyes

The Violin Trade, Money, Power, Corruption & Sex

Roger Graham Hargrave

Copyright © 2024 Roger Graham Hargrave

The moral right of the author has been asserted.

Apart from any fair dealing for the purposes of research or private study, or criticism or review, as permitted under the Copyright, Designs and Patents Act 1988, this publication may only be reproduced, stored or transmitted, in any form or by any means, with the prior permission in writing of the publishers, or in the case of reprographic reproduction in accordance with the terms of licences issued by the Copyright Licensing Agency. Enquiries concerning reproduction outside those terms should be sent to the publishers.

This novel is a work of fiction. The opinions expressed by the book's characters should not be confused with the author's own sentiments. Although its form is that of a biography and sometimes even an autobiography, it is neither the one nor the other. Occasionally, space and time have been rearranged to suit the narrative. Consequently, while certain long-standing institutions, agencies, public offices and events are mentioned, all the names, characters, businesses, places, events and incidents in this book are either the product of the author's imagination or used in a fictitious manner. Any resemblance to actual events, or actual persons, living or dead, are purely coincidental.

However, as recorded here, information about instrument identification was for the most part correct for the period described. Even so, since those times, much new information has come to light. Suggestions for further reading will appear at the end of this work.

Troubador Publishing Ltd
Unit E2 Airfield Business Park,
Harrison Road, Market Harborough,
Leicestershire LE16 7UL
Tel: 0116 279 2299
Email: books@troubador.co.uk
Web: www.troubador.co.uk

ISBN 978-1-80514-202-7

British Library Cataloguing in Publication Data.
A catalogue record for this book is available from the British Library.

Printed and bound in Great Britain by 4edge Limited
Typeset in 11pt Minion Pro by Troubador Publishing Ltd, Leicester, UK

I dedicate this book and indeed all of my other written works, to my wife Claudia, who since the early 1980s, has continued to support this financially costly hobby.

1

There was a lull in the proceedings. For as long as she could remember it had been the same. Grandpa Scott and her father had always made a brave effort to help Angel celebrate her birthday, but there was no escaping the atmosphere. Angel had been born in the city of Chicago, on Saint Valentine's Day, the 14th of February 1929; a memorable day. It was the day that Al Capone's mob had machine-gunned seven members and associates of Chicago's North Side Gang, an event that came to be known as the Saint Valentine's Day Massacre. But for the Scott family, this day was memorable for two rather more poignant reasons. Not only was it Angel's birthday, it was also the anniversary of her mother's death.

Years later, when her father had also died, Angel discovered her mother's death certificate amongst his papers. Mary MacGregor Scott had died of postpartum haemorrhage; excessive blood loss, aggravated by exhaustion following an exacting three-day labour.

Presumably to prevent Angel from feeling responsible, the two men, who were now her only family, had never spoken about the incident. And perhaps their tactics had worked, because although Angel was aware that her mother had died in childbirth, she had never felt even remotely culpable. The most likely explanation for this apparent indifference was that she had never started to remember that which her father and grandfather could never forget.

In spite of the men's refusal to discuss her mother's passing, Angel was reminded of her every time she looked in her dressing table mirror. According to both men, Angel had inherited her shock of unruly red hair from her mother. This, at least, was something she could understand. She had always been proud of the way her hair shone in sunlight, like the fine gold wire windings that her grandfather Scott used on high-quality violin bow grips. In addition, within the beautiful hazel colouration of her irids, several minute gold flecks sparkled, as if someone had sprinkled them with tiny grains of genuine gold leaf. Here again, her father and grandfather assured Angel that her mother had borne this same rare distinction. In deference to this distinctive colouration, for as long as she could remember both men had taken to calling her Angel Eyes, or simply Angel.

From an early age, Angel had been aware that her hair and eyes were special. Everyone scrutinised them, from neighbours to teachers, to street cleaners and shopkeepers. Sometimes folk would stare unashamedly for several minutes, but as a young girl, she was never perturbed by this attention; in fact, she revelled in it.

Angel's Grandfather Scott had been born Hermann Schott in 1883, in Markneukirchen, a small town in the Kingdom of Saxony. At that time, Saxony was the fifth state of the German empire. In spite of its size, the town had a rich musical instrument-making tradition dating back to the seventeenth century, but around 1900, instrument production had reached its zenith. So much so that eighty percent of the world's musical instruments, from grand pianos to mandolins, were being manufactured in the town.

In 1897, Hermann Schott was apprenticed to a violin maker in Markneukirchen. On finishing his initial training, having lied about his age, he left his place of birth and travelled north with a consignment of pianos.

Arriving at the German seaport of Bremerhaven in 1903, Hermann had boarded a ship bound for New York. Unable to speak a word of English, on Ellis Island, a helpful official recorded his name as Hermann Scott. Later that year, Hermann Scott moved to Chicago with Innis Stuart, an Irish orphan he had met while being processed on Ellis Island. It had been love at first sight.

In Chicago, with Innis Stuart's help, Hermann began importing musical instruments from his hometown. In 1904, less than six months after a rather hasty but happy marriage, Mrs Innis Scott gave birth to a bouncing blond-haired boy, who was christened Randolph Scott, a true American child, with a true American name.

Initially, the Scotts' import business was highly successful, but in 1917, on the eve of the United States' entry into World War I, reports by James Watson Gerard, the US Ambassador to Germany, suggested that 500,000 German reservists living in the US were ready to revolt if war was declared. As a precaution he had called for their internment. Less than a month later, the US entered the conflict, and although he was not actually interned, Hermann Scott was subjected to severe government restrictions. As a result, Randolph, now thirteen years old, had been forced to begin working full time in the family's shop.

Foreign imports having ground to a halt, with the help of his young son, Hermann reverted to his original trade of making violins, and by the 1920s, the Scott family business had become heavily reliant on the sale and repair of instruments and bows of the violin family. It turned out to be a fortuitous change of direction.

Gradually, the Scotts' violin making and restoration workshop gained a reputation for good work and fair prices. Young Randolph in particular was an industrious and gifted worker. This was a blessing, because lingering resentment towards his father's strong German accent meant that by the 1920s, Randolph was soon travelling extensively in the US, in a quest to find high-quality instruments and bows for the company's growing trade in fine antique violins.

After a few early mishaps, Randolph quickly developed a connoisseur's eye and a shrewd business acumen. From the start he had been popular with his colleagues, many of whom, like his father, were recent immigrants from Europe. Perhaps because of his friendly nature, his youthful exuberance and his father's European connections, several violin and bow makers provided helpful snippets of information and advice. They also outlined the methods and salient features of the various violin making traditions in their hometowns and cities, and what better way was there to learn than from craftsmen who had actually constructed instruments in those places?

Having quickly developed his own shorthand system for recording information about violins and violin making, Randolph gradually transferred these notes to a series of beautifully illustrated journals. These journals were essential, because at that time, reliable publications about violin identification were virtually non-existent. The one truly magnificent exception had been Randolph's favourite book, *Antonio Stradivari: His Life and Work (1644–1737)*, by the violin makers W. E. Hill and Sons of London.

The most celebrated violin maker of all time, Stradivari had lived and worked in the northern Italian city of Cremona. Published in 1902, this handsome leather-bound volume contained beautiful colour prints and photo-etchings of the master's work. It would be 1931 before the Hills published a second, equally magnificent volume, *The Violin Makers of the Guarneri Family (1626–1762)*. Eventually, these two works became paragons of twentieth-century violin literature. But for Randolph, it was not simply the illustrations and information that these magnificent volumes contained; it was the manner in which the material had been collected and recorded. Definitive works in every respect, at a pivotal moment in Randolph's career they had demonstrated the importance not only of seeing and studying instruments, but of understanding the context in which they had been made.

It was no accident that the Hills chose to write about these two Cremonese violin-making families. From the mid-sixteenth century, Cremona had been celebrated for its school of violin makers. Founded by the Amati family, among others, the school would eventually include the Guarneri, Rogeri and Bergonzi families, and of course, the most famous of them all, the Stradivaris.

Together, these makers produced the most sought-after instruments ever made. Players valued them for their tonal qualities, makers for the inspiration they provided, and collectors for their sheer beauty and perfection.

It is fair to say that after reading *Antonio Stradivari: His Life and Work*, Randolph's passion for antique violins gradually developed into an obsession for instruments made in northern Italy; in particular those made in the city of Cremona.

By the 1930s, for Randolph and his father, the intrinsic beauty of Cremonese instruments, their undeniable sonority and their stylistic authority made them irresistable. The fact that their monetary value was also increasing dramatically was important in one respect only; in order to hear and see these wonderful works, rather than buying and selling cheap instruments for a mass market, Randolph and his father chose to become dealers in fine Italian violins.

It had been rumoured that the Hills were working on a third volume about Cremona's Amati family, the fact that it had never materialised was particularly unfortunate, because Randolph was infatuated by the Amatis. In the first half of the sixteenth century, Andrea Amati had founded a dynasty that would continue making instruments in Cremona for more than two centuries. Eventually, Andrea's grandson, Nicola Amati, would be responsible for teaching a new generation of makers, that in due course would pass the art of violin making to the entire world.

Moreover, as Randolph was fond of telling anyone prepared to listen, although ultimately instruments by Antonio Stradivari and Joseph Guarneri del Gesù became more famous and more valuable, aesthetically, the most beautiful instruments ever made were those produced by the Amati family.

Hermann was the classically trained violin maker. He was certainly the better craftsman, but by the time Randolph had reached twenty-one, the age of majority, he was already a genuine connoisseur and was destined to become one of the all-time greats. Meanwhile, Innis, his mother, was the rock on which the business was founded. Being initially the only one able to read, write and speak business English, Innis had been crucial to the company's early success. In addition to running the household, she organised the arrival of imports, and was often called upon to carry out assembly and simple repair work.

When Innis died on the last day of December 1925, after a six-month fight with tuberculosis, the event traumatised both men. Hermann had lost the love of his life, and Randolph his wonderful mother. For weeks, Hermann had been so bewildered that he had wandered around his atelier not knowing which instrument he was supposed to be working on next. Even when Randolph had placed work on the bench in front of him, for minutes on end he would stare vacantly at his tools, as if trying to remember what they were for.

Randolph was struggling himself. Watching his mother slowly waste away had been bad enough, but seeing her coffin being lowered into the frozen ground had disturbed his sleep for weeks. Ultimately, however, it was thanks to his mother that they did not lose the business altogether. From her sick bed this remarkable woman had organised things so well that even after this huge psychological setback, the Scott family business had continued to run like clockwork. Initially Randolph had taken the reins, but realising that his son needed his support, Hermann had slowly followed, and together they learned to manage their grief.

The following year, a beautiful red-headed violinist walked into the Scotts' shop and Randolph was immediately smitten. If protocol had allowed, he would have proposed on the spot, however, in a sincere effort not to upset his father, his wooing had been discrete. Nevertheless, within weeks it was clear, even to the old man, that the pair were head over heels in love. And, after the heartache of Innis's prolonged illness and passing, even Hermann welcomed this intelligent and vivacious young woman, and life gradually returned to the Scott establishment.

Mary MacGregor was a Chicagoan with one foot in either camp. As a classical violinist she could be as demure, traditional and conservative as the occasion required, but she was not averse to enjoying the wilder side of life that the city of her birth had to offer.

In a strange quirk of history, from January 1920 to December 1933, the United States of America, the world's most prosperous and dynamic country, prohibited the sale and consumption of alcohol. Although prohibition had been almost 200 years in the brewing, from the moment of its introduction, the Volstead Act had been weak and badly policed. It quickly became clear that the federal government had neither the will nor the wherewithal to enforce it. Prohibition's big winners were the nation's gangsters, and by far the most celebrated of these was Al Capone, a New York-born hoodlum who controlled much of Chicago's underworld.

Around this same time, thousands of African Americans were fleeing brutal oppression in the Deep South. Hoping for a better life, many found their way to the ghettos of Chicago's South Side. Along with these desperate souls came a rich musical tradition in the form of southern blues and hot Dixieland jazz, but even this legacy was destined to be exploited by white businessmen.

Dance music in particular came to dominate all forms of popular music. Ballrooms, theatre halls, speakeasies and night clubs sprang up everywhere, serving up a heady mixture of alcohol, music and dancing. In downtown Chicago, many of these clubs were also owned and controlled by Al Capone and his mobsters.

This period came to be known as the Roaring Twenties. For white Americans, it was a time of considerable prosperity.

Mary was a classically trained violinist, but she loved everything about contemporary American culture.

Having a slender willowy figure, she was a *flapper*, a party woman who wore make-up, danced, smoked and exercised her newly acquired right to vote. And, like her father, William MacGregor, better known as Pay Dirt Bill, she also enjoyed an occasional glass of illegal liquor. By comparison, Randolph Scott was as conservative as they come. It was a love match made in heaven.

When it came to dancing, Randolph had two left feet, and although he would occasionally allow Mary to lead him onto the floor, his greatest pleasure was simply watching her dance the Charleston alone.

Characterised by its toes-in, heels-out twisting steps, the Charleston could be performed solo, with a partner or in a group. Even amongst the many talented performers in the city, Mary's uninhibited routine stood out. She had many admirers, both men and women, but Randolph always knew that she only had eyes for him, and that when she danced, each performance was for his benefit alone.

Hermann was delighted with his son's choice. Mary MacGregor was as talented on the violin as she was vivacious on the ballroom floor, and on the 1st of June 1928, she and Randolph Scott were married; unfortunately, their happiness was short lived. Nine months later, on the same day that Al Capone's mob gunned down seven members of Chicago's North Side Gang, Mary Scott died. Not in a hail of bullets, but while giving birth to a baby girl.

Neither Randolph nor his father had time to grieve. From that moment they were responsible for raising a new red-headed edition to the Scott family. It was never easy, but it was a task they would savour every day for the rest of their lives.

2

Having been obliged to specialise in the making, repair and sale of violins, the Scotts discovered that this was a business for which they were ideally suited. It took time, but with diligent effort and hard-won expertise, the two men gradually monopolised the Midwest violin trade.

In spite of the Great Depression, by 1937, some four years before the Japanese bombed Pearl Harbour and the US entered World War II, the Scotts had become wealthy enough for Randolph to enrol his daughter at an exclusive private academy; the Chicago Latin School for Girls. Initially, with no mother or any other female relative, the shy eight-year-old was beyond happy. The school, with its female staff and pupils, was everything she could have wished for.

Designed to provide students with a rigorous college-preparatory education in the time-honoured tradition, the school boasted a curriculum that was heavily influenced by the classics, including the study of the Greek and Latin languages, hence the name *Latin School*. Consequently, although she had started life speaking the Great Lakes dialect, within a year, Angel was already a refined, well-educated young lady. She was even encouraged to play her beloved violin. Gradually, however, as the outside world changed, Angel also changed, and she changed in ways that her two male guardians either could not or would not rationalise.

In 1940, the early onset of Angel's menstrual cycle immediately distanced the young redhead from the other girls in her class; paradoxically it also proved expedient. At the tender age of eleven, Angel was able to accept an alert teacher's help and sensitive explanation, without the kind of embarrassment that would almost certainly have come had she already been a teenager.

In view of the family's circumstances, Angel's father received notification that the school would continue to provide all necessary support for as long as required, and no more was said about the subject. Unfortunately, in spite of regular 'health and hygiene' lessons in the classroom, Angel's knowledge of sexual matters was still woefully inadequate and would remain so for many years. This deficit was aggravated by the ill-informed gossip of her classmates, whose own knowledge of the subject was, to say the least, questionable.

Three days after the bombing of Pearl Harbour in December 1941, Nazi Germany and Fascist Italy also declared war on the United States and shortly thereafter Angel's personal problems were exacerbated. In spite of wartime rationing, Angel not only grew taller, but her body was rapidly changing shape. Her hips became wider and her bosom heavier. Of course, this development was the natural process of becoming a woman. But the curvaceous body she was developing did not match the slender appearance of her heroines, nor did it come close to the figure of the ideal American woman, as envisaged by the girls in her school.

As a prepubescent girl, Angel had been sylphlike; like the delicate, satin-draped fairies depicted by her favourite children's book illustrator, Arthur Rackham. Following her penchant for heroines, Angel had also become a devotee of the female aviator Amelia Earhart, who had recently disappeared while flying across the Pacific Ocean. She daydreamed about the women her father so often talked about; women who delivered new aircraft to front-line fighting squadrons, and above all, she thought about her own mother. In Angel's imagination, these women were all slender and long-limbed, like the flappers of the 1920s, who had worn their hair and skirts short and listened to jazz and blues in smoky night clubs and speakeasies.

Angel had wanted to fly above the world on gossamer wings, but instead, she was beginning to resemble a chubby Rubenesque cherub, whose stunted embryonic wings would never lift her off the ground. Even from herself, there was no hiding the fact that she was turning into a buxom redhead, and she gradually became self-conscious and withdrawn. In these times of war, Angel's voluptuous curves created some resentment amongst her fellow pupils, many of whom had not yet reached puberty. They accused her of being unpatriotic and of buying food on the black market. Actually, nothing could have been further from the truth. With her grandfather's help, Angel had been one of the first to plant a Victory Garden. She had also spent many hours collecting scrap metal, aluminium cooking pots and rubber for the war effort. Once again, added to these unfair accusations was the fact that Angel's grandfather was German and that her father had been exempted from military service.

Because of his woodwork and management skills, and the fact that he was a single parent, Angel's father, Randolph, had been seconded to do war work at Orchard Place. Orchard Place was a huge plot of agricultural land, which the government had acquired in 1942 to construct a massive two-million-square-foot plant for the manufacture of Douglas C-54 four-engine transport aircraft.

Initially, Randolph had been employed to work on the construction of the all-wood building, but by the time the first C-54 rolled off the assembly line, his organisational skills had been recognised and he was promoted to a senior management position. Even in the face of his important contribution to the war effort, Randolph was often subjected to disparaging comments, especially from women. The most frequent being, 'Why are you not fighting for us? My husband is out there fighting for you.'

Although Angel continued to immerse herself in projects to help the war effort, this resentment of her father's reserved occupation status only served to increase her sense of alienation in the school that she had once revered.

Hermann, Angel's grandfather, who had initially taught her to play the violin, was particularly fond of a melancholy piece he called *Trauriger Sonntag*. They had often played this piece together, until one day Randolph had asked them to stop. Years later, after hearing Billy Holiday's version, called *Gloomy Sunday*, Angel had finally understood her father's objection, and also why this tragic melody was referred to as *The Hungarian Suicide Song*. Nevertheless, in spite of her father's opposition, whenever they were alone Angel and her grandfather continued to play the piece. Remarkably, rather than confusing her, each man's reaction to this melancholic work somehow helped her to understand them better as individuals.

As for Angel, far from feeling depressed, the melody served to sooth her soul. Indeed, although she would occasionally feel a little despondent, for the most part, she was a resilient young woman. She was solitary rather than lonely, and like many solitary children, at such times she would retreat into her own fantasy world. Allowing her mind to roam, she would spin intricate stories in which she became a heroine of ancient Greek legend; her favourite being Aphrodite, the goddess of beauty, passion and procreation. Alternatively, she would play the violin for hours on end, gradually losing herself, as the instrument and the music worked their magic.

In addition, every evening without fail, Angel and her grandfather listened to the war's progress on their large Wurlitzer radio. On Tuesday, the 6th of June 1944, they had followed the D-Day landings in Normandy. In January the following year, they had listened as the Battle of the Bulge ended, marking the start of the German army's retreat. Night after night, they listened impassively, trying to piece together the complex series of events that were happening around the world.

The day before Angel's sixteenth birthday, a massive Allied bombing raid on the city of Dresden had begun. In four raids between the 13th and the 15th of February 1945, 1,249 heavy bombers dropped almost 4,000 tons of high-explosive bombs and incendiary devices on the city. That year, the death toll of almost a quarter of a million even managed to overshadow the anniversary of Al Capone's Valentine's Day Massacre.

Angel's sixteenth birthday should have been a special day, but with the news about Dresden having not yet broken, she was convinced that nothing monumental was about to happen; simply because on all her previous birthdays, her father and grandfather had made sure that nothing monumental *would* ever happen.

At school, only one child had acknowledged Angel's birthday. Amanda Kowalski, the shy daughter of a Polish immigrant, had slipped a card into Angel's school satchel. Like Angel, Amanda was something of an outsider. In view of this, and also in view of the fact that Angel's grandfather was German and that the war in Europe had started with Germany marching into Poland, the gesture was remarkable. But the two girls were intelligent enough to realise that they were both from recent immigrant stock, whose families had experienced enough problems assimilating, without becoming involved in the kind of troubles that ethnic groups often carry with them from their native lands.

On discovering the card, Angel had mixed feelings. She was pleased that someone had remembered her birthday, but she was also aware that Amanda was afraid to be seen associating with her; afraid of being ostracised herself. Like the Scotts, Amanda's father was a prosperous self-made man, but like Angel's own father, he was also trade.

It was not that the other girls were openly aggressive; mimicking their parents, they merely ignored anyone they considered inferior. In this brave new world, with no established nobility, the fathers and especially the mothers of these privileged private school girls saw themselves as persons or families with lineage; members of a *de facto* aristocracy. As such, they took pains to emphasise behavioural and cultural distinctions between themselves and the rest of society.

Angel was not resentful of Amanda's behaviour. She understood her motives better than anyone. Amanda was shy and fearful, especially of those girls that decided who sat where and who was allowed to express an opinion. Depending on their perceived position in the hierarchy, most of Amanda's classmates used her to run errands or simply to perform sycophantic acts of servitude. Angel did none of these things. In spite of feeling self-conscious, she was not afraid of these pseudo-aristocratic snobs. Indeed, the one advantage of her size was that she was hardly afraid of anything, but although she had no wish to be friends with these girls, like everyone else, she longed for some form of recognition and inclusion.

3

It being February, the journey home from school had been cold, and Angel was pleased to find a log fire burning in the parlour. Her father was waiting. Dressed in his best Sunday clothes, he was fussing over the cake and lemonade he had spent all morning preparing for his daughter's sixteenth birthday. For a while the two sat together, quietly absorbing the heat, until suddenly her father leaned forward and without looking at her directly, he said, 'Grandpa and I have something we need to show you. He's on his way here now.'

A strange silence followed before Angel heard her grandfather's voice at the back door. In a strong German accent, the older man was calling to his son. 'You're gonna have to help me wiz zis dam ting Randolph.'

Briefly placing a hand on Angel's shoulder to prevent her from standing, Randolph rose quickly and left the room. A few moments later both men returned carrying a large chest. The chest was clearly not heavy, but it was large, unwieldy and extremely dirty, and since the men were dressed for the party, they were struggling to keep the box away from their clothes.

They set it down in front of the fire and stood there for several minutes, one either side of the chest, until eventually her grandfather spoke: 'You neffer knowed your mutter, Angel,' he began. Recently his German accent had become even more pronounced. 'She voz a beautiful girl like you; same red hair, same gold eyes.'

At this point her father took up the story. 'Do you remember your mother's father… your Grandpa MacGregor?' Without waiting for an answer, he continued: 'His name was William, although most folks called him Pay Dirt Bill, or just Pay Dirt.'

Somewhere in the back of her mind, Angel could remember a loud, large, unhappy man, with a huge bushy red beard. He had occasionally rubbed it against her cheek. What had he called it? A chin-pie kiss. Yes, that was it… 'Now then Angel,' he would say, 'would ya like a chin-pie kiss from ol' Pay Dirt?'

Interrupting her thoughts, her father continued: 'Bill was a Scotsman. He was a real joker and a fun guy to be with. Before your ma died, he used to drop by on a regular basis, but her passing knocked the stuffing out of him. He drank himself to death before you were five years old. Anyway, Bill left you his chest, to be opened, in his words, "when you reach sweet sixteen". We've kept it safe ever since. Neither of us has any idea what's inside.' He paused, then as if suddenly remembering, he added, 'There's a key.

Here!' he said, dusting his hands before reaching into the hip pocket of his trousers.

The key was rusty. A small cardboard label was attached with a piece of frayed hessian string. Written in faded blue ink were the words, *Not to be opened until 14 February 1945*. Angel's heart was thumping like a steam hammer as she took the proffered key from her father's hand. She spoke her grandfather's name, 'William MacGregor,' before asking, 'Why did they call him *Pay Dirt*?'

'He voz a gold prospector,' Grandpa Scott answered. 'And like yor papa says, he voz a very funny man. In some vays, he voz also a very smart and very generous man. But ze viskey made him crazy. Even during prohibition, he drank like ze fishes.'

Again, Angel's father took up the narrative. 'We offered to make him a shareholder in the violin business, but Bill had gold fever. Admittedly, at times he found a lot of pay dirt. He certainly had the Midas touch.'

'The Midas touch,' Angel recalled. 'Midas, the king of Phrygia.'

From an early age, her father had read to her from Nathaniel Hawthorne's *A Wonder-Book for Girls and Boys*. The edition had been illustrated by Arthur Rackham. One story, 'The Golden Touch', told how the Greek god Dionysus had granted King Midas his wish; that everything he touched should turn to gold. At first, the king had been delighted, until his food, drink and even his daughter were turned to gold. This beautifully illustrated book became Angel's introduction to the legends of Ancient Greece which she grew to love with a passion.

Her father continued: 'Sometimes this chest was so full that Bill could barely lift it, but from the feel of it today, there is nothing of any value left. Even before your dear mother died, old Bill always lost money as quickly as he found it. Bad investments were inevitably followed by gambling and whiskey. He generally recovered, but when your ma died, he lost interest in everything. Occasionally, he would talk about a secret stream he had discovered, where he only had to dip his beard in the water for it to come out looking like the Golden Fleece of Jason and the Argonauts.'

Again, Angel remembered Jason's quest for the Golden Fleece, another magnificent story from Ancient Greece, and soon, she was picturing her maternal grandfather's huge bushy beard shimmering with gold dust; Grandpa Pay Dirt's very own *Golden Fleece.*

The chest looked more than a hundred years old. Although outwardly calm, as she inserted the rusty key into the lock, Angel felt her heart racing once again. In spite of its obvious age, the key turned with surprising ease. Lifting the iron latch, she raised the lid and looked inside. In the fire's flickering light, she could see two circular wooden sieves, each with a wire net base. Below these were two shallow copper bowls of the kind used for panning gold. From illustrated dime novels and stories about the California Gold Rush, Angel knew immediately what these curious objects were.

There were several more tools in the chest, including a small pick and shovel set, a trowel, a large round magnifying glass and a number of small tin boxes, one of which rattled. Beneath everything was a stiff leather pouch, dried and cracked with age. Having carefully laid out the tools and most of the boxes on the hearth rug, under the watchful eyes of her father and grandfather, Angel carried the pouch and the one small box that rattled over to the table. Pushing the cake and lemonade to one side, she attempted first to open the tin box, but its lid was rusted fast.

After a short but fruitless tussle with the box, Angel turned her attention to the cracked leather pouch. She was impatient now, and as she quickly lifted the flap, an almost invisible cloud of golden dust fell slowly onto the table's polished mahogany top. With considerably more care, she removed several folded papers that were tucked inside the pouch, but as she attempted to unfold them, her movements across the polished surface dispersed the shimmering dust. In less than a second the gold was gone. It had simply vanished; it had been there, she had seen it, and now it was gone. She was momentarily devastated, until her eyes focused on the documents.

There were two well-thumbed folded sheets of poor-quality paper. The first appeared to be a simple map drawn in faded brown ink. The outlines of a lake and several rivers were clearly visible, but there were other shapes and configurations that Angel could not identify. The map, if that is what it was, showed no recognisable buildings or features. Instead, certain points were marked by the letters of a curious alphabet, some of which appeared to be of Greek origin, including the letters Alpha and Omega.

The second sheet was filled with a densely packed, extremely fine and beautiful crafted script. It had clearly been written by a steady hand using an exceptionally thin nib. Again, the ink was brown and faded. Angel retrieved the large magnifying glass from the floor and walked back to the table. Under the glass's strong magnification, the script appeared even more striking, nevertheless it remained stubbornly illegible. There were no discernible punctuation marks and no gaps to indicate the end of a word or phrase. It was just an endless ribbon of unidentifiable symbols. Angel turned to her father who was now standing beside her.

'What is it, Papa?' she enquired.

'I have no idea,' he said. 'Perhaps Grandpa knows.'

'Vell, it is surely not German, or Polish… or Russian,' he added after a short pause. 'But I'm sure you vill work it out, although I vuddent bother. Dat Pay Dirt Bill, he voz crazy.'

And perhaps she would have left it at that, had she not managed to open the small rattling tin box later that night. Once she was sure that her father and grandfather were sleeping, with the help of a little paraffin oil and an old screwdriver, Angel loosened the lid and tipped the contents of the box onto her small marble-topped dressing table. The sight took her breath away. A dozen or more gold nuggets of various sizes skittered across the marble top, their dazzling appearance amplified by the dressing table's silver mirror.

The largest nugget resembled a dimpled haricot bean; one that had been dried a little too long. The smallest was the size of a mustard seed. But their size was unimportant. Together they were simply magical. Barely able to restrain her excitement, Angel carefully placed the nuggets back in their box and closed the lid. After hiding the box under her bed and sliding the leather pouch with its strange papers under her pillow, she closed her eyes and dreamed of *striking it rich*.

The following morning, as she showed her father and her grandfather the contents of the small tin box, Angel was bubbling with enthusiasm. All thoughts of the war were gone.

'They're gold nuggets!' she exclaimed. 'Grandpa MacGregor must have found them, and I think he left the map and instructions to show me *where* he found them!'

'That's very nice, Angel,' her father replied, without reciprocating her enthusiasm. 'But right now, you need to eat something before you go to school.'

Somewhat deflated, Angel looked to her grandfather, who without lifting his head, simply said, 'Dat Bill, he voz a crazy son—'

'That's enough, Grandpa,' said Randolph, interrupting the old man's flow. He didn't approve of his father using bad language in front of his daughter, especially when he swore in English. Somehow his German accent made the old man's swear words seem even more offensive.

Unlike Angel, who had been preoccupied with her gold nuggets, both men had heard the news about the Dresden bombings. Hermann had been devastated by the reports. Dresden, the second largest city in the Kingdom of Saxony, had been a cultural icon. As a young man Hermann had visited the city several times to hear concerts in the magnificent Frauenkirche, or the Semperoper, the Saxon State Opera House, both of which had been destroyed by the fire storm that had followed the Allied raids.

That day at school Angel found it impossible to concentrate. Still unaware of the bombings, all she could think about was Grandpa MacGregor's papers and his – *her* – glistening gold nuggets. Unfortunately, there was no one in whom she could confide. Even Amanda Kowalski was out of the question; the other girls would eventually squeeze it out of her. Her grandfather had quickly dismissed the glittering pieces as fool's gold, and although her father had been vaguely impressed by the nuggets, he also believed that their value was negligible. He even suggested that Angel should save them in a small purse as a nice keepsake. Either way, neither of them was prepared to waste time even discussing the subject, let alone helping her to interpret the papers.

At first, the men's lack of enthusiasm had annoyed Angel, who was so preoccupied with the contents of the chest that it was almost three days before she finally heard the terrible news about the Dresden raids. Her grandfather had supported the war against Nazi Germany and Japan, but this action seemed not only unnecessary, but vengeful and unworthy of the country he had come to love. Although for his granddaughter's sake he tried to hide his true feelings, Angel had caught him quietly weeping at his workbench.

Hermann Scott was not the only one to react in this way. However, other than through the reaction of her grandfather and other adults, Angel was incapable of understanding what had happened in Dresden or why. Like most Americans, although she was aware of the deportation, torture and murder of Jews and other minorities in German death camps, so far, in Angel's teenage brain, information and comprehension remained mercifully far apart. Indeed, for their perceived part in finally bringing hostilities to an end, most Americans had even welcomed the two nuclear bombs that were eventually dropped on Hiroshima and Nagasaki. It was only after the Soviet Union conducted its first nuclear test in 1949 that fears were raised about nuclear war somehow reaching the United States of America, but by that time, Angel's world had already changed beyond all recognition.

In the meantime, interpreting her Grandfather MacGregor's strange document became a suitable distraction from the horrors of the war. Deciphering its cryptic text was made even more difficult by the diminutive size of the beautifully crafted symbols and characters. The magnifying glass had proved useful, but other than showing the manuscript's true beauty, it made no contribution to understanding the message that Angel was now convinced her Grandfather MacGregor had sent from beyond the grave.

4

For several months Angel attempted to decipher the enigmatic script. As she scoured her school and local libraries for information on foreign language alphabets and calligraphy, almost unnoticed, the war in Europe ended. Meanwhile, in complete secrecy, the Manhattan Project had succeeded in exploding the world's first nuclear bomb in the state of New Mexico.

Knowing that her Grandfather MacGregor was of Scottish origin, Angel even researched Celtic runes, in case the language he had used was a form of ancient Gaelic. Again, using the magnifying glass, she examined the various characters for repeats and patterns, but although many of the symbols looked vaguely familiar and were often repeated, nothing made sense. It was all just a back-to-front jumble.

Angel also examined the tools, the tins and the cracked

leather pouch for clues but found nothing helpful. She looked for hidden messages, both inside and outside the chest. She searched for secret panels and compartments but found none. Basically, it was just a plain old wooden box, with a lid and an iron lock. There was no place to hide a cipher or clue of any kind. The whole process was becoming extremely frustrating, but whenever she started to feel despondent, Angel would remove the nuggets from the small leather drawstring purse in which she now kept them and roll them through her fingers. This simple act always lifted her spirits and drove her on to greater efforts.

Angel soon realised that she was neglecting her schoolwork, and more importantly, her father's illustrated journals on instrument identification; not to mention studying the works of W. E. Hill and Sons. It was not that she was bored with school or violin expertise; it was just that, for the moment at least, her Grandfather MacGregor's papers seemed so much more urgent. At school, Angel was still an outstanding student, and even at the tender age of sixteen, she already had a good theoretical knowledge of instrument identification. In addition, having spent most of her life surrounded by violins, she had been privileged to hear some of the country's greatest players, playing some of the world's finest compositions, on some of the world's greatest instruments.

Angel was hard-working and keen, and Randolph knew that one day his daughter would be ranked amongst the greatest connoisseurs in the violin business. His only worry was her business acumen. Angel was naive about the ways of the world. Although this made her a wonderful person, it also made her vulnerable. He was afraid that if and when she took over the Scott family business, unscrupulous people would quickly take advantage of her trusting nature.

Indeed, Angel's childlike naivety was already manifesting itself each night. In the vain hope that she would somehow receive inspiration from them, before sleeping, Angel placed her Grandfather MacGregor's papers under her pillow. In the end however, it was not her pillow but her dressing table mirror that solved the puzzle. While brushing her unruly red hair in front of the mirror one morning, she caught a glimpse of the manuscript, which she had left lying on the dressing table's marble top. Although the script was still illegible, somehow it made more sense. Until now, the script had been a back-to-front jumble. But in the mirror, although clearly still a jumble, it was no longer back to front. Angel remembered reading about how Leonardo da Vinci had used mirror writing to record his private deliberations. 'Could this be mirror writing?' she asked herself out loud. But before she had completed the question, she already knew she had found the answer.

Within minutes Angel had assembled pen, ink and paper and laid them on her dressing table. Peering into the mirror, she started to copy the reflected manuscript. Even with the help of the magnifying glass, the script's diminutive size made the process difficult; nevertheless, the first few words were already taking shape. It soon became clear that her Grandfather MacGregor had left out all forms of punctuation, but it was also clear that it was only a matter of time before his cryptic message would be revealed.

The matter of time that Angel had envisaged quickly stretched into several days. Reconstructing words and sentences proved more difficult than she had imagined. This was mainly due to the size of the text, but in some places the ink had faded almost entirely away. In addition, several folds and creases in the poor-quality paper were causing problems.

As Randolph and Hermann quietly observed these developments, it soon became obvious that Angel was having difficulty managing her schoolwork, her work on the violin journals and her household duties. And it was not long before they also noticed the effect that lack of sleep was having on her normally fresh appearance.

The map proved slightly easier to decipher. It too had been drawn as a mirror image. Angel had already started copying the map's reflection, before she suddenly realised that a far more effective method would be to trace the map on a transparent sheet of paper and then simply turn the sheet over. Although this revelation pleased her, she was angry with herself for not having considered the idea while working on the manuscript.

In view of their reaction so far, Angel decided to wait before showing her father and grandfather what she had discovered. She had something to show now, but there were still a few loose ends to tie up. The manuscript contained two groups of six numbers. From the manuscript's layout and from her school geography lessons, Angel realised that these numbers were almost certainly grid references for a map. The problem was that her Grandfather MacGregor's simple hand-drawn map had no grid. She would need to find the map to which the grid reference belonged.

Fortunately, there was a clue as to where such a map might be found.

Long before she had finished interpreting the manuscript, Angel realised that it was a personal letter addressed directly to her. One easy to read section read, 'You're one quarter Scottish blood, and Robert the Bruce should help you find the place you require. If not, complete James Boswell's famous quote, *I hated the English; I wished from my soul that the Union was broke and that we might give them another...*'

Was Grandpa MacGregor playing some elaborate game? Or was he deliberately trying to hide information from prying eyes? Angel had heard of James Boswell, but not of Robert the Bruce. Boswell was a Scottish author who had famously written about Samuel Johnson, the man who had completed the first dictionary of the English language. In her well-stocked school library, it had not been difficult to find Boswell's quote: 'I hated the English; I wished from my soul that the Union was broke and that we might give them another battle of Bannockburn.'

Inspired now, Angel turned to the library again. Thinking about her grandfather's reference to her Scottish blood, she found two books on Scottish history, one of which contained the legend of Robert the Bruce and the spider. The story instantly fascinated Angel. It was like a tale from Greek mythology. At one point, Robert Bruce, King of Scotland, had been forced into hiding when King Edward of England had invaded his land. The story recalled how, while hiding in a cave, Robert had watched as a spider tried over and over again to build a web. The final success of this humble spider is said to have inspired

Robert to continue fighting, until against overwhelming odds, he had eventually beaten the English at the Battle of Bannockburn.

'Bannockburn' was obviously the key. Angel reasoned that it was not the Bannockburn in Scotland, but the small village of Bannockburn in Lake County, Illinois, some forty miles away from the Scotts' violin shop. The village had been founded by a Scottish real estate developer in the 1920s and was already one of the most expensive and exclusive residential areas in the Chicago region. But what had this to do with Grandpa MacGregor's map?

After a protracted search in the Chicago Public Records Office, Angel eventually found what she was looking for. Along with a recently printed map of Chicago's waterways, that had been compiled by the US Army's Corps of Engineers, she found a large-scale development plan of the Bannockburn area. Although they were drawn to different scales, using the six-number grid reference, Angel compared these visual documents against her tracing of Grandpa MacGregor's map. On Bannockburn's north-eastern side, she finally found a perfect match; one that included both the line of a stream and the outline of a small lake.

Before leaving the records office, Angel purchased a new government map of the district. When she arrived home, again using the manuscript's two six-digit references, she pinpointed two positions on the new map. The points indicated a 200-yard stretch of stream that drained into the west fork of the north branch of the Chicago river.

Angel now had an official map with references showing where the gold nuggets had been found. She also had a manuscript that explained how to extract and refine the pay dirt. She was almost beside herself with excitement. The following day was Saturday; the shop would close at one o'clock and she could finally tell her father and grandfather the news. Exhausted, she finally fell asleep, clutching her tiny bag of gold nuggets.

Having wound her clock and set the alarm, Angel was awake bright and early. She prepared breakfast and put coffee on the stove. Hermann and Randolph arrived at the table together. As usual, they had washed and shaved before coming down from their respective rooms.

Angel greeted them proudly: 'I've done it! I've found the gold.' When the two men gave her a blank look, she repeated her words. 'I've found the gold.'

'What gold?' her father finally managed to ask.

And then she realised. They had no idea what she was talking about. It had been almost six months since she had opened the chest, during which time she had more or less kept herself to herself.

'Grandpa MacGregor's gold,' she declared.

'Had you lost it?' her father asked. 'I told you to put it in a purse.'

Angel was almost sick with frustration now. 'I'm talking about Grandpa MacGregor's map and manuscript. I know… I know what they mean!'

'Zat ol' fool, he voz crazy,' was Grandpa Scott's only comment.

The war in Europe was over and both men were busy with the task of revamping the shop in preparation for the war ending in Asia. It took all morning and much of the afternoon before Angel could persuade her father that she had actually managed to decipher both the map and the coded manuscript. In the end, even Grandpa Scott seemed impressed by her logic, but when she tried to persuade them to take her to the stretch of river she had identified, their enthusiasm rapidly disappeared.

'Let's check everything through carefully before we make any hasty decisions,' her father suggested. 'Look! Here, for example, it says that you should beware of snakes.'

With a fluttering heart, Angel had read Grandpa MacGregor's warning about water moccasins. She hated snakes, but the lure of gold had quickly driven them from her mind.

'Let's just go and scout the area,' she suggested. 'We could drive out there tomorrow in the Studebaker.' She was almost pleading now, which was something she hated doing, but for one brief moment she noticed her father beginning to soften.

The ploy worked. Randolph loved his four-door Studebaker Commander, and other than for official business, it had been years since they had driven anywhere for pleasure. He considered the small amount of rationed gas that he had saved from the previous months. They would not be allowed to exceed the wartime speed limit of thirty-five miles per hour and the site was almost forty miles away, but Angel's enthusiasm was impossible to ignore.

'What do you think, Gramps, do you fancy giving the Studebaker a run tomorrow?'

'Only if I'm at the wheel,' his father answered. And the deal was done.

5

The following day was Sunday, but Angel was dressed for work, not church. The deaths of both Innis and Angel's mother had put paid to any residual religious belief the men might otherwise have had. These days, the internal combustion engine had far more pulling power than the local preacher.

Looking like a farm girl in her boots and blue denim overalls, Angel quickly filled a gunny sack with some of the tools from Grandpa MacGregor's chest: the trowel, a sieve, a zinc bucket and the smallest copper pan. Along with a quickly prepared picnic hamper, she placed everything in the car's large trunk.

'Why are you taking all that stuff along?' Her father laughed. 'Wasn't this supposed to be just a scouting mission?'

But he too was wearing overalls with a bib and straps.

Angel could not remember having seen her father in such clothes. Her grandfather yes, but as a manager her father was always a snappy dresser. Even when working in the shop, he had always worn a suit under a white doctor's coat. With this coat his intention had always been to present the image of a violin surgeon rather than a repairman. He had borrowed the idea from a Rolls Royce workshop he had once visited with a wealthy client before the war.

For more than an hour they drove north along the Skokie Valley Road, before turning west for a mile or so, and then south along a dirt road. The area was a strange mixture of affluent building projects, old settlements and parkland. It was not what Angel had expected. The landscape was more urban than rural, but there were plenty of lakes and streams, so she remained optimistic. Having parked the Studebaker at the very end of the dirt road, they walked a few hundred yards more down an almost overgrown track. With Grandpa Scott holding the map and leading the way, Randolph followed carrying the picnic hamper, while Angel and her gunny sack brought up the rear.

It soon became clear that the area was being developed and there were already several plots staked out with red painted poles and 'for sale' notices.

Angel was pleasantly surprised when Grandpa Scott found the stream. It was in a quiet, peaceful spot. Indeed, it was the ideal place for a picnic, and much to Angel's frustration, the men insisted they should eat before checking out the stream. But Angel had come too far with this project to be side-tracked now.

Still carrying the gunny sack, Angel walked over to the

edge of the stream. It was only about fifteen paces wide. On either side, rich vegetation overhung its steep muddy banks, which she quickly realised she would be forced to slide down. The main body of water was shallow and slow-moving, its level clearly much lower than normal. There were several gravel banks with small pools and numerous boulders rising up from the riverbed. On the far side, almost lost in the rich undergrowth, a small notice indicated that this plot was also for sale.

Seeing Angel struggle with her load, Randolph gallantly walked over in his brand-new overalls and gave her a helping hand, but they both ended up sliding down the muddy bank in an inelegant manner. As they landed in knee-deep cloudy water, they looked at one another then burst out laughing. Angel had not seen her father laugh so freely in years, and it was infectious. She eventually managed to reach out and drop the gunny sack on a nearby gravel bank. This was fortunate, because they were soon holding onto each other and giggling uncontrollably. They had slowly managed to regain a little decorum, when they heard Grandpa Scott, only a few yards away, setting out the picnic somewhere above their heads. Quickly exchanging conspiratorial glances, the laughter began again.

It was some time before they managed to find a suitable spot on the riverbed where they could excavate a little silt, sand and gravel. Working together they passed scoop after scoop through the sieve and into the zinc bucket. Each time Angel checked the remaining stones for signs of gold before casting them aside. As she did so, she recalled what the manuscript had said: 'Climb into the stream at low water (dry season) and dig silt from the bed. Pass the silt through a sieve into a zinc bucket. As you do this, check the sieve for nuggets. Larger nuggets are rare, but pea-sized nuggets are fairly common; you can expect to find several dozen each day. Any smaller nuggets will fall through the sieve. When the bucket is full of fine sand and silt, place a small amount in the copper pan and carefully agitate and wash it. Keep adding fresh water to the pan, while slowly washing the lighter material out and back into the river. Being heavier, any small pieces of gold will always sink to the bottom of the pan. This is a slow process, but with care you will eventually find your pay dirt. Most of the pieces will be tiny, but they all mount up.'

Having sieved several loads, the bucket was soon full of fine sand and silt, which little by little Angel started to wash. At first her father had been good with advice, showing her how to hold and agitate the pan, but he had soon grown tired. So, when Grandpa Scott peered over the edge and suggested they should climb out and eat some lunch, he was quickly on his way. However, Angel was not hungry, and having politely told them so, she returned to the pan.

To avoid wasting valuable prospecting time, Grandpa MacGregor had advised Angel to practise the washing process before going to the site. He had even suggested using nuggets from the tin. Unfortunately, Angel had no time to learn how to avoid wasting time. The consequence of this was that progress now was both slow and tiring. With almost an hour already gone, Angel was barely halfway down the first bucket and her arms were beginning to ache. As she worked, she had listened to the two men chatting over lunch; now however, everything had suddenly become eerily quiet. Even the birds appeared to have stopped singing. Needing to rest her arms, Angel climbed part way up the bank. Hermann and Randolph had already finished the picnic and the beers that she had cleverly slipped into the wicker basket, and they were now snoring peacefully in the shade of an American Elm that had conveniently established itself at the stream's edge.

Angel turned and slid back down the bank. Alone now, she thought briefly about spiders and snakes, but as soon as she hit the water, there was only one thing on her mind. Using the trowel, she removed another small scoop of sand and silt from the bucket. Placing it in the pan, once again, she started the washing process. Slowly, she swished water over the grey slick, until almost all of it had been washed back into the stream. Just as she was about to tip out the remainder, she saw it, nestling in the seam at the bottom of the pan. It was barely the size of a pin head and yet it shone with unmistakable intensity, like a lighthouse beam reaching out across miles of desolate ocean.

The physical jolt that Angel felt was not the usual rush of adrenaline that a body experiences in response to a stressful, exciting or dangerous situation. This was something else, something that hunters, speculators and gamblers have felt since the beginning of time. That incomparable rush of turbo-adrenalin, the kind that is directly linked to the successful pursuit of materialistic goals; the kind that is a precursor to serious addiction. Even the excitement of discovering and translating her grandfather's papers could not compare to her encounter with this tiny fragment of pure gold.

Her mind was racing and her body trembling, she

wanted to scream, but shock had taken her breath away. Besides, the men were sleeping and surely there was more to come. She needed to regain control. She needed to prove to them and to herself that she could remain calm and not miss the next nugget. Fifteen minutes later, Angel found two golden rice-sized grains lying side by side in the bottom of the pan. She was already dreaming of all the possibilities when the last measure of silt from the bucket yielded a fourth nugget. It was as big as a sunflower seed.

She was about to begin digging again when her father looked over the edge. 'How much longer are you going to be down there, Angel?' From the tone of his voice, he was getting restless. 'It's already five o'clock. We need to be getting back.'

Although it seemed as if she had been in the stream only a short while, she had actually been standing knee-deep in water for three and a half hours. This revelation made her feel unexpectedly tired, but the truth was that hunger and lack of sleep over many weeks had finally caught up with her.

Her father climbed down and helped her retrieve and wash the tools, before they both scrambled back up the muddy bank. Grandpa Scott offered Angel a towel and a change of clothes, but all she wanted to do was show them her finds. The two men were sympathetic, but both insisted she should remove her wet clothes and have something to eat and drink before they would look at anything. Being a dutiful child, Angel did as she was told, but once again she was crestfallen at their lack of enthusiasm.

'We can come back next weekend,' she helpfully

suggested, as she dried and dressed herself. 'And soon I will have my autumn holiday.'

But the mood amongst their little group had suddenly grown sombre, and in spite of the warm day, Angel felt a distinct chill in the air. Holding up his right hand as if he was about to swear an oath, with his free hand, her father offered her a sandwich. With an upward flick of his chin he urged her to eat. When she was finished, he poured homemade lemonade from a stone flask, and lifting his chin again, he urged her to drink. By now she was obeying his unspoken commands rather like a small child who has misbehaved. Up to this point they were still standing, but as they sat down together, her father grew ever more serious.

'Angel,' he began, 'your grandpa and I want you to see this.' He handed her an official-looking report. It was an Illinois State Geological Survey. 'You don't need to read all of this right now,' he said, once she had registered what it was. 'But basically, what it says is that there is no gold in this region.'

'Well they're wrong about that!' she countered, opening her fist to show off the four gleaming gold nuggets. She was triumphant now.

'No, Angel! They are not wrong.'

Something in her father's voice made her realise that he was telling the truth.

'I don't understand… Are you saying this gold… is not real?'

'It's real enough.'

'So, I found real gold, right here where Grandpa MacGregor's map said it would be.'

'That's right, Angel, but you didn't find it all.'

'What you mean?' She was uneasy now; something was clearly happening that she did not understand.

'I dropped eight grains in your bucket, but you only found four. I made these, and all those nuggets in the tin box, from melted scraps left over from bow repair work.'

There was a long silence before Angel spoke again. 'Are you saying that you tricked me?' She looked to her grandfather, but he was staring at the ground. Turning back to her father, with a note of desperation in her voice, she pleaded, 'But what about the maps and the chest? They were real… weren't they?'

'I'm sorry, Angel. We bought the chest with the prospecting gear at a yard sale last year. They were what gave us the idea.'

'What idea? And what do you mean *we*? Are you saying that Grandpa was involved in this trick?'

'I did the research. Your grandpa drew the map, wrote the manuscript and made the label that was attached to the key. He's better with his hands.' He paused then finally added, 'I'm afraid they were all fakes.'

But Angel was not about to give up so easily.

'They called him Pay Dirt; Pay Dirt MacGregor. I heard people call him that lots of times, even after he died.' She was struggling to hold back tears now.

'It was an old joke, Angel. Bill was a gardener, and until your mother died and he turned to drink, he had an excellent reputation. He worked for the folk who lived in that wealthy residential district that borders Lake Michigan. In fact, it's such an affluent neighbourhood, it has been known as Chicago's Gold Coast for years. But, as you will see, according to the Illinois State Geological Survey, there were never any gold deposits, either here or there. As for your Grandpa MacGregor, because he worked on the Gold Coast, and because as a gardener he was paid for working with dirt, they called him...'

'Pay Dirt,' Angel obligingly answered.

'Yes!' her father said. 'Good lies always contain some element of truth.'

'But why? Why did you do this?' she pleaded, as the tears that had been waiting started rolling down her cheeks.

'Let's get in the car, Angel and we'll explain everything on the way home.'

6

The previous year, 1944, on her fifteenth birthday, Angel had received a copy of *Burnt Njal's Saga* from her father. Translated from the Icelandic by George DaSent. It was typical of the perfect stories that Randolph somehow always managed to find; stories that allowed his daughter's mind to roam free. Having started her with heroes and heroines of Greek mythology, he had gradually expanded her repertoire to embrace epic tales of valour and adventure from many different cultures, especially ones that included powerful or influential women. Angel had already devoured accounts of Pocahontas, the Native American princess; Boudica, the Iron Age warrior queen; Cleopatra, the last pharaoh of Egypt; Calamity Jane, the Wild West frontierswoman; and most recently of Amelia Earhart, the American aviator who had disappeared while flying across the Pacific Ocean when Angel was just eight years old.

Opening *Njal's Saga*, Angel read the following lines and was immediately hooked: 'There was a man named Mord whose surname was Fiddle; he was the son of Sigvat the Red, and he dwelt at the Vale in the Rangrivervales. He was a mighty chief, and a great taker up of suits, and so great a lawyer that no judgments were thought lawful unless he had a hand in them. He had an only daughter, named Unna. She was a fair, courteous and gifted woman, and was thought the best match in all the Rangrivervales.'

Burning to know more about Unna, Angel had quickly excused herself, leaving the men sitting in front of the warm log fire. As she closed the door, Randolph had turned towards his father and smiled, but the look on the old man's face had quickly turned his son's smile upside down. Realising what was about to come, Randolph's body stiffened slightly.

'Ve need to talk, Randolph,' his father had begun. 'Ve cannot put ziss off no longer. Angel is growing into a voman and someday soon, zee vil be alone in ze world. My Innis and your Mary are gone. Ve need to do something now.'

Hermann sat back and waited for Randolph's response, but it was slow coming.

'I am trying my best to teach her the business,' he eventually said. 'She is a smart girl, and she is already proficient at identifying various schools of violin makers, but she needs more hands-on experience. Much of what she knows has been taken from my journals and is therefore theoretical. Someday I would like to take her on the road with me, but for now, perhaps you could involve her more in the workshop. I know you have shown her how to re-hair violin bows, but maybe you could teach her how to make a violin as well?'

'Vimmen do not make violins,' Hermann said emphatically. 'Occasionally zay put new horse hairs on bow sticks, but zay are used to vorking with combs and hairs. Zay cannot do violins. Zay neffer haf und zay neffer vill. It's not right!'

'Look around you, Papa, while men are away fighting, women are doing everything. In my factory they're building complex engines and even flying aircraft to where they're needed. There is no such thing as men's and women's work anymore. It's all just… work. Anything Angel wants to do, she can do. Anything she wants to be, she can be.'

'She cannot make violins. Zis is men's vork. And even if I could teach her, musicians vud never accept her. Anyvay, when ze vor ends – and it vill end – men vill take back zer jobs and the vimmen vill have babies and look after ze houses. Zis is what happened last time and it vill happen again.'

Randolph knew this was true. It had certainly been the case after the first war with Germany. And now, although women were proving they could do 'men's work' just as well as men, Randolph feared that once the war was over, federal and civilian policies would quickly replace women workers with men. In addition, he could already envisage American society pressurising women to become feminine stay-at-home moms, cleaning, cooking and taking care of children. As soon as an armistice was signed, the dice would be loaded. However, what he could not see was his daughter doing any of these things. Marriage and a happy family were almost certainly what she wanted, but they were probably not what she would be getting.

Randolph hesitated before saying what he felt needed to be said: 'You're probably right, Pa, men will want their jobs back and women will return to the home and have babies, but that is exactly the problem. We both love Angel; she is our flesh and blood and she has a truly beautiful face but…' Randolph stopped. He was close to tears now as he lowered his voice. 'She's fat!' he said.

Suddenly horrified at having voiced his innermost feelings, he nevertheless continued: 'She is also extremely clever, and most men are intimidated by large clever women. I'm just afraid that no eligible young man will look at her twice; especially now that fewer young men will be returning after this stupid war.'

'But she is kind and ven ve are gone she vill also be rich,' his father said.

'Do you want someone to marry Angel for her money?'

'No ov course not und zat is not vot I meant.'

'I know!' Randolph answered quickly, realising that he had pushed his father too far. 'I'm sorry. I'm just worried about Angel's future. That's why I think that she should learn the art of violin making.'

'Listen, Randolph, that vill neffer work. It is a culture ting. It neffer happened and it neffer vill happen. You must accept dat. You can teach her to become an expert. Dat she *can* use. Dis knowledge vill be accepted. You can teach her vot very few people knows. And there iz real money in dealing. There iz no money in making and repairing violins. You know dis, Randolph, vy you keep pursuing zis idea?'

'I keep pursuing it because I know that she will be

eaten alive in the violin dealing world. She is too nice; too naive.'

'Zen ve need to provide her with ze means to sneak up on zem, vissout zem ever knowing vot hit zem until iz too late.' And for the first time that evening he gave a raucous belly laugh. 'Iz true,' he gasped, 'zay von't know vot hit zem,' and he continued laughing. 'And because she'z a voman and young, even if she iz a big girl, she vill have great advantage. She haz beautiful face and great innocence. Most men, especially older vonz, vill fall over backvards trying to impress her. And, zay von't suspect a ting. But zat von't last forever. She vill need to keep learning until she iz zo good zay cannot ignore her. Zen zay vill come to *her* to ask *her* opinion. And ven dat happens, she vill be queen of ze violin business.'

After weighing his father's words, Randolph spoke again: 'You are right, Pa, and with our help, I am convinced that she is capable of achieving this. She could even be the best of the best, but that will not make her a businesswoman. I'm still afraid that her niceness and naivety will lead to her downfall.'

'Randolph, vee can even teach her zat. Vee don't need to take ze niceness out of her, just ze naivety. I know a vay. It vill be very hard on her, but she is strong.'

That evening and for much of the year that followed, while Angel slipped into her various fantasy worlds, Hermann and Randolph gradually planned and compiled their own Scottish saga in the shape of Grandpa MacGregor's gold prospecting chest.

And sure enough, just as Hermann had predicted,

following the Normandy Landings, and the liberation of Paris, once victory seemed assured, the US government began urging women to return to working full time in the home. Indeed, in spite of having made strong advances towards equal rights, within months of the war ending, the number of women in paid employment had fallen by almost ten percent. For American women, marriage, children and homemaking would quickly become as much a part of the national agenda as they had been in the homemaking lessons at Angel's school. A genuine college education for women would remain a rarity for a considerable time. In fact, by the time Angel would have been old enough to attend college, less than one percent of white women would be receiving degrees; and discrimination meant that for racial minorities, statistics barely existed. In reality, most young women still viewed higher education as a means to meet eligible young men with a view to marriage. In fact, it was still widely believed that if a woman had not walked down the aisle by the time she was twenty, she was in danger of becoming an 'old maid'.

Unfortunately, as much as she might have wanted to, Angel simply did not fit the image of an ideal American housewife; tending to hearth and home, sporting a feminine hairdo and wearing a delicate dress. In particular, her full figure and her undoubted intellectual ability were seen by most people, including her menfolk, as a serious handicap.

On the eve of Angel's sixteenth birthday, Hermann was convinced more than ever that their ruse would work, but

Randolph worried that it would drive a wedge between himself, his father and his daughter. He had thought carefully about how Angel might react. He had even considered the hour-long drive back home during which, confined in the back of the Studebaker, Angel would be obliged to listen to his explanation. He was just not sure if she would accept what he had to say. Neither was he sure exactly what he would say. He and Hermann had discussed the topic over and over, but now he was no longer convinced that it was the right thing to do. Indeed, in retrospect it all seemed unnecessarily cruel.

7

Angel pressed a handkerchief against her closed eyes as she sat in one corner of the Studebaker's long back seat. She looked and felt very small, and for the first time in her life she was seriously angry with the two men.

'That was a really horrid trick,' she eventually blurted out.

'It wasn't a trick, Angel,' her father replied, as the car moved off with Grandpa Scott at the wheel. 'It wasn't a trick,' he repeated, 'it was a lesson; quite possibly the best lesson you will ever have. You are a young lady in a big man's world. The violin trade can be ruthless, and when Grandpa and I are no longer around, no one is likely to help you. You will need to have your wits about you all the time. You are as smart as paint, Angel, and at least theoretically, you know more about instrument identification than I knew at your age, but that will not help you with the Al

Capones of this world. And believe me, Angel, they may not have Tommy guns and scarred faces, but there are plenty of serious gangsters in the violin business.'

While his father drove slowly home, Randolph half turned in his seat to face Angel. Her head was down, and the handkerchief was still pressed firmly against her eyes.

'Angel, your grandpa and I will not be around forever. Someday we are both going to die, and you will be left to run the shop alone.'

Talking about death was a bad start, and in trying to correct his mistake, Randolph only made things worse. 'We don't know what might happen. I mean, neither of us is planning on dying any time soon, but even without this war, the world is an uncertain place and both Grandpa and I know how easy it is to lose someone you have come to depend on, and how hard it is to recover when they are gone. If and when that time comes, you will need to be ready.'

Randolph could see that his daughter was shocked by this statement. He took a deep breath and tried to recover his purpose. On hearing her father's remarks, Angel had raised her head and through damp, red eyes, she was now studying her father's face. She had never seen him look so miserable. He was normally fun to be with; Grandpa could be grumpy from time to time, but her father was always bright and gay, and now here he was talking about dying.

'It really wasn't a trick,' her father repeated again, but this time more gently. 'Your grandpa and I deliberated long and hard about what it might be like for a woman to be working in the violin business. And, as far as we are both aware, there are no independent women violin makers working anywhere in the world.'

From behind the wheel her grandfather called back, 'Zer neffer ver any und zer neffer vil be.'

Randolph was about to reply to his father, but his daughter answered first and there was more than a little anger in her voice.

'That's what they said about women flying aeroplanes until Amelia Earhart flew solo across the Atlantic Ocean.'

'Jah, und see vot happened to her?' Hermann interjected. 'Sie crashed to death in ze Pacific Ocean.'

'That's enough, Father!'

'Sie needs to know ze truth!' he replied forcefully.

'And what *is* the truth?' asked Angel, suddenly raising *her* voice.

'That's enough, you two!' Randolph was shouting himself now. His loud retort shocked them both. Neither had ever heard him raise his voice, certainly never in normal conversation. 'The truth is that we are worried about you, Angel. You are a highly intelligent, well-educated young woman and should you decide to continue with the shop, as a connoisseur, you will certainly be knowledgeable enough. It's just that, after careful consideration, your grandpa and I came to the conclusion that when it comes to buying and selling instruments, unless you learn how to become vehement and vigilant, you will lose out to the bandits and sharks. Perhaps not every time, but with the price of top violins rising so high, it would not take many mistakes for you to lose everything. You're too trusting, too naive and too nice, Angel, which is why we devised this scheme. We both realised that simply telling you to be careful would not work. You needed to be given a painful lesson; one that you would never forget.'

Randolph had tried to say these words with conviction, but he was still having trouble finding a way to voice his concerns without appearing mean-spirited. And the sad truth was that he *was* conflicted. Like his father, Randolph was convinced that very soon most women would be expected to remain in the home and raise children, which was unquestionably work, but it was not a well-paid career. He was torn between worrying that Angel would never find a husband and wanting her to be completely independent; a self-sufficient woman with more than just a job. He wanted her to become a successful violin dealer, and that would require something more than the commitment, energy and spirit that she so obviously already possessed.

Randolph was wary now as he began again: 'Every day, someone comes to the shop, wanting to sell a precious Italian violin. They all appear to be nice genuine folk, and no doubt many of them are. They certainly have interesting and plausible stories, but unless I can identify their instrument, these stories are merely a distraction. In every case, I need to be sure what their instrument is, or at least what it is not. Only with that knowledge can I begin to think about the possibility of making a purchase. I then need to check the instrument's condition and judge whether the people wanting to sell are in fact the rightful owners.'

'You mean that the instrument has not been stolen,' Angel intervened.

'Exactly! In many cases, they will have documents proving the instrument's provenance and that they are indeed the legitimate owners of the instrument they want to sell, but as you now know, such papers can be faked. So, if I don't know what I'm looking at, I might end up buying their stories and their papers rather than the instrument.'

After an extended pause, Randolph continued: 'There are thousands of ways to sell someone a worthless or a stolen instrument, and it takes a good detective to make the right judgment. By cracking the codes that your grandfather and I devised, you have already proved that you can do the detective work, but you were blinded by the gold. And, if that piece of land *had* been for sale, you would have done your best to persuade your grandpa and I to buy it.'

Having reflected for a moment, Angel realised her father was right. She had seen the 'for sale' notice and was embarrassed to realise that she would have done everything in her power to convince them to purchase the plot.

'Angel, several times a week, my mother would tell me that the old English term "fiddle" not only means "violin", it also means to swindle, cheat or defraud. The expression comes from the poor reputation that people who bought and sold fiddles had earned back in the nineteenth century, and the sad truth is that nothing much has changed since. You will need to remember this if you are ever going to buy and sell instruments.'

'Then why not let me work in the workshop if you think I'm too naive to buy and sell instruments? Teach me how to make and repair them. The only thing that you've attempted to teach me so far has been the history and lives of the classical Italian violin makers and how to identify their works.'

At this last remark Angel's grandfather started to turn his head, but before he could open his mouth, her father answered: 'Your grandfather is right, Angel, at least for the moment, there is no such thing as an independent female violin maker. In the past, women no doubt assisted in their husbands' workshops. And of course, at the end of the nineteenth century, in the factories of Mirecourt in France and Markneukirchen in Germany, women and even children were employed on violin-making assembly lines; just as they have been throughout this war on automobile assembly lines in Detroit, or aircraft assembly lines, right here in Chicago. But that must have been soul-destroying work for anyone with an artistic bent. It would certainly not have been work for a young woman with a creative imagination.'

Her father paused before adding, 'Although hypothetically, it would still be possible to teach you the art of violin making, realistically I suspect that simply trying to gain acceptance as a female violin maker would cost you more time and energy than you could ever recoup. Nevertheless, in order to understand how expertise works, you will need to know how and why different violin making groups used different materials and methods of construction, and how these differences help us to identify specific makers. And to be honest, your grandfather can teach you this better than I can.'

At this point Hermann gave a reluctant grunt. 'OK!' he eventually said. 'I can do zat!'

After another short pause, believing that he had found

a suitable analogy, Randolph suddenly turned back to his daughter and looked at her intently: 'Angel, your mother was a truly exceptional violinist, and there were many women like her, but none of them were able to find work as professional musicians. Even today, there are almost no women in American orchestras. In fact, it was a year after your mama passed away before a woman was finally offered a position in a major American orchestra. In 1930, Edna Phillips was employed as a harpist by the Philadelphia Orchestra. Unfortunately, Edna's appointment did not start a trend; even the war was unable to challenge that particular status quo. It would seem that women flying four-engine transport aircraft was quite acceptable but playing the violin in an American symphony orchestra was not.

'As talented as she was, your mother was obliged to give private lessons to other young ladies; ladies that would also be unlikely to find employment in a professional orchestra. It's not that women are incapable. For centuries young ladies from high society were expected to play an instrument and to perform at private *soirées*, and many were genuine virtuosos. At the other extreme, in the eighteenth century, Antonio Vivaldi is said to have led an all-girl orchestra; one of several. These were made up of orphan girls who were taught by rote, and although they were almost certainly exceptional musicians, they were probably mistreated if they did not make the grade.'

Her father had been about to add that at least they were not castrated, like many of their male counterparts, but changing his mind, he eventually said, 'It's not much better for black musicians, especially in the world of classical music. As you well know, Angel, lots of black musicians are extremely gifted, and some, like the composer William Grant Still and the jazz pianist Nat King Cole, were even classically trained. In fact, in the 1930s, Still was the first black man to conduct a major American orchestra, but in spite of his individual achievements, even today, there is apparently no room for full-time black musicians in American symphony orchestras. I'm afraid it's the way of the world.

'Now, I am not suggesting that being a white woman in the violin business would be as difficult as being a black man in an orchestra, but prejudice of any kind is a hard thing to shake off ,Angel. Which,' he rather magnanimously added, 'is what your grandpa was trying to say. He was certainly right to suggest that becoming a connoisseur would be the lesser of two evils.'

Angel could not recall her grandfather having said any of these things, but she had not only understood her father's message, she had already taken its implication a stage further. If breaking into the violin business was that difficult for a black man, what chance would a black woman have?

While Angel contemplated this scenario, her father continued his sermon: 'In spite of what your grandpa says, I believe women will eventually be accepted both as professional players and as violin makers, but for now, your best chance of an independent career is to become a serious connoisseur and, if possible, a violin dealer. As things stand, even for male violin makers, there is not much money to be made doing run-of-the-mill repair work and almost none making new instruments. One day it might happen, but right now, in order to make a reasonable living, everyone in the business needs to do *some* dealing.

'Of course, if you insist on becoming a violin maker, your grandpa and I will help you...'

At this point Angel's grandfather gave another rather more disgruntled grunt, but her father continued: 'But, as a connoisseur, they would be forced to accept you simply because, if you continue learning the way you have been, they would not be able to ignore you. You are already better than most of our colleagues, and if you so wish, your grandpa and I will do our utmost to make you the best in the world. And I do mean the best, Angel; you are quite capable of that.'

After another short pause her father added, 'Even your grandpa is convinced of that.'

In reply, Angel lowered her eyebrows and gave the back of her grandfather's head a sceptical look.

When they finally stopped outside their Chicago townhouse, Randolph turned completely in his seat and looked directly into Angel's eyes. Although *her* eyes were no longer red, he knew that *his* were.

'Before we get out of the car, I want to finish by saying that you are all that we have, Angel, your grandfather and I love you more than you can know. We just want you to be successful and happy and we want to somehow protect you, even after we are gone. Our hope is that from now on, whenever you pick up a violin, you will remember the intensity of those feelings you had when you believed that Grandpa MacGregor's gold was going to make you rich. We want you to remember how *gold fever* set your heart racing; how it made you restless during the day and sleepless at night. How you neglected the ordinary business of your life and how you were prepared to risk everything, even the snakes and spiders that you are normally so afraid of. You have a wonderfully vivid imagination, Angel, but this time, powered by the irresistible urge to find gold, it simply careened out of control.'

Randolph studied Angel's face as he spoke these words. He could see that she was already contrite and once again he started to feel remorse welling up in his heart.

'Look,' he said finally, 'you are not alone. Thousands, possibly hundreds of thousands of people have experienced such feelings, even back into antiquity; just think of Jason and Midas. With some it's gold, with others it might be a valuable painting or a beautiful violin. It really doesn't matter. It's *gold fever* and you must learn to recognise it in yourself and eventually in others, because it can make anyone blind.'

Angel was silent now. She could see that the things her father had said about gold fever were valid and she was not proud of herself, but on one point at least she remained defiant. She may be a dreamer, but she was also a pragmatist. She recognised that in some awful way, the negative words of her grandfather were true. For the moment, she could never make a living as a violin maker, at least not enough of a living to provide her with true independence. Nor did she trust herself to become a suffragette for that particular cause, especially since she knew in her heart now that she really could become a successful connoisseur, and if necessary, a dealer. She would just need to be more careful about trusting people. She was already aware that being a woman would hinder her from time to time, but she also knew that her femininity might help her achieve those goals.

Angel was about to open the car door when she suddenly stopped. 'So, you both want me to approach life with a little more cynicism; to be less naive,' she said in a voice strong with emotion. 'In other words, to be more grown up.' Before either of the men could answer she continued, 'In which case I want you both to start addressing me in a grown-up manner. My mother wanted me to be called Grace and that is how I was christened. Angel Eyes is a baby name, and now that I am sixteen, I find it a little demeaning. So, from now on, I would like you to call me Grace.'

She was about to reach for the rear door handle again, when to her surprise, her grandfather addressed her. 'I agree, but I've been calling you Angel for zoh long I may not alvays remember.'

'That's alright,' she replied, 'I may not always remember that I'm a grown-up.'

The tension having been relieved, everyone laughed and the incident with the gold was forgiven; but it was never forgotten.

8

From this moment, with Grace's full cooperation, both men dedicated themselves to the task of turning her into a world-class connoisseur. She was an exceptionally gifted young woman, but neither Hermann nor Randolph were about to underestimate the task that lay ahead.

Randolph had long since recognised that to become a violin connoisseur, the student must be given the opportunity to see as many fine instruments as possible and to record their features in meticulous detail. He was convinced that the very process of compiling, analysing and correlating such information will eventually heighten the connoisseur's perception. In another context, such a state might well be termed *enlightenment*, but he was also aware that enlightenment of this nature is not an innate gift. Natural talent may be helpful, but it is total dedication to any discipline that creates outstanding ability, and such dedication is invariably the product of passion. In Randolph's opinion, there never had been, and never would be, a truly great connoisseur who was not obsessed with fiddles. Although he was convinced that his daughter already had these attributes in abundance, she would still need good guidance. Moreover, in spite of his own father's help, Randolph was well aware that secrecy in the business and a scarcity of reliable information had meant that his own research had often been a difficult and rather hit and miss process.

Nevertheless, having studied the works of W. E. Hill and Sons, and having developed his own series of beautifully illustrated journals, Randolph was convinced that the task of identifying violins could be tackled systematically. Over the following weeks and months, Randolph prepared a series of guidelines that he felt sure would help Grace to identify virtually any instrument, regardless of its origin, and he was determined to show his daughter how that might be done. Even so, he was aware that most of what Grace had learned so far was theoretical, and that what she needed now was hands-on experience.

Taking these factors into account, and considering the post-war reality that women were now facing, in September 1945, only a few weeks after the Japanese surrender, Randolph decided to take Grace out of school; the idea being that she could travel with him, whenever and wherever he went on business. In the meantime, she would spend the remaining intervals with her grandfather in his workshop. It was a decision that the Scott family would never regret.

9

Having stocked the Studebaker with provisions, Randolph and his daughter drove north to Milwaukie then west to Madison, before returning to Chicago via Rockford. This first four-day trip was something of a fishing expedition, not only to test the market and their ten-year-old mode of transport, but to see how Grace would adapt to conditions on the road. Randolph needn't have worried, even when the going was rough, Grace had revelled in the experience.

The Studebaker also played its part well. Initially designed and built to cope with poor roads, the Studebaker was rugged and loaded with torque. In a land where journeys are measured in hundreds rather than tens of miles, this quintessential American automobile swallowed distances as easily as a hungry kid sucks up a strand of spaghetti. Its coach springs softened the ride just enough for comfort, but not enough to lose the sensation of travelling, and once the wartime speed limit had been lifted, even Randolph's cautious forty-five miles per hour top speed was intoxicating.

Using the argument that reports on weather and road conditions would make their journeys easier and safer, her doting father fitted the automobile with a second-hand Motorola radio with push-button station settings, and Grace quickly became another statistic in America's love affair with the car.

Grace's experience with Grandpa MacGregor's maps and her infatuation with Amelia Earhart's adventures quickly turned the young sixteen-year-old into a keen and proficient navigator. Rather like the references she had recorded on her *gold-map*, on her growing collection of state maps Grace now recorded the location of interesting violins, prominent musicians, music teachers, orchestras and even museums.

For almost two years, whenever she was not working in her grandfather's workshop, Grace and Randolph toured the northern and Midwestern states, occasionally even venturing south. They would often be away for days on end, visiting violin makers, county fairs, music schools and concert halls; in fact, anywhere they might find violins, violas, cellos and their accompanying bows. Even the endless hours spent travelling between venues were not wasted. Most of their time was spent learning.

Grace loved these sessions with her father. He had an uncanny ability to paint wonderful pictures of the past, simply by presenting dry facts in an interesting and easily digestible way. Although she had studied the publications of W. E. Hill and Sons, her father's journals were far more personal. Whenever she read them, she could hear his voice speaking the text. Years later, often in the most out of the way places, reading and recalling his soft baritone provided comfort and security. By the time she'd left school, Grace had read and transcribed his journals so often that, rather like an actress memorising the lines of a play, she could recite most of their content word for word. This simple fact had been amply demonstrated on their first tour. Milwaukie, Madison and Rockford may not have yielded much in the way of instruments and bows, but as they travelled along, Randolph had been both pleased and surprised by his daughter's ability not only to summon the contents of his journals, but to discuss them with understanding.

On their maiden voyage, as soon as the Chicago skyline had begun to recede behind them, Randolph's opening line had been, 'To understand the science of violin identification, you first need to understand a little basic history. So, before we start to put some flesh on the bones of theory, Grace, let's see how much basic history you can recall.' At this point his daughter had smiled with mischievous anticipation, but before she could begin, Randolph continued. 'The first violins appeared in Europe, in the early sixteenth century, at the height of what we now call the Italian Renaissance. As you know, the Renaissance was a period of cultural and artistic revolution, in which the violin and its music played an integral part.

'The violin was not an invention as such; it was

probably the culmination of ideas and developments by many musical instrument makers. Eventually two important and highly profitable violin-making centres were established in what is now northern Italy.' Randolph laughed before adding, 'If you did not neglect your studies while prospecting for gold, you should be able to recall the names of these places, Grace?'

Without hesitation Grace answered, 'The first was the city of Cremona, where the Amati family was active. The second was the nearby city of Brescia, where Gasparo da Salò, Gio Paolo Maggini and several others were working.'

'That's right, Grace. Although barely thirty miles apart, Cremona and Brescia were separated not so much by distance as by political boundaries. From the end of the fifteenth century to the middle of the sixteenth century a series of violent wars were waged for the domination of Europe. Largely fought between France and Spain, these wars eventually resulted in Spain dominating most of the Italian peninsular for almost two hundred years. The only exception was Venice, which at that time was the largest trading power in the world.'

'Are you saying that Amati, Stradivari and co. were Spanish?'

'Not exactly, but their lives were heavily influenced by what happened at the Spanish court. As a result, in spite of their close proximity, Cremona was controlled by Milan, which was in turn controlled by Spain, while Brescia fell under the jurisdiction of the Venetian state. Although for the most part relations remained peaceful, politically and commercially these two musical instrument-making centres were fierce competitors.'

Before continuing, Randolph quickly glanced sideways, to see if his daughter was still paying attention. He needn't have bothered; his daughter was hanging on every word, waiting for her father to make a mistake.

'At that time, Cremona's population was around forty-one thousand. Considering the fact that in 1927, more than a hundred and twenty thousand people attended a single football game in downtown Chicago, by today's standards Cremona was small and Brescia smaller still.'

'That's right,' Grace exclaimed, before paraphrasing the words of her father's journals, 'but surely in those days, Cremona would have been considered a large and important city. It certainly had flourishing commercial, cultural and artistic traditions, isn't that right, Papa?'

'Indeed, it did.' Randolph was both amused and impressed, even so he continued his discourse. 'Cremona occupied a dominant position on the vast fertile plain of the Po River, which, along with its tributaries and canals, was also a major European highway. This navigable system extended some two hundred and fifty miles from west to east across northern Italy. From the mid-fifteenth century, Milan and Venice, the two controlling powers, were situated at either end of this waterway, while Cremona lay midway between them on the banks of the river Po itself. The city had several important libraries, with manuscripts and books on mathematics, astronomy, history, philosophy and theology. I'm sure you would have loved it, Grace.' Randolph smiled, before adding, 'That is, always assuming that your father had been a wealthy nobleman!

'In spite of its rich cultural traditions, because wars and skirmishes flared up at regular intervals, like most towns and cities of the time, Cremona had strong defensive walls capable of withstanding a long siege. As a result of its position and strength, the city dominated and controlled all traffic moving across and around this important network of roads and rivers. Theoretically, all products and wares passing through this system would have been available in Cremona. As well as the usual goods and chattels, they would have included ancient artefacts and manuscripts, and inevitably musical instruments. And along with these things came fragments of civilisations and cultures from as far away as Byzantium, Arabia, India and even China.

'Eventually, manufacture and trading made northern Italy the richest area of Europe and one of the richest in the world; much like the United States is today. As a result, Cremona's leading citizens became extremely prosperous. Not least among these were the Amati family with their lucrative violin exporting business.'

'Whose praises *I* was supposed to be singing,' Grace interjected, with just enough irony to disturb her father's flow.

'Right again, Angel... I mean Grace,' Randolph replied, half-embarrassed, half-amused. 'So, why don't you tell me about the Amati family, while I try to keep quiet? You have about an hour before we reach Rockford, will that be enough time?'

'Almost!' said Grace, barely able to suppress a smile. 'I know that Andrea Amati is your favourite maker and that he was born in Cremona sometime around 1505, a dozen or so years after Christopher Columbus discovered America.' She paused briefly. 'Actually it was the Bahamas. The truth is that Columbus never actually made it to the North American mainland.'

10

Eager to prove herself now, Grace was bubbling over with enthusiasm. 'And,' she added, 'the idea that scholars and seafarers of the time believed the world was flat, cannot be true either. Even the ancient Greeks knew that the earth was round.'

'You and your ancient Greeks!' Randolph replied, waving his hand as if to say, 'Get on with the story.'

'Yes, sir!' Grace answered with a cheeky salute. 'Around the time of Andrea Amati's birth, Leonardo da Vinci was busy painting the *Mona Lisa*, while Michelangelo was completing his sculpture *David*.'

Grace paused for effect, before taking a deep breath and continuing: 'By the end of Andrea Amati's life in 1577, Niccolò Machiavelli's most important work, *Il Principe*, had been published, Martin Luther had posted his *Ninety-five Theses*, Giorgio Vasari had written his *Lives of the*

Most Eminent Painters, Sculptors and Architects, Nicolaus Copernicus had published *De Revolutionibus*, and in spite of the enormous loss of ships and lives, Ferdinand Magellan's expedition had circumnavigated the world. And, somewhere in the midst of all this activity, Andrea Amati had become a master instrument maker, and by 1539, he had opened his own workshop in Cremona.

'Although Brescian makers did not date their instruments, according to your journals, in 1938, the Cremonese historian Carlo Bonetti established that Brescia's first known violin maker, Gasparo da Salò, was born in 1542, by which time Andrea Amati was already about forty years old. So, it seems reasonable to suppose that it was not the Brescian school, but Andrea Amati and his sons that developed the violin, which then became the prototype for virtually every violin that followed, up to and including the present day.

'When Andrea Amati died in 1577, his two sons, Antonio and Hieronymus Amati, were named as his heirs. By that time, the Amati workshop was already a highly sophisticated international business, mainly producing and exporting instruments of the violin family. In turn, Hieronymus Amati had a son called Nicola. Nicola was not only the greatest maker of the Amati dynasty, but directly or indirectly he was responsible for teaching the art of violin making to several Cremonese artisans, including the Guarneri, Stradivari and Ruggeri families. From these makers the secrets of violin making quickly passed to the rest of the world. This same Nicola also had a son called Hieronymus II, who became the last member of the Amati dynasty. All told, the Amati family produced instruments in Cremona for more than two centuries. How am I doing so far?'

Randolph was seriously impressed, but he could not stop himself from making a further comment. 'You are almost certainly right about the Amati family's role in developing the violin. However, I would also argue that although successive Cremonese makers like Antonio Stradivari and Guarneri del Gesù managed to improve the violin in terms of power and tone, Nicola Amati fashioned the most aesthetically beautiful instruments of all time. Furthermore, the consistency of his craftsmanship was second to none.'

This was something new. Grace took her eyes off the road ahead and turned to her father. 'Are you saying that Nicola Amati was actually better than Antonio Stradivari?'

'Aesthetically I believe he was,' her father replied. 'In order to achieve certain practicalities, the Stradivari and Guarneri families were prepared to sacrifice the purity of line and balance that the Amatis had so carefully perfected. Of course, for people like us, such changes were fortunate, because it is the subtle differences between the Amati family's designs, and those of their Cremonese pupils and followers, including Stradivari, that are the key to instrument identification. And it did not stop there, because once the influence of classical Cremonese instruments became almost ubiquitous, this same rule applied to every subsequent violin maker, up to and including the present day. Indeed, the simplest definition of instrument recognition is how much a particular maker's method, materials and style deviates from that of the Amati family. I hope that this will become apparent as you accompany me on the road, Grace.'

11

Barely three weeks later, towards the end of October, Grace and her father were on the road again. Following rumours that a member of the Lincoln Little Symphony Orchestra was about to sell his 1672 Francesco Ruggeri violin, Randolph and Grace made their way across the Great Plains of Illinois, Iowa and Nebraska, stopping at Cedar Rapids, Iowa City, Des Moines, Omaha and many points in between. The Ruggeri may have provided the initial incentive, but Randolph was experienced enough not to pin too much hope on rumour alone. Accordingly, he had instructed Grace to place advertisements in several local newspapers on their route. She had also written letters and sent out flyers to orchestras, music societies and teachers. These notifications proudly announced that the famous Chicago violin connoisseur, Mr Randolph Scott, would be visiting the area and would be valuing instruments for insurance purposes. It was made clear that this service was free of charge and that there would be no obligation to purchase cover. Randolph was mindful of the fact that although the general population was still euphoric about the recent news of Japan's unconditional surrender and the end of World War II, for working people, times were still hard, and few jobbing musicians could afford insurance premiums. Nevertheless, this was of little concern, because the main object of this exercise was not to sell insurance, but to locate instruments that might eventually be for sale.

When they arrived at their Lincoln hotel, there was a veritable clamour of musicians waiting in the lobby to consult the famous Chicago violin connoisseur, Mr Randolph Scott.

The Ruggeri turned out to be an interesting find. According to its label, the instrument had been made in Cremona, in 1672. It had been purchased from a well-known dealer in New York and was accompanied by a large portfolio of papers and certificates from several respected authorities. It was an attractive violin, and considering its age, it was in a remarkably good state of preservation. After briefly examining the instrument, Randolph handed it to his daughter and asked her to consider its authenticity and condition and say whether they should make an offer.

'Take your time, Grace,' he said. 'Take it to your room. Use your dentist's mirror and your small electric torch to look inside. Write a comprehensive condition report; this is an important instrument, so we don't want to make any mistakes. Try and think about everything you have learned about Francesco Ruggeri: who he was, where he worked and what features you might expect to find. And remember, if you have any doubts, write them down and we can discuss them together over lunch. In the meantime, I will be assessing a dozen or so violins and a cello that people have brought along in response to your advertising campaign. I've already had a quick look. There doesn't appear to be anything spectacular, but there may be a couple of pot boilers.'

Grace was excited. At the shop, her father had often asked her opinion, but this was the first time he had invited her to make a full written assessment on her own. She already knew that Francesco Ruggeri was one of the most important makers working in the Cremonese tradition, and that his works closely resemble those of Nicola Amati. Indeed, the Hill brothers of London, the world's most famous violin connoisseurs, were convinced Nicola Amati was Francesco Ruggeri's teacher.

Grace sat down at a small table and quietly composed herself for the task ahead. After laying the violin on a soft cashmere cloth, she took out her notebook, a newly sharpened pencil, a tape measure, a short boxwood ruler, and a veneer calliper. A jeweller's eyeglass, a dentist's mirror and a small electric torch completed the ensemble. She would need to systematically check every known feature before reaching a conclusion.

Having already washed her hands, she picked up the violin and began by recording its vital statistics. Her father had taught her that gradually working through this measuring process helps to order the mind before the real examination begins. 'A good routine is essential when examining any instrument,' he had always told her.

'Without routine you can easily miss something of real importance.'

After recording more than one hundred predetermined measurements, Grace checked the instrument for damage. Her grandfather had taught her how and what to look for. He had been a strict but fair teacher. Using examples of his own invisible repair work, he had shown her how a skilful repairman can glue cracks, then make them disappear by carefully retouching the varnish. She had been astounded to see that even looking with her jeweller's eyeglass, cracks that her grandfather had repaired were often virtually invisible. Watching her reaction, the old man had said, 'Iz not so difficult. Given enough time you can repair almost any damage on a violin.' Although Grace knew that this was probably true, she also knew that such work required the kind of skill and experience that few violin makers possessed.

'Zee best vay to find an invisible repair is to look behind it, inside ze instrument. To prevent a repaired crack from reopening it needs to be reinforced. Zis can be done in several vays. The qvickest and easiest vay is to place a number of small vooden studs at intervals along ze crack… Inside ze violin of course, zay vud look stupid on ze outside,' he had added, laughing at his own joke. 'Zeese can usually be seen through ze violin's soundholes, although you vill need to use a dentist inspection mirror to see zem on ze belly. Probably ze easiest tings to see are patches. Patches are applied to support places where zehr are lots of parallel cracks, or cracks running across ze grain, or areas of ze back or belly zat are too dunn—'

'You mean *thin*,' Grace interrupted.

'Ya! Und patches can also be disguised, but zay can almost alvays be detected at ze edges, where ze grain lines do not match up. Patches are not easy to hide.

'Owever, sometimes ven ze sides of a violin have been smashed, because zees strips of vood are extremely thin, ze repair man vill occasionally reinforce ze broken piece wiz a veneer of ze same size, made from similar material. If zis work is done vell, it can be undetectable both inside and out. It takes lots of experience and a good eye to spot such a repair. A connoisseur usually finds such repairs only after noticing some other *apparently unrelated abnormality*.' Grace smiled to herself; her grandfather had struggled with these final unfamiliar words. She knew that he was repeating words and phrases that her father frequently used. 'But wiz time you vill learn zees things too,' he had concluded with reassurance.

Grace had often been privy to discussions between her father and grandfather on the subject of violin expertise. Although never heated, these discussions were often protracted and intense, especially during Chicago's icy winter months when the three of them would sit in front of a blazing log fire.

Probably because of his own proud violin-making apprenticeship, Grace's grandfather always maintained that violin makers everywhere, including the great Italian craftsmen, are not so much artists as highly skilled artisans. Although he conceded that the work of the great classical Italian makers often transcended simple craftsmanship, he insisted that all musical instruments are the product of a systematic and business-like approach to a sophisticated but repetitive craft. He argued that the powerful master craftsmen of each town or city determined which type and pattern of instrument could be constructed and which materials and method were to be employed. Their aim being simply to reproduce identical high-quality instruments every time.

According to her grandfather, centuries ago towns and cities were far more isolated and autonomous than they are today. This meant that in each place, groups or schools of artisans developed their own unique and often secret methods of working towards the same goal. Grace already knew that being able to recognise which method was used to make an instrument helps connoisseurs to identify where an instrument was made. And, once you are able to identify where an instrument was made, then the individuals within that school can be further identified by the singular way they used their tools and the materials they employed. He insisted that even though craftsmen in a particular school used the same plans and templates as their colleagues, the repetitive nature of their work causes each maker to develop specific idiosyncrasies or personal traits; in other words, their own individual style.

Together in her grandfather's workshop, Grace and the old man would hypothetically disassemble instruments into their various parts. One of her favourite lessons had been when he had tackled the instrument's head. He had told her how this part of the instrument provided one of the most important clues for instrument identification, while at the same time posing some of the most difficult questions.

He explained how this part of the instrument is intricately carved from a solid block of maple and that like much of the violin itself, it is a complex amalgam of utilitarian and decorative features. Within this structure, a simple box is created to hold the wooden pegs with which the instrument's strings are tuned. This *peg-box* then terminates in a carved form known as the scroll. According to her father it was given this name because it resembled the ancient rolls or scrolls of paper, or papyrus, upon which knowledge was recorded before the development of printing.

Her father had gone on to explain how the ancient Greeks had carved variations of the scroll motif on the tops of the massive stone columns; the ones that supported the roofs of buildings like the Parthenon in Athens. He explained how Greek and later Roman architects had gone on to develop many stylised spiral forms, all derived from natural objects, including shells, ferns and the horns of certain animals. He concluded that these forms were later taken up and developed by Renaissance artisans, like the Amati family of instrument makers. But her grandfather had insisted that the German word *Schnecke*, meaning snail or spiral, better described the violin's scroll.

Occasionally, a violin's pegbox was finished in the shape of a lion's head, the finest examples of which were created by another early instrument maker, Jacobus Stainer. According to Grace's father, although Stainer was of German origin, his method indicated that he must have been taught violin making by the Amati family in Cremona. These rare lion-head examples may have been one of her grandfather's favourites, but from Andrea Amati onwards, the overwhelming majority of violin makers completed the peg box by carving a scroll. And, for violin makers working within strict traditional boundaries, these carved scrolls became a kind of artistic statement, a signature.

Having carefully recorded the Ruggeri's measurements, Grace perused the instrument's various component parts to see if their features corresponded with what she had learned about the work of Francesco Ruggeri. Remembering what her father and grandfather had taught her, she began with the head and neck. The first essential was to establish if the head had been made by the same person that had made the main body of the violin, and whose label was fixed inside the instrument, or if it had been carved by someone from the same school, a relation perhaps or an apprentice, or whether the head was simply a later replacement, having nothing to do with the Ruggeri school. Grace was well aware that a replacement head would devalue the instrument considerably.

After several nervous minutes Grace was relieved to see that everything seemed just right. The wood from which the head was carved was definitely of Cremonese quality. Moreover, although the scroll's form and flow followed an Amati design, the workmanship was unquestionably in the style of Francesco Ruggeri, especially the undercutting of the volutes, which were characteristically flat around the first turn.

Satisfied, Grace moved on to the main body of the instrument. After checking the black and white inlaid strips around the edgework and corners, she eventually examined the shape of the instrument's arched back and front, together with the form and cut of the F-shaped soundholes.

Grace already knew that the arching and soundholes

are what make a violin resonate and function the way that it should. Without their complex curves, no violin would be able to withstand the pressure of the strings. Furthermore, a good arching amplifies the string vibration, enabling the instrument to fill a large concert hall with sound.

On completing her examination, Grace was convinced that, as with the head, the main body of the instrument also conformed to all the usual Ruggeri criteria. All the features that she might have expected to see were present; the shape of the outline, the cut and form of the soundholes, arching and the materials and application of the inlay.

The corners and edgework were somewhat worn, but not inconsistent with an instrument of the Ruggeri's age. The archings of the front and back were almost perfect, which *was* somewhat unusual for a Ruggeri, but not for an instrument with no visible damage.

The varnish itself was shiny and highly polished. Although her father had taught her to be wary of shiny fiddles, the instrument's provenance papers indicated that the Ruggeri had spent some time in New York City, and her grandfather had always said that because New Yorkers liked bright shiny things, they had a tendency to over-polish their violins. In any case, Grace was convinced that the violin had been made by Francesco Ruggeri in Cremona, in or around the year 1672, and she was almost right.

When her father returned from assessing the other instruments, Grace was putting the finishing touches to her notes. She was pleased with her morning's work and ready for the sandwiches and coffee her father had ordered from room service. Although Grace was keen to talk about her findings, her father refused to say anything about the Ruggeri, or any of the other instruments, until they had finished eating. Only when the cutlery and crockery had been taken away did Randolph begin, but he started not by asking about the Ruggeri, but about its owner.

'He seems a nice old man,' Grace had replied with a broad grin. 'He was almost certainly an exceptional player, but I think he is struggling to keep up the required standard. He probably should have retired years ago. Is that why he's selling the Ruggeri?'

'So I've been told,' Randolph answered, before asking Grace if she had brought her notes.

'Yes!' she answered with enthusiasm, as she pulled several papers from her satchel.

'I don't mean those notes,' her father said. 'I mean the ones you've collected over the years. Do you have them with you?'

'Certainly!' she answered again, but this time more slowly.

'Tell me what they say about the grain structure of Francesco Ruggeri's belly wood?'

A little unnerved, Grace pulled out her ledger and fumbled through the pages. Eventually, she found what she had been looking for. 'It says that Francesco Ruggeri's belly wood is similar to that used by Nicola Amati. It is of high quality and perfectly quarter sawn. The year rings are usually narrow, straight-grained and evenly spaced. A second note says that the year rings are not as narrow as the wood used by the violin makers of the Mittenwald school, in the German Alpine region.'

'And what do your notes say about the shape of Ruggeri's archings?'

Again, it was several seconds before Grace found the relevant section. 'It says that archings on Francesco Ruggeri violins are often distorted. The bellies have a tendency to collapse, especially on the soundpost side.'

'And the belly arching on this particular Ruggeri?' Randolph asked.

'The instrument has no cracks or repairs and is in such good shape that I figured… Well it all just looks so pure.'

'What about the corners and edges? Do they seem pure and unworn?'

'They are consistent with the instrument's age?' she said, as if she were asking herself the question.

She was nervous now.

'And the varnish?'

'I admit that it is very over-polished, but according to the provenance papers, it was in New York for several years.'

'So, do you think it's worth buying?'

'I had thought so, but you're starting to worry me.'

'OK! So, let's look at it together.'

Without fuss Randolph took the Ruggeri from its case and laid it on the cashmere cloth. Placing a jeweller's glass to his eye he examined the area around the soundholes. Having done so, he turned to Grace.

'This belly wood is typical high-quality Cremonese wood. It is exactly what you would expect to find on a Francesco Ruggeri. The reason why Cremonese violin makers chose this kind of wood is because it was grown in the mountains at high altitude. Being so high up, the climate was cold, and because the trees were covered with snow for much of the year, the growing season was very short. As a result, the year rings are always extremely narrow and very close together. This kind of growth pattern makes the best tone wood for musical instruments. It is exceptionally strong and light, and it vibrates freely. By comparison, because the climate is mild, and the growing season longer, timber from trees of the same species that are grown in lower regions are heavy and more resinous, and as a result, the sound that such timbers produce is often muted and dull. The year rings are much thicker and more widely spaced. Looking carefully at the growth pattern of such trees, you can easily see which summers were good and which were bad. It's almost like looking at a retrospective weather forecast. Unfortunately, mountainous terrain makes it extremely difficult to harvest these fine high-altitude trees. This means that tone woods of this nature are expensive, and they were always expensive, even centuries ago when this particular piece of wood was harvested.

'But the thing is, even up in the high mountains, growing seasons varied. If it was a good year in the valleys and plains, it was usually a good year in any nearby mountains too. And, although these differences can be difficult to see with the naked eye, with a jeweller's glass they quickly become obvious. For this reason, on all violin bellies, however good the quality, there will always be one or two year rings that stand out, even to the naked eye, but of course, you know all this, Grace.'

'I'm not sure I understand what you are saying though,' she answered. 'Are you trying to tell me that this is not the work of Francesco Ruggeri?'

'In all its essential parts it would seem to be correct, but… take a look at this stronger year ring here,' her father said, pointing with a pencil to a slightly wider grain line. 'This was obviously the product of a good summer. Now, since this piece of belly wood is probably less than one-eighth of an inch thick,[1] this wider line should also be visible on the inside. Do you agree?'

Grace nodded her agreement.

'Then please, using your dentist's mirror and your torch, look through the soundhole and see if you can find it… No wait!' he said. 'Use *my* mirror. It has a slight magnification. It's not good for general observation work, but it is useful if you are looking for something specific.'

Grace took the mirror. She had seen it before; the glass was slightly dished, like a shallow bowl. After spending several minutes with the mirror and the torch, Grace turned to her father.

'I can't seem to find it.'

She felt cold sweat on the back of her neck.

'What should that tell you, Grace?'

'I…' she began, but she was struggling even to speak now. She was not afraid of her father, but she was afraid that she had missed something vital. She started again, 'Well, I guess it suggests that something is wrong. At first, I had assumed there must be a patch on the inside, but I can't see any patches. What am I missing?'

'Look again, Grace. The entire belly is covered by one huge patch. This patch has been feathered out at the edges, so that if one uses a mirror in the normal way, the patch

---

[1] One-eighth of an inch = 3,18 mm.

cannot be seen. At some point, this belly suffered some serious damage, and once the cracks had been fixed and made invisible, a full-sized patch was inserted, rather like fitting one belly inside another. The damage is well hidden, but the violin no longer sounds like a pure Ruggeri should. It is rather like playing on an instrument made of plywood. It is not the musician's age that's causing him problems. It's the violin itself. In my opinion, he is neither ill nor about to retire, what he is trying to do is provide a reason for the instrument's substandard sound.'

'But how did you see this so quickly? You barely looked at it when we arrived.'

'I didn't see it, Grace,' her father replied, 'I already knew about it. This violin was repaired in 1910, by an exceptionally gifted French colleague of Grandpa Scott. He was two years younger than your grandpa when he arrived in Chicago in 1905. He had been taught violin making in Mirecourt, the French violin making centre. Your grandpa and grandma helped him to settle and they quickly became good friends and business partners. When America entered World War I, he enlisted and was sent back to Europe, where in 1918, he was killed at the Battle of the Lys. Losing a close friend in this way was hard on your grandpa, especially since their home countries were fighting each other.

'This Frenchman was a talented restorer, but he was working for a dubious dealer, who persuaded him to do this work. According to your grandfather, there was never any doubt that this work was carried out with the intention to deceive. The New York story was invented later, to explain the instrument's highly polished finish, which had been done to help hide the violin's extensive repair work.

'I had the chance to see this violin in the 1920s, when it repeatedly came into our shop for adjustment. The sound was always a problem and the violin had already been sold several times before it finally left Chicago. So, when Grandpa heard that the violin was for sale, we decided that it would provide you with another excellent lesson.'

'Are you saying that you drove us halfway across America just to give me another lesson? Aren't you both being a bit extreme?'

'I don't think so, Grace. There are few better examples of how to lose money fast. Your friendly violinist may appear to be a nice doddery old man, but I assure you he is still an exceptional player. He was pretending to be frail so that we would not question the violin's inferior sound. He is fully aware of the Ruggeri's condition and if we had not known the fiddle's history, he would have sold it to us without batting an eyelid.

'The thing about information is that usually the more you know the better off you are. Nevertheless, no matter how all-inclusive your information might appear to be, in itself it does not constitute wisdom. You have reached a difficult stage in your education, Grace. Theoretically, you are as well versed in the essential characteristics of fine violins as any top connoisseur, but moving from theory to practice is never easy. Familiarity with such details may be an essential part of a connoisseur's schooling but relying on them entirely is the mark of a novice. Accordingly, it is the novice who will take fright if a feature that is normally associated with a specific maker is not present on a genuine instrument. In the same way, it is the novice who will accept a fake, simply because it includes *all* the salient features of a maker's work. And, as you have just discovered, missing or ignoring details that should have set off alarm bells might have cost Scott's a lot of money.' Her father was smiling broadly now. 'Look, Grace,' he said, 'if it is any consolation, when your grandfather first showed me this instrument, I made the same mistake. But so far, I have never made that particular mistake again and neither will you.'

'But it has already cost us money,' she replied. She was clearly concerned. 'We've come all this way for nothing… or are we going to buy it cheap? After all, it's still more or less a Francesco Ruggeri.'

'No, Grace! Even if we could knock the price down, I would never want to sell this fiddle. No matter how honest we were about its condition, this kind of restoration work is dishonest in its intent, and our name would always be associated with it. We've talked about this before, Grace, it would damage the family's hard-earned reputation, and in this business, reputation is everything. Anyway, I have uncovered one or two minor gems among the rest of the lots. We can buy and sell them with impunity, and they will more than cover our expenses. And didn't we have a good time?'

12

Grace had smiled at her father's last remark. Even though fate had not always been kind to him, her father had always had a positive attitude. From time to time she had tried to put herself in his shoes. In 1917 the United States had declared war on Germany. As a result, Grandfather Scott's movements had been severely curtailed, and from the age of thirteen, Randolph had been forced to work in the family business. By the age of twenty-one, he had not only experienced the lingering death of his mother, but he had also been obliged to take on the day-to-day running of the family business that in his grief, his father had become incapable of managing.

Following this, in quick succession, Randolph had met, married and lost the love of *his* life, before being left alone to raise a new-born baby girl. Grace had tried to understand her father's predicament, but like most young people, the world of her parents and grandparents was as much ancient history as were her heroes of Greek and Norse mythology. She could rationalise her father's and grandfather's stories, just as she could rationalise the war and her own mother's death, but she could not easily empathise with things she had never experienced. And yet somehow, her father had survived these tribulations, and until her grandfather had recovered enough to return to his workshop, he had gone on to rescue and develop the company's commercial business alone.

Travelling the length and breadth of the United States, Randolph had gradually learned the ins and outs of violin dealing and expertise. By the time the Great Depression had deepened, following the Wall Street Crash of 1929, young Randolph Scott was already a recognised and respected name in the violin world. By the time he turned thirty in 1934, he had made several trips to Europe, where in London, Paris and Rome, he had purchased several classical Italian violins from well-established but hard-pressed dealers.

In London, one of his best contacts had been Horatio Montague. Horatio Montague's shop in London's West End was a bastion of English tradition. An imposing marble pillared door led to an interior that was all glass chandeliers, polished wood and gleaming brass handles. The whole building smelled of beeswax. It was a place primed to receive royalty. As a result, notwithstanding his fine clothes, Randolph always felt somewhat out of place. Compounding this feeling, on his first visit to Montague's in 1933, Randolph had also been introduced to Edward Montague.

Edward Montague, Horatio's only son and heir, had

attended Eton College before joining the family firm. Aged twenty-one, Edward was eight years younger than Randolph, but this tall, healthy-looking young man had an air of superiority about him that had immediately unsettled Randolph. The younger man's Old Etonian accent was also a puzzle. It was almost a parody of King's English, with many additional words and phrases that Randolph had failed to find, even in a recently published *Oxford English Dictionary*.

In spite of his initial discomfort, within months of their first meeting, Randolph had purchased several fine violins, initially from Horatio and later from Edward Montague. Indeed, had he but known it, Randolph was Montague's most valued customer. His dollars may not have been essential to keep Montague's afloat, but in those times of austerity, they helped keep up appearances; and appearances meant everything to the Montagues.

Notwithstanding his importance, Randolph was led to believe that, by allowing him to purchase their beautiful Italian violins, the Montagues were doing him a personal favour. Even so, on returning to the United States, Randolph was still able to turn a handsome profit. Indeed, after one such trip, he had allowed himself the luxury of returning to the States on the Cunard-White Star Line's new flagship, the RMS *Queen Mary*. He had been accompanied by two Nicola Amati violins, a Peter Guarneri of Venice and a fine Golden Period violin by Antonio Stradivari. It had been Randolph's richest haul so far, and he was bubbling with pride as he settled back in the *Queen*'s lavish concert hall to hear the ship's resident musicians play Beethoven's String Quartet No. 14 in C-sharp Minor.

In 1936, Edward Montague had married the daughter of his father's best friend, Daphne Fortescue Smythe; a beautiful debutante who had recently been presented at the English court. A respectable nine months later, a new heir to the Montague family empire was born. His name was James.

In 1939, following the outbreak of World War II in Europe, travel between the United States and Britain was severely restricted. Although the United States was still neutral, Randolph's wonderful trips on the *Queen Mary* abruptly ceased when she was converted into a troupe transporter.

For Britain, 1939 marked the beginning of five years of suffering and adversity. Leaving his wife and child at home, Edward Montague had entered the Infantry Officer Cadet Training Unit at the Sandhurst Royal Military Academy. In 1940 he received an emergency commission and joined his father's old regiment, the Coldstream Guards. His first and only involvement in the war came when he was sent to join the British Expeditionary Force in Europe, just as it was retreating to Dunkirk. On the 29th and 30th of May 1940, the defence of the Dunkirk perimeter had held, allowing the Allies to fall back to the evacuation beaches. However, on the 31st of May, Edward's Coldstream Guards were sent to reinforce a break in the line, where British troupes were threatening to abandon their position. The Guards eventually restored order, by shooting some of the fleeing troops and turning others around at bayonet point.

Eventually, the German assault was beaten back, and the British troops returned to hold the line. Somewhat ironically, having never raised a weapon in anger, the first and only shots that Edward fired in World War II were over the heads of his own countrymen. But, since Eton had been organised like a minor military regime, Edward had already learned that however bizarre, orders were never questioned. In any event, Edward did not regret his actions at Dunkirk; as far as he was concerned, these runaways were cowardly working-class guttersnipes. Instilled in him at his exclusive private school, it was an attitude that would remain with him for the rest of his life.

This evacuation came to be known as the Miracle of Dunkirk. But for Edward the greatest miracle happened when he arrived back in the UK. While disembarking, he fell from a jetty in the Thames estuary and suffered a badly fractured femur. As a result, he spent the rest of the war initially in a series of plaster casts and later learning to walk with the aid of crutches.

While Edward was convalescing in rural England, on the 7th of September that same year, the London Blitz had begun. It continued for fifty-six of the following fifty-seven days and nights. After one daylight raid, amid the rubble of a bombed Mayfair house, an auxiliary fireman was surprised to find Edward's three-year-old son, James, unharmed beneath his mother's lifeless body. Her remains were buried before Edward had the chance to see her again.

Like Randolph, Edward Montague had been left alone to raise a child, but circumstances affect people in different ways. Edward's attitude to life had simply hardened. Somewhere in the back of his mind, he blamed his son for the death of his wife and thereafter avoided all physical contact with the boy.

Edward returned to the family's violin business with a slight limp, which gave credence to the idea that he had been wounded in action and was therefore a war hero. Making the most of this assumption, he started to affect a military bearing in everything he did. Eventually, this included organising the violin shop and its staff as if they were part of a military campaign. The problem was that most were heartily sick of conflict and being told what to do. Moreover, being somewhat emotionally unstable himself, Edward found it difficult to sympathise with other people's problems, which only made matters worse.

In an effort to keep his employees at a distance, Edward endeavoured to communicate through military-style briefings, during which he was fond of quoting cheesy lines from popular songs; one of his favourites being 'Pick Yourself Up' from the 1936 film *Swing Time,* starring Fred Astaire and Ginger Rogers. On the first full working day after VE Day, Edward gave his staff a pep talk, which concluded with him quoting extensively from the song's lyrics, until everyone but himself was cringing with embarrassment.

As well as Edward's wife, many of the Montague workforce had been killed, or had lost loved ones themselves, either in the London Blitz or fighting with British forces somewhere in the world. Directly or indirectly almost no one had survived unscathed. Remarkably however, in spite of Hitler's protracted bombing campaign, the Montague family's West End premises and their extensive stock of instruments were still intact.

After the war, for reasons beyond Randolph's control, the violin business in America had changed radically in his favour. Holding out alone for so long had left Britain virtually bankrupt, and now America was reaping the harvest. Its businessmen had already profited handsomely from World War II, and in its aftermath they continued to do so. Whereas before the war Randolph had been expected to travel to European violin shops, from October 1945 these same dealers began arriving cap in hand, seeking *his* custom. Chief amongst them was Edward Montague.

Edward hated the idea of having to deal with the Yanks in this way. They had arrived late on the scene in World War II, just as they had in World War I. He certainly concurred with the current British opinion that GIs were *over paid, over sexed and over here*. Already tens of thousands of British women were in the process of marrying GIs and emigrating to the United States. What chance did a man with a war-damaged leg and a young child have of finding a suitable wife now?

Nevertheless, after the hardship of London, the United States and Chicago in particular offered Edward a welcome respite. Being removed from the sombre atmosphere of London's painful post-war recovery, he gradually found himself able to relax in the Windy City.

As far as was possible between such diverse characters, Randolph considered Edward a friend. Indeed, the first time Edward had crossed the Atlantic, in October 1945, Randolph had invited him to stay at the Scotts' comfortable family home. It was a perfect arrangement. For Edward, it saved on expensive hotel bills. For Randolph, it meant having first choice of the instruments that Edward was offering. Desperate for sales to replenish the Montague family coffers, Edward was carrying instruments of the finest quality only. His first foray into the new world was so profitable that in spite of the increased risk of storms, in December he was back again. The following year, as regular as clockwork, he returned every three months.

Since the round trip took at least two weeks, ostensibly this was a considerable feat, however, Edward was very much a man of leisure, and as well as the Scotts' hospitality, he made good use of his time on board ship. The truth was that there were a great many distractions to occupy Edward's highly attuned senses of indolence and pleasure.

By comparison Grace was a workhorse. Returning from Nebraska, following their first serious road trip, Grace barely had time to spruce both herself and the Studebaker before her father had driven off to collect Edward Montague from Chicago's Central Station. In fact, she was still recording the trip's meagre pickings in the company's inventory when her father introduced them.

Although only sixteen, Randolph Scott's daughter looked and acted like a much older woman. She was heavily built, with a rounded stomach, full hips and ample breasts; nevertheless, she was elegant and as she walked every part of her swayed rhythmically. A shock of fiery orange hair surrounded a soft, friendly and strikingly beautiful face.

A devotee of Hollywood films, in Grace Scott, Edward recognised something special. She not only resembled Ginger Rogers, albeit somewhat heavier, but she also appeared to be a woman without fear, like Vivien Leigh's character Scarlett O'Hara in *Gone with the Wind*. *Can she dance?* he'd wondered.

Grace herself had been immediately smitten by this tall, handsome, thirty-two-year-old man. With the consummate ease of a man well versed in the social niceties, Edward had bowed his head and raised her hand, almost, but not quite, to his lips. He had an accent like the British actor David Niven, who Grace had seen in a 1942 film about the development of the Supermarine Spitfire fighter aircraft. Like Niven, Edward had been a British Army officer, moreover, from his slightly awkward gait, it was obvious that Edward had been wounded in action and was probably a hero. In addition, he was a senior partner at Montague Fine Violins, and as such, he was almost certainly a violin aficionado. What more could a girl want?

In spite of being a widower, Edward had very little experience with women; Eton and the Guards had been strictly men-only environments. The rare contact that he had had with womankind had been limited to events in the debutantes' calendar. These events, which included the Henley Regatta, Royal Ascot and similar social gatherings, had all been heavily chaperoned.

Fundamentally, in manner and appearance, the young debutantes Edward was permitted to meet were virtually identical. They were placed on pedestals and their only physical contact with men came while dancing at various invitation-only balls. Of course, Edward had been schooled to wear the right clothes and behave in the correct manner, but as was the case for most of his male friends and acquaintances, women largely remained a mystery. One or two of his Eton school comrades had experienced prostitutes and loose women of the town. Their stories were eagerly awaited in the dorms, but they were always exaggerated, embellished and embroidered, long before being rehashed ad infinitum.

Although convinced that he had met his young debutante wife entirely by chance, Edward's marriage had been carefully prearranged while the pair were still prepubescent teenagers. At first the union had been amicable. In fact, until war had been declared in 1939, their relationship, including their courtship and marriage, had been a succession of parties, balls, concerts and trips to West End theatres.

Even after the birth of their child, nannies and servants made sure that the couple's busy social calendar was not disturbed by their offspring. Like most debutantes, Edward's new wife was a wonderful dancer and Edward genuinely loved dancing. His Eton schooling had included dance lessons and he had quickly become a skilled and passionate dancer. Unfortunately, it soon became apparent that his new wife's love of expensive social events also included many of the young men who attended them.

13

The day after war had been declared, sports and popular pastimes were immediately suspended, but because of their value to morale, cinemas, theatres and dancehalls quickly reopened. This proved to be a wise decision, because from that moment, every week in Britain, between 25 and 30 million cinema tickets alone were sold.

Following Dunkirk, Edward's 'war damaged' leg and the loss of his wife had initially prevented him from stepping out. Instead, he had become a devotee of dance films, especially those with Fred Astaire and Ginger Rogers in starring roles. But the war was over now, and he was back in America, a thirty-two-year-old cripple, being confronted by a confident young woman with hair like spun gold and eyes to match. Edward was acutely aware that Grace was the last of the Scott family dynasty. She was well educated, and according to Randolph Scott, she was well on the way to becoming the world's first female connoisseur. And, as if this were not enough, she was a Ginger Rogers lookalike, with the confidence of a Scarlett O'Hara. She would certainly fit the bill; in fact, she was almost too good to be true.

That night Edward danced in his dreams.

The following morning Edward and Randolph completed their business with remarkable speed. Not only were the instruments fine and genuine examples, but they were all reasonably priced. Even Hermann, Grace's normally sceptical grandfather, was pleased. In the meantime, while the men attended to business Grace had prepared a veritable feast for their house guest. Not wishing to appear voracious, Edward had attempted to restrain his appetite, but having survived years of draconian rationing in the UK, the sight of this richly laid American table had proved impossible to resist.

Later that same evening, Grace was still clearing the kitchen after their rather prolonged meal. Randolph had returned to his office to finish the paperwork pertaining to his latest purchase, and Hermann had gone upstairs to his room for a quiet nap. Keen to appear useful, Edward offered to help Grace with the washing-up. This was something he would never have considered back home in England but having observed Grace's father and grandfather working in the kitchen the night before, he felt no sense of shame as he picked up a towel and started drying the dishes. In the relaxed atmosphere of the Scott household, things were quite different from anything he had experienced in London.

As Edward and Grace worked silently together in the kitchen, a large Wurlitzer radio played American dance music in the adjacent living room. And, just as they had finished putting the dishes away, Glenn Miller and His Orchestra began playing 'Moonlight Serenade'. Having wiped the surfaces clean, Grace was standing with her back to the sink, looking to see that nothing had been forgotten. Absentmindedly, she tapped her foot to the 4/4 time beat and visualised the step sequence of a slow foxtrot.

'Do you dance?' Edward said suddenly.

It was an invitation rather than a question and it surprised even himself.

'I do a little,' Grace replied.

Without another word he stepped forward, took hold of her hand, and placing his other arm around her waist, he drew her close. Grace felt herself merge with the curves of his body as if she had always belonged there. Edward's limp magically disappeared and soon, quite naturally, they were drifting effortlessly around the small space as if they were in a vast ballroom. Grace felt elegant and weightless as she wheeled and turned, following Edward's lead as if she had been doing so all her life.

Edward felt the soft volume of her orange hair against his cheek. 'You don't just look like Ginger Rogers...' he said, but just as he was about to add, 'you dance like her as well,' he suddenly became acutely aware that he was dancing and flirting with a sixteen-year-old girl in her father's kitchen. Leaving the sentence incomplete Edward relaxed his hold, but Grace was not about to let that happen. Tightening her grip on his hand, she pulled herself into his arms until he could feel her muscular strength.

She may be a little round, he told himself, *but she is a powerful woman.*

There were no more excuses now. As they turned and twirled in the enclosed space, Edward could no longer deny the curves of her body moving rhythmically against his. It had been a long time since he had held a woman so close, but in that moment, he could feel the danger as keenly as he sensed the cocktail of hormones that were coursing through Grace's body.

Mercifully the music ended, but as he stepped away and thanked her for the dance, he could not prevent himself from saying, 'We must do this again some time.'

As Edward spoke, Grace's legs abruptly lost their strength. They did not give way entirely as she walked into the living room and sat by the fire, but having skipped so elegantly around the floor, she was having to concentrate hard now to avoid stumbling over her own feet.

Very little was said as they waited for her father to return from his office. When he arrived, the two men shared a bottle of red wine and small talk, while Grace quietly drank a glass of sarsaparilla. At some point, Randolph casually suggested, 'Seeing that this is your first visit to Chicago, Edward, would you like to see or do anything special while you are here?'

Edward reflected for a moment. 'Actually, this may sound silly, but I would love to see a movie.'

'Oh, I'm sure that we can arrange that,' Randolph answered. 'What would you like to see?'

'If it is really no problem, I would love to see Fred Astaire and Ginger Rogers in *Top Hat*. The last time I saw it was in London, before the war, and I noticed they are showing it again here in town.'

Randolph was more than a little dismayed. After his

wife's untimely death, he had lost interest in both dancing and dance music. These days he preferred the more ordered format of serious classical works, where audiences are expected to remain quiet for the duration of each piece and not to applaud between movements. He certainly did not relish the prospect of watching a beautiful dancer like Ginger Rogers, reminding him of what he had lost.

On seeing her father's hesitation, Grace suddenly intervened.

'Oh yes, Daddy! I would like to see that too. If you don't have the time, I could accompany Mr Montague.'

Wanting to appear helpful rather than excited, Grace attempted to control the eagerness in her voice, but without much success. However, although her excitement was palpable, her father put it down to youthful enthusiasm.

'I'm not sure that Mr Montague...' her father began, but he did not finish the sentence.

'Oh, I don't mind if Grace comes along,' Edward said gallantly. 'I believe it's a matinee showing so we would be back in time for tea.'

Randolph briefly considered the ethics of allowing his sixteen-year-old daughter to go to the cinema with a man twice her age, but Edward was an ex-officer and presumably a gentleman. Furthermore, it being an afternoon performance, neither he nor Grandfather Scott would have either the time or inclination to see Fred Astaire dressed in top hat and tails.

By now, however, Grace's already fertile imagination was running wild. She was aware that Edward had worn top hats and tails at Eton and probably on many formal occasions since, and that even with his bad leg, he was a good dancer. Moreover, he had an accent that was quintessentially English. Fortunately, in the nick of time, she noted the precarious nature of the situation, and quickly regained her composure.

'Well, if you don't mind?' she heard her father say.

'Not at all,' Edward replied. 'It will be my pleasure.'

The following afternoon, Grace and her chaperone, Mr Edward Montague, handed their outdoor coats to the hat girl in the foyer of the Music Box Theatre in downtown Chicago. The Music Box was a magnificent art deco picture palace, whose auditorium had an enchanting dark blue ceiling, with twinkling stars and moving cloud formations.

As Edward and Grace entered this ultra-modern environment, they could not have appeared more out of place. Edward's 1930s double breasted suit, waistcoat, and regimental tie were already dated, but Grace's outfit was even more passé. She wore a plain white silk blouse buttoned to the neck and a thick tweed dress that finished just above her ankles.

It being an afternoon matinee, the cinema was less than half full. Ignoring the usherette's guiding light, with the merest touch of her elbow, Edward steered Grace to the far side of the theatre. He selected seats towards the back and close to the far wall. From here, without having to turn his head, he could observe everyone in the theatre, including the young usherette in her sky-blue and gold uniform.

This smartly dressed woman scrutinised this curious couple for a while, but when nothing untoward appeared to be happening, she relaxed and was soon studying Ginger Rogers's dance routine instead. She had watched this film many times, but she was still captivated by the speed and elegance of Rogers's movements. She had read somewhere that Rogers did everything that Astaire did, but she did it wearing high heels and travelling backwards. What's more, as a cinema aficionado, she could see that the sequences had been filmed with barely any cinematic cuts.

As Irving Berlin's song *Cheek to Cheek* reached its finale, the usherette watched intently as Rogers hung submissively on Astaire's arm. But as the dancers made their way over to the balcony and for one magical moment stared into each other's eyes, for some unaccountable reason, this young star-struck picture palace attendant turned and glanced across at Grace and her companion.

She was shocked by what she saw. The pair had not moved. They appeared as still and stiff as two cardboard cut-outs. It was simply not possible. How could anyone remain unmoved by such beauty, such elegance, such rhythm? And for one horrific moment it occurred to her that they might actually be dead; but they were not dead. Like a line of highly disciplined foot soldiers facing an oncoming cavalry charge, outwardly they seemed calm, but inwardly they were both emotionally charged; the one with raw sexual energy, the other with the thrill of the chase. Having no other outlet, in an action designed to create warmth by expending their pent-up energy, their skeletal muscles had begun shaking uncontrollably. Normally, the natural release for such energy would have been an intense sexual coupling, but the auditorium of this large and very public picture palace was hardly the place for such niceties.

As the lights in the auditorium dimmed, almost as a gesture of reassurance, Edward had placed his right hand on Grace's left thigh. Had anyone been watching, they would not have seen his upper arm or shoulder move. Nor would they have noticed Grace's reaction, because for several minutes she had remained perfectly still, while both her hands remained linked together on her lap. Eventually, almost imperceptibly, she slid both hands down her thighs. Sensing the movement, Edward swiftly and smoothly removed his hand from the coarse woollen material of her dress. He was mortified; he had gone too far, and within seconds he felt a hot blush reach his face and neck.

Several more minutes elapsed before Edward realised what was happening. Slowly but surely, Grace had been gathering her dress with her fingers, until she had rolled most of it up around her waist. Her legs and thighs were exposed now, so that even in the cinema's half-light, Edward had full view of her stocking tops and suspenders. He'd had no idea that she was even wearing stockings. In Britain stockings were still rationed. They were therefore both expensive and rare, and although no longer rationed in the United States, as far as Edward was aware, they were still scarce. Indeed, on both sides of the Atlantic, nylon stockings had become a kind of currency. Being a businessman, Edward was curious to know how this sixteen-year-old girl had managed to obtain these valuable items, but he said nothing; instead, his eyes were no longer fixed on the silver screen, but on the silver sheen of Grace's legs.

14

At the age of ten, Grace had discovered part of her mother's wardrobe, neatly stored in a large leather suitcase. Unable to discard these items, her father had squirreled away four flapper-style silk dresses and several pairs of stylish matching shoes. Grace had been enchanted.

These delicate costumes reminded her of the magical satin-draped nymphs and fairies she had always dreamed of becoming, and having found them, she started to imagine herself wearing them at some magnificent ball.

From the moment of their discovery, whenever she was alone in the house, Grace would slip into one of these elegant silk dresses. Unfortunately, as she grew older and her breasts and hips started to develop, she quickly realised that although she had her mother's hair and eyes, she would never have her mother's figure. Her own curves were already way beyond the flat-chested boyish silhouette that her mother must have enjoyed in order to wear these beautifully slender 1920s costumes.

Being a motherless child, Grace had obtained assistance from school personnel with regards to intimate requirements, including underclothes. The results were usually practical but not always flattering. Determined to improve her appearance, immediately following VJ Day, Grace had visited a Chicago department store, where she had been measured for a new brassier in their recently reopened women's fitting area. Apart from the fact that she had realised that her breasts had become full and heavy and in need of support, Grace had an overwhelming desire to look attractive.

Along with the bra, she had purchased two pairs of soft cotton panties and a suspender belt, but there were no stockings available anywhere. Throughout the war, the US government had been calling for women to donate nylon and silk stockings and clothing to manufacture such items as parachutes, mosquito netting and hammocks. As a result, stockings had quickly become a black-market commodity to rival sugar, butter and even gasoline.

Fortunately, a few days after Grace had purchased the bra, Du Pont, the sole manufacturer of nylon stockings, announced that it would be resuming their production. The following morning, newspaper headlines declared, 'Peace, It's Here! Nylons on Sale!' And, from that moment, the merest rumour of stockings being available created chaos in department stores all across the United States. Between August 1945 and March 1946, in what came to be known as the Nylon Riots, stores were overwhelmed by women determined to buy such items. The demand created queues far bigger and more hostile than those for essential foodstuffs, but Grace was up for the challenge. Eventually, her intimidating size and her obvious determination had won through, and at considerable personal risk, she had managed to come away with not one but two pairs of Du Pont nylon stockings. She had also been startled to find that fighting her way to the exit with her spoils had proved almost as exhilarating as finding gold nuggets.

And now, for the first time, Grace had dared to wear her new nylon stockings outside the confines of her own room, and if the sound of Edward's breathing was any guide, they were about to become a huge success. She had considered wearing a more alluring dress, but she had calculated that as well as passing muster with her father, the long tweed skirt she had chosen would create a better surprise for Edward.

Even with his lack of experience Edward was not about to let such a chance go by. Slowly and deliberately, he placed his hand back on Grace's thigh. The heel of his hand and his palm lay on her smooth naked flesh, while his fingertips touched the soft lustrous fabric of her stocking tops. They were reminiscent of high-quality suede, but with a lighter, smoother and more lavish feel.

Grace was utterly convinced that men were excited by ladies' stockings and in turn this was exciting her. She would have been disappointed to know that other than their fiscal value, Edward's interest in Grace's hard-won Nylons was practically zero.

15

In spite of his age, Edward was only vaguely aware of the moral and ethical minefield that was closing in around him. He had no idea what the legality of his situation was, but he suspected that any repercussions would be severe. All he had was the vaguest notion that he was playing with fire. Grace, on the other hand, was well aware of her legal status with regard to sex and marriage under the age of consent.

Through most of the 1800s the age of consent in America had been between ten and twelve years. In the 1920s, depending on the state, it had been raised to between sixteen and eighteen. Nevertheless, as the Eunice Winstead case had proved, in many states, marriage between consenting adults still had no statutory age limit.

Grace had not seen the controversial film *Child Bride* that had initially been released in 1938, and being far too young, she had missed the original newspaper stories in 1937. The film had been based on the marriage of nine-year-old Eunice Winstead, who had been legally married to a twenty-two-year-old man in Tennessee. The story had been covered by most major newspapers and periodicals, including *The New York Times* and *Life Magazine*, whose reporters had visited and photographed the young couple in their cabin.

Less than a month after the wedding, *Life*'s photo-article and the film that followed sparked a national debate, during which it soon became apparent that child brides were not uncommon in the United States. By the time the film was released Grace had already turned fourteen. As usual, without ever having seen the film or read an article on child brides, the girls at Grace's school had been free with their opinions on the subject, but she was of a different mettle. A born academic, Grace had combed through back copies of various publications at her local library. As a result, she knew exactly how far she could go with Edward, if he were to avoid a prison sentence for the statutory rape of a minor.

While Grace was thinking on these things, having already considered his plan of action, the ex-soldier in Edward launched his first sortie. Emboldened by her tacit acceptance of his hand on her thigh, he gradually advanced until his palm was enveloping her mons. Beneath the thin cotton of her panties, he could feel the soft bushy growth of her pubic hair. It was a dangerous move, but Edward was resolute now.

Grace herself was at a crossroads. She was not sure how much further she could allow Edward's hand to roam, but the decision was taken from her. Reaching across the delicate fabric, Edward pulled the panties to one side and placed the flat of his hand directly onto her golden bush.

To suggest that they remained completely motionless during these final moments would be an exaggeration, nevertheless, their actions continued to pass unnoticed. While the usherettes were studying Fred and Ginger's *on-screen* moves, in this half-empty auditorium, most of the audience were performing their own *off-screen* moves.

Having realised that she was completely safe in this surprisingly intimate public space, following Edward's lead, almost imperceptibly, Grace opened her legs. As Edward took advantage of this action, Grace's moan was clearly audible, but such was the magnetism of Astaire and Rogers that no one in the place turned a hair.

Two days later, in another downtown cinema, the couple sat through *Gone with the Wind*. Grace had pleaded with her father, but because it was Edward's last day before starting his journey back to London, Randolph had been reluctant to give his consent.

'Mr Montague has enough to worry about,' he had argued, but Mr Montague quickly put Randolph's concerns to rest, by saying that a film would help him relax. And, in confidence, Edward had admitted that he might even fall asleep during the film's four-hour long screening. Although for most of the film, Grace's eyes had in fact been closed, in spite of being both physically and mentally exhausted, neither she nor Edward slept, not even for a second.

Knowing how long the film would run, Grace had

taken precautions. To prevent her new and rather delicate cotton panties from being torn, she had simply left them at home.

The film's unusual length had nevertheless taken Edward by surprise. Long before the halftime interval, his fingers were aching badly, but the convulsing of Grace's thigh and buttock muscles were urging him to re-double his efforts. There had been some initial resistance, but Grace's natural secretions were providing more than enough lubrication and Edward had no difficulty inserting his fingers deep inside her vagina.

Grace was vaguely aware what an orgasm was. From an early age she had played with herself. It had started while she was wearing one of her mother's silk dresses. Placing her hand over her crotch, she had rubbed her new growth of pubic hair through the delicate material. The pleasurable sensation had been short lived, and a little mild embarrassment had caused her to quickly fold the dress away. Nevertheless, for several days, Grace continued to think about this curious new sensation. Finally, exactly one week later, she opened the suitcase again and buried her face in the soft material. It felt warm, smooth and soft, like the skin of her newly developed breasts.

Laying back on her bed, she spread the dress over her otherwise naked body like an ultra-thin bed sheet and through the flimsy silk she rubbed herself again. Almost immediately she was rewarded with a tingling sensation in her lower abdomen that caused the muscles around her vagina to contract.

The idea of touching herself again in this way felt

vaguely improper, but the fact that there was no direct skin-on-skin contact somehow vindicated her actions. From overheard conversations between older girls at school, Grace was aware that addiction might be a possibility. The idea had alarmed her, but she could no longer stop herself. The sensation was simply too intense to ignore.

Soon she found herself waking up at night with her hands between her legs. She was even starting to caress her breasts. In the beginning, these actions were not related to fantasies about men They were simply actions that provided feelings of intense pleasure. At times she was almost overcome by the plethora of mixed emotions that this behaviour engendered. As usual she was not fearful, but she was nervous, especially when she started to realise that by adjusting the position and pressure of her fingers, she could control the intensity and duration of her pleasure. In spite of these revelations, nothing was helping her come to terms with what was happening to her body and mind; and in particular with the guilt she was beginning to feel after each session.

The worst was having no one to talk to. In her school hygiene lessons, nothing had been mentioned that even remotely hinted at this phenomenon. Thanks to a sympathetic teacher, Grace was aware of the reason for her monthly periods and after a clandestine search in her local library, she had even managed to find details relating to the menstrual cycle and the development of babies in the womb, but she could find no references, either positive or negative, about the feelings she was now experiencing almost every night. In the end, she came to the conclusion that, if medically nothing negative had been recorded, then nothing serious was likely to happen. Indeed, the only helpful information she was able to glean from the overheard ill-informed conversations of senior girls was that this was neither an uncommon, nor apparently abnormal act.

That there were unlikely to be any negative medical consequences made continuing her experimentation that much easier. For some time, a portion of guilt had remained, but eventually, the pleasure she received from her nightly sessions had gradually resolved any lingering inhibitions.

The film's unusually long running time required a prolonged interval, during which Edward had left the auditorium to relieve his bursting bladder. However, when long after the film had resumed, Edward had still not returned, Grace's imagination was soon running wild. Had he left in a huff. Would she have to make her own way home; in which case her father would be furious? He would almost certainly blame her for persuading Edward to take her out. She was afraid now and close to tears, but it was not fear of her father, it was fear of losing Edward and her carefully laid plans for the future.

Like Grace, Edward was also confused. Sitting in a cubical with his trousers around his ankles, he had glanced down at his right hand and seen traces of blood on his fingers. Realising what he had done, a curious mixture of guilt and pride welled up inside him. It was almost as if he had successfully completed an unpleasant military assignment.

Although things were developing much as Grace had

hoped, when Edward eventually returned to his seat, she quickly became aware that something had changed. She was experiencing a distinct coldness. It was almost as if Edward was rebuking her, and she did not know why. Her understanding was that not only had he taken part in this event, but surely, he had also taken pleasure from it, and yet now…

16

Twenty-four hours later, Edward was ensconced in his cabin, on a ship bound for Southampton. As he had boarded the train for New York on the first stage of his journey to England, while her father was looking the other way, Edward had given Grace a playful Clark Gable wink. This sly wink was just enough to banish any uncertainty she had been having since the previous day, and from that moment Grace wanted Edward Montague with body and soul. Even so, she was clever enough to realise that neither her father, nor the authorities, would be happy about a sixteen-year-old girl having an intimate relationship with a man twice her age. Nevertheless, Grace had no intention of losing the love of her life through inaction. She was aware that in England, Edward would be a long way off, with who knows what temptations. She also believed that she was not the greatest catch, and the more she considered these things, the more determined she became to prepare herself for Edward's next visit.

Equally keen to seize the moment, Edward had already indicated that he would return before Christmas 1945, with even more beautiful instruments. Although only a few weeks away, for Grace it would be a long hard wait, and the worst would be having no one to talk to about her feelings for this wonderful aristocratic English gentleman.

Grace had long since accepted that once her father and grandfather were gone, she *would* be entirely alone, and just as her grandfather had indicated, she was not sure if she would be able to survive in a man's world. A young girl accompanying her father on his business trips was one thing, but in years to come, being an older single woman would be an entirely different story.

Right now, her father and grandfather were offering her the chance to become the world's first female violin connoisseur. It may not be as glamorous as Amelia Earhart's solo flight across the Atlantic but at least it was a start. Although Montague's was a company with an exceptional reputation for expertise, Grace believed that if she worked really hard, perhaps in some small way, she could prove herself useful. In any event, working with her father and grandfather would help her pass the time constructively until Edward's next visit. In the meantime, she needed to convince Edward that this union was both right and proper. In fact, the more she considered her position, the more she was persuaded that with a little careful preparation, she could marry Edward and enjoy the best of both worlds.

Even before Edward's train rolled out of sight, Grace had developed a plan of action. Had Edward known how her mind was working, as a military man, he would have been impressed by her foresight and tactics. Grace herself would have been shocked to know that *his* plans and *hers* were virtually identical, albeit driven by entirely different motives.

The voyage home gave Edward time to think, and the thing he thought most about was Grace's age. He had been genuinely surprised to find out that she was only sixteen. Intellectually and physically, she had seemed much older. Even without make-up he had been convinced that she was at least eighteen.

Although Edward did not understand the finer points of women's anatomy, to his way of thinking he had taken Grace's virginity. Right now, if her father were ever to find out, it would be a serious matter. It would certainly ruin the new and highly profitable business arrangement that was once again developing between the Scotts and the Montagues. For a moment, Edward had even considered the possibility that Randolph might shoot him; after all, Chicago was the city of Al Capone. Although on reflection he considered this highly unlikely, if, as his plan entailed, Grace were to become pregnant with his child, perhaps in a year or so, marriage would be more acceptable, even desirable. Her father and grandfather would certainly not want Grace to go through life as an unmarried mother. Nevertheless, in order to avoid any unpleasant repercussions, he would need to bide his time. Likewise, even though Edward's father had been urging him to remarry for some time, here again he was not sure the *old boy* would approve of a sixteen-year-old bride.

As Edward lay in his cabin contemplating these things, he concluded that in spite of everything, marrying Grace was one of his better ideas. Although he had a live-in nanny to take care of his young son James, he was still a single parent. He did not love Grace; of that much he was sure, but it had been the same with James's mother who'd been killed in the London Blitz.

It was true that Grace was somewhat overweight, but that would only concern others. For the most part, his few social acquaintances would understand his need to find a mother for his young son, and even he had to concede that at least her stunningly beautiful face would be an asset in the shop.

17

As the new year turned and the months rolled on, Grace and her father continued to travel and chronicle the lives and times of the great Italian violin makers, until gradually she began to make sense of who had worked where and when and who had influenced who. At times these family stories were extremely complex, often horrific and almost never easy. In addition, reliable information was scarce. In many instances, as was the case with Giovanni Baptista Rogeri, other than a name, a date and a place on a label, little more was known. Although Grace diligently recorded whatever information she could find. She soon found out even knowing the difference between the Rogeri and Ruggeri family trees did not always provide an answer.

Randolph had a series of mantras that he was fond of repeating to his daughter, including, 'The more I know, the more I know how little I know,' and, 'Question everything, especially that which you most fervently believe.' But Grace's favourite was, 'Most people in this business do not want to hear what I am about to tell you.' Whereupon Grace knew exactly what was coming. She had heard this particular mantra so many times that she had memorised it word for word: 'Many eminent musicians and a few bootlicking violin makers claim that Cremonese instruments can be identified by their unique tonal qualities. Some even believe they can discern a typical Stradivari or Guarneri timbre; but this is nonsense. The simple truth is that while players can occasionally be recognised by their style and technique, no one has yet proved capable of identifying the instruments of a particular maker purely by their sound. The idea of a tonal fingerprint, unique to a specific maker, is pure fiction. The process of instrument identification, as with all other objects of art and antiquity, is essentially a visual one, which is why, Grace, people like you and I will always be needed.' Her father would then end by saying, 'Now this does not mean that players cannot tell the difference between bad, good and exceptional sounding instruments, because they can. It just means that they cannot tell you who made a particular instrument, simply by playing and listening to it.'

Grace loved this particular mantra because it exposed one of life's fundamental dangers; that of overestimating your own ability.

For Randolph, these road trips with Grace were essential; not only did they further his daughter's education, they also provided valuable stock for the Scott family's day-today business. However, apart from high-quality German, French and English instruments, thanks to Edward Montague the Scotts were now able to offer a constantly expanding selection of Italian masterpieces, including some of the finest examples by Stradivari and Guarneri del Gesù.

While impoverished Europeans were looking to convert their assets into cash, flushed with their victories over Germany and Japan, affluent Americans were hungry for culture. Although not such an obvious investment opportunity as fine paintings, boosted by the demand from musicians, museums, the recording industry, and a growing number of private collectors, there was a strong and steadily developing niche market for antique violins.

By the summer of 1946, Edward had already visited the Scotts' household four times. On each occasion, he was carrying Italian instruments of the finest quality; instruments that were still not readily available in the United States. Coupled with Randolph's expert eye, this unique selection quickly established the Scotts' reputation for excellence, even at an international level.

Whenever he was in America, Edward continued to stay at the Scotts' comfortable family home. It was a perfect arrangement for both parties. For Randolph, it was the chance to purchase some of the world's finest instruments without leaving his own front parlour. Edward's motives were a little more convoluted. Of course, the Scotts' offer of free board and lodging was attractive, but although the Montagues were no longer strapped for cash, by this time, Edward was looking at the bigger picture.

Having established a precedent, whenever Edward

was in town he and Grace would go to the movies. Although they mostly watched song and dance films, on one occasion they sat through a crime thriller called *Lady on a Train*. At some point, in mock fear, Grace had thrown her arms around Edward's neck and left them there until the credits had started to roll.

Between Edward's visits, time in her grandfather's workshop, road trips with her father, keeping her journals up to date and learning the ins and outs of the violin business, there was no further time for Grace to socialise. In fact, even though she was devoted to the business, Grace was often physically and mentally exhausted. Typical for that period was an unusually strenuous road trip in the fall of '46; fortunately, this time, their reward far exceeded all expectations. Over a fourteen-day period, the pair clocked more than 2,000 miles, mostly along Route 66. Having stopped at several towns and cities on the way, they had eventually reached their final destination: Santa Fe in New Mexico. In order to avoid the extreme temperatures of summer and winter, Randolph had chosen mid-October for the journey. Unfortunately, conditions on the road were unseasonably hot, dry and dusty.

Once again, following her father's instructions, as well as placing adverts in local newspapers, Grace had sent out letters and flyers, informing orchestras, music societies and teachers of their imminent arrival. As a result, father and daughter had also been invited to attend a recital organised by the city's Concert Association. In spite of the fact that Santa Fe was noted for its artistic leaning and its eye-catching Pueblo-style architecture, this was

New Mexico and they were not expecting too much. Consequently, Grace had been surprised by the size of the audience. In this somewhat out-of-the-way place, she could only imagine that half of the town's population must have purchased tickets.

After the performance, outside the theatre, Grace and her father were approached by a man wearing dirty overalls. The man had a long, white and rather unkempt beard, and as he walked towards them, he waved a piece of paper. It was one of Grace's flyers.

'Scuse me, sir,' the man asked. 'Are you the gentleman what's doin' the valuin'?' When Randolph indicated that he was, the man added, 'And are ya also buyin'?'

'That depends on what you have, sir,' Randolph answered respectfully.

'I got a chella. It's on the flatbed,' said the man, pointing a few yards down the road to where an old flatbed Ford was parked up against the sidewalk. 'Back then, my pa played the chella, but he's been dead for years now. I don't play and I don't have no relatives what do. So, I figured on valuin' Pa's chella, so as I can sell it.'

With sinking hearts Randolph and his daughter followed the man, who was already apologising for the cello's condition.

'It's the climate here,' he said. 'Freezin' in winter, 'n hotter than hell in summer... if y'all excuse me, Miss.'

As he apologised for his bad language, he lifted the cello off the truck and removed the oily sheet it was wrapped in. Randolph's heart stopped. *Sometimes, instrument identification is almost too easy*, he said to himself. But in doing so, he was denying the years of careful observation that had heightened his perception and given him the ability to see many things at a glance. In the blink of an eye, he had registered the patina of genuine age, the cut and quality of the wood, the instrument's very distinctive modelling and above all, its rich, dark varnish.

Instruments were not always so easy to identify. Often, he would study an instrument for weeks on end without reaching a definitive conclusion; this time however, he was certain. All that remained was to assess the damage and how much restoration work would be needed.

'It's the damned climate,' the man started again.

'Well, yes, but maybe it's just old age,' suggested Randolph with a merry chuckle. 'I believe it's a Gio Paolo Maggini cello, which would make it at least three hundred years old.'

'Do you mean… it's what it says it is on the label?'

'I haven't seen the label yet, but if it says *Gio Paolo Maggini in Brescia*, then the label is probably right.'

'Yea, that's right… That's what the label says, but how did you know that?' the man replied, clearly impressed.

'That's my job.'

'That's amazin'! And you recon it's three hundred years old?'

'The truth is, Maggini never dated his labels, so it will be impossible to say exactly how old it is, but he died of bubonic plague, in a pandemic that swept through Lombardy around 1632. So, it must have been made before that,' said Randolph chuckling again.

'Is it still infectious?' said the man, suddenly holding the instrument out at arm's length.

'Oh, I think you are more likely to die of heat stroke

here in Santa Fe,' Randolph said jokingly, and then more seriously he asked, 'what do you want to do with it now?'

'Well it's no use to me, so I'd still like to sell it, but it'll be expensive, it's more than three hundred years old, y'all know.' And now he was laughing too.

'You forgot to mention that Maggini cellos are also extremely rare,' said Randolph before adding, 'so, where can we talk business?'

'Yea, that's right, his chellas *are* extremely rare,' said the man, repeating Randolph's words.

18

Having come to a fair and amicable agreement, the two men drew up and signed the necessary paperwork, after which the cello spent its last night in Santa Fe, in Grace's room at the El Rey Court Hotel.

'I'm sure you know what you're doing, Papa,' said Grace, as the man left with his pockets full of cash.

'But?' her father asked, sensing dissent.

'I'm sure you're right, but that cello is pretty beat up. There are lots of cracks, especially in the spruce top. The neck is loose, the sides are no longer firmly attached to the front and back, and the double lines of inlay are loose almost everywhere.'

'That's all true, but there are no pieces missing and a skilled restorer will be able to fix it up as good as new.'

'A skilled restorer?' said Grace. 'You mean Grandpa.'

'Yes, I mean Grandpa. It will take him a while, but we will still make a handsome profit.'

'You could have made more,' said Grace. 'He had no idea what it was worth.'

'You know that's not our company's policy, Grace. We have earned a reputation for fair business and that is what keeps us *in* business.'

'Yes, but are you really sure it's right? I can see that it's not a Saxon factory copy, that's obvious, but according to your ledgers, there were a lot of unknown makers working in Brescia and labels do get swapped around… I don't mean…' Grace began.

'No, no, you are right to ask, but this cello is the real thing and it will be magnificent when it's finished.'

That night, as Grace laid her head on the hotel pillow, the realisation of what had just happened finally caught up with her. There had been no sudden rush of adrenaline, nothing that compared with discovering that first tiny fragment of gold in the bottom of her prospecting pan. The high had been slower coming, but its arrival was no less intense and this time she knew it was real. There was no doubt in her mind now that her father had been right. This was the real route to her independence.

The following morning, having no proper case for the cello, Randolph wrapped the Maggini in two second-hand woollen blankets he'd managed to find at a local thrift store. The blankets had a strange smell, one which Grace would occasionally recall for the rest of her life.

With the additional cello, it was more than a little cramped in the back of the Studebaker. Soon after leaving Santa Fe, Randolph checked his rear-view mirror, half expecting to see Grace uncomfortably asleep between the instruments. Instead, she had her head up against the open window, her red hair was flashing like a beacon in the warm wind. Her father had assumed she was cooling off. It was certainly hot, both inside and outside the car, but in fact, she was desperately trying to disperse the musty odour of the thrift store blankets.

Somewhere outside Amarillo, unable to tolerate the smell a moment longer, after a short but heated discussion with her father, Grace ditched the blankets in an oil-drum trash can at a roadside gas station. Having decided that her body was soft enough to cushion Maggini's handywork, the pair had simply driven on.

With the blankets gone, the thousand-mile return journey no longer felt quite so daunting. Even so, the blankets' lingering smell had left Grace feeling vulnerable, and although she no longer felt like talking, she needed the security of her father's voice. He did not require much prompting. Already knowing the answer, she asked, 'Wasn't Maggini a pupil of Gasparo da Salò?'

'That's right, Grace, but in spite of Brescia's undoubted success with a wide variety of instruments, it is still true to say that it was Cremonese rather than Brescian workshops that represented the cutting edge of violin-making technology. As you indicated a couple of months ago, from Andrea Amati onwards, Cremonese makers virtually monopolised the violin business. Not only did they set the standards, they quickly became famous and highly productive. It may be hard to believe, but from the outset, the manufacture and export of violins was at least as important to the economy of Cremona as General Motors, Chrysler and Ford are to the economy of Detroit today. And in the end, Grace, it is *always* about the economy, whether it be national, local or personal.

'In fact,' Randolph continued, 'in order to prevent their hard-won export businesses from being exploited, since medieval times, towns and cities across Europe had systems in place to protect their merchants, tradesmen and artisans. As your grandfather and I have often pointed out, these professional associations, usually known as guilds, were created to govern each occupation, including musical instrument making.

'Such guilds were often extremely powerful, and in the autonomous walled cities of Europe, the master craftsman of each group controlled who could work when and where, and which methods and materials could be employed. Within these structures, the traditional technologies of each trade, such as formulas, designs and methods, were handed down from generation to generation, not only unchallenged and unchanged, but in complete secrecy. Anyone who revealed such information, or did not comply with guild rules, would be severely punished.'

Randolph paused before speaking again: 'Actually, although we no longer have guilds, it was much the same where I worked at the aircraft factory. Secrecy was everywhere. The members of the board of directors were the only people allowed to see the whole picture. Various aircraft parts were given to different shop-floor workers to complete. These parts were then brought together and assembled by other workers, who had no idea how these parts had been designed or made. In this way, the right hand never knew what the left hand was doing, and neither the enemy nor our competition could copy our finished aircraft.'

At this point Grace interrupted her father. 'But, if you are a skilled woodworker, unlike aeroplanes, violins are easy to copy. I know that just from watching Grandpa.'

'That's only partly right, Grace,' he answered. 'Obviously, some secrets could be copied, but others could not. As you know, even today, the famous Cremonese varnish recipe remains a mystery. Because of the guild system, violin makers working in other cities were forced to develop and use their own varnishes. And, as you also know, although both Venetian and Brescian violin makers had fine varnishes, they were quite different from Cremonese varnish. With practice they are easily identifiable, but so far no one has been able to successfully reproduce any of them.'

'Yes,' Grace agreed. She was still feeling a little unwell and once again she prompted her father to continue. 'Isn't Brescian varnish a rich dark brown colour, whereas Venetian varnish is reddish and Cremonese varnish has a more orange hue?' Then, as an afterthought, she added, 'And, isn't Cremonese varnish usually thinner and more transparent, while Venetian and Brescian varnishes are generally thicker? And aren't Venetian and Brescian varnishes often wrinkled and cracked, especially on cellos?'

'Well, those are simple descriptions, but I know what you mean... By the way, Grace, painters and violin makers call such cracking and wrinkling *craquelure*.'

Suddenly Randolph changed tack. 'Talking of painters reminds me. Only members of a guild were allowed to practise their trade within a city and its territory, and these guilds were operated exclusively by and for male workers.

Although occasionally the wife or daughter of a member would be allowed to continue in business after his death, such arrangements were extremely rare, which makes the presence of a successful female painter in Cremona all the more remarkable. Her name was Sofonisba Anguissola, and I bet you've never heard of her.'

'I haven't,' said Grace. She was palpably impressed now and lifting her head, she studied her father's eyes as he watched her in the Studebaker's rear-view mirror. 'Tell me more.'

'I only heard about her recently myself,' he replied. 'She is hardly mentioned in books on art history. In part, this is because her works have often been attributed to other artists, including Titian. It's also the reason why she is not mentioned in my journals.' He was smiling now, as he added, 'I had hoped that her story might help persuade your grandpa to teach you violin making, unfortunately I think his opinions are too deep seated.' Mimicking his father's voice Randolph added, 'Zer neffer ver any und zer neffer vil be vimen violin makers…'

They were both laughing as her father continued. 'Sofonisba Anguissola was born in Cremona, sometime around 1532. She was the daughter of a modest but aristocratic Cremonese merchant. She began her training as a painter in Cremona, just as Andrea Amati and his two sons were busy developing the violin family. At the age of fourteen, she also travelled briefly to Rome, where Michelangelo is reported to have been so impressed by her work that he contributed towards her instruction.

'In 1566 Giorgio Vasari stopped off in Cremona while revising the second edition of his *Lives of the Most*

Eminent Painters and Sculptors. He was also impressed with Sofonisba and he mentioned her in his treatise. In her ninety-second year she was drawn by the Dutch master Anthony Van Dyck, who reported that she was erudite and amiable, and that she gave him useful advice about light. Just one year later, Sofonisba died at the age of ninety-three. At the time of her death, Andrea's grandson Nicola Amati was almost thirty years old.

'In view of the way things are in America right now, although it may seem unusual, in the first half of the sixteenth century, largely as a result of the Renaissance Humanism movement, the education of women was considered desirable among the aristocracy.

'Like the Amati family, this talented Cremonese woman was famous throughout Europe. Unfortunately, like so many phenomenal women, from the nineteenth century onwards, Sofonisba Anguissola was more or less written out of history.'

Grace suddenly sat bolt upright. 'Why?' she said. 'That's not fair.'

'Oh, come on, Grace! With your knowledge of history, this should come as no surprise to you. You know that historically women have often been discouraged from certain activities. What's more, even when they were successful, their achievements were often ignored, attributed to someone else, or simply erased from the records altogether.'

Once again, her father was back on the subject of fascinating women in history. As far back as Grace could remember, he had quoted or alluded to powerful, artistic or courageous women. Although this was something she had always cherished, she was also aware that such references were a thinly veiled attempt to compensate for the loss of her mother.

While noting her father's words, without looking up, Grace interrupted again. 'Were there ever any female violin makers that were erased from the records?'

Randolph half turned towards his daughter. 'Sadly, there is not much documentation, but in 1906, in his book about the Cremonese violin maker Joseph Guarnerius, Horace Petherick mentioned the violin label of a woman called Katarina Guarneria. Petherick was not sure if she was the widow of the great Joseph Guarneri del Gesù or some other female relative. But with your knowledge of Latin, one day you might find out that some of the world's most revered violins were in fact made by a woman. That would sure wake up your grandpa. I know he doesn't believe in women violin makers, but I'm pretty sure they existed, and not just in nineteenth-century violin-making factories.

'Anyway,' her father said, returning to his theme, 'this young Cremonese woman, Sofonisba Anguissola, eventually moved to Madrid and became court painter to King Philip II of Spain and a favourite of his wife, Isabel. Isabel was the eldest daughter of King Henry of France and his Florentine wife, Catherine de' Medici. Although she was now living in Paris, this same Catherine de' Medici ordered an entire orchestra from Andrea Amati, who was still living and working in Cremona.

'This orchestra was intended for Catherine's son, King Charles IX of France, who was also the brother of Isabel of Spain. And, by the way, Grace, this orchestra was of the finest quality. On each instrument the King's coat of arms was painted and embellished with gold leaf and Latin phrases. What is perhaps even more remarkable is that four hundred years later, a number of these instruments are still being played.

'The patronage of such powerful people helped make the Amati family seriously wealthy. That said, as you should know from your schoolwork, Catherine de' Medici was a crafty political schemer and a highly skilled poisoner. She was a clever woman, but she was not a nice person. I'm sure Sofonisba Anguissola would make a much better addition to your scrapbook of heroic women.' And again, her father chuckled to himself.

'So, as you can see, Grace, it was a much smaller world back then and even though there were no automobiles, steam ships, trains or planes, when they were not fighting wars, there was plenty of interaction between the various ruling powers of Europe. Europe's elite even shared a common language.'

'Latin?' Grace interjected.

'Latin!' her father confirmed.

'So that's why you sent me to the Chicago Latin School?'

'That's right,' Randolph replied, laughing. 'Latin was the main language of diplomatic communication, but an equally important diplomatic strategy was marriage. In spite of enjoying splendid isolation behind their defensive walls, as had been the case with both Catherine de' Medici and her daughter Isabel, highly complex alliances between families and states were forged through the auspices of arranged marriages. These occurred at all levels of society.'

'Is that what you have planned for me?' she asked playfully, not realising that she would soon be arranging such a marriage for herself.

Already feeling guilty for believing that Grace would never find a suitable husband, this question struck a chord with Randolph, making him even more determined that she should become an independent woman.

Doing his best to ignore the tease, her father went on: 'As I was saying, in spite of alliances and allegiances, the world outside these fortified cities could be highly dangerous. At night, city gates were secured and barred, as were the homes of the families living inside. Securing each household, including any live-in servants and apprentices, was often the task of the chief matriarch. Anyone left outside, whether friend or foe, would be refused entry until daybreak.

'Tragically, the one thing that locks, keys and high walls could not keep out was disease. In the Po valley, the river, its surrounding wetlands, and even city moats harboured and transported diseases such as typhoid, cholera and malaria. Domestic water was largely drawn from communal wells. It was seldom pure and rarely drunk neat. In fact, the importance of wine as a means of barter had more to do with its antibacterial qualities than with its flavour or its inebriating effect. In towns and cities people of every status relieved themselves in streets and alleyways, and latrine hygiene was often ignored altogether, especially in the poorer areas, which inevitably resulted in contaminated wells and groundwater. Tanners, weavers and dyers used chemicals, excrement and urine in the preparation of their wares and this effluence was simply dumped into rivers and streams. Meanwhile, below the stone floors of cathedrals and churches putrefying corpses slowly added themselves to the soup.'

At this last remark, the expression on Grace's face reassured her father that she was still listening intently, and he continued unabated: 'Nicola Amati's craftsmanship was phenomenal, and by the 1620s, his hand was clearly the ascendant one in the Brothers Amati workshop. Theoretically, at this point the stage was set for the Amati family to continue its dominance of the violin business, not only in Cremona, but throughout Europe. Unfortunately, shortly after this time, a series of dramatic events altered the course of the Amati family tradition and the history of violin making forever.

'Apart from waterborne diseases, tuberculosis was a prolific killer, and at regular intervals various plagues raged through northern Italy. But, in the 1630s, already weakened by the Thirty Years War and successive widespread famine, the population of Europe was decimated by an outbreak of bubonic plague. On the Italian peninsular, within weeks, twenty-five per cent of Lombardy's inhabitants were dead, and the area's entire social structure had all but collapsed. Some cities, including Verona and Milan, lost around fifty per cent of their inhabitants. Remarkably, although the population of Cremona was reduced to one third by death and flight, Nicola Amati somehow managed to survive. Fortunately, not only was Nicola the finest maker of his generation, but by killing off his competitors, this plague ensured the pre-eminence of Cremonese violin making for a further century. In fact, among those who died was our old friend Gio Paolo Maggini of Brescia; one of Nicola's biggest rivals.'

19

Having reflected on the virtues of the Amati family, Sofonisba Anguissola and the plague, just outside the town of Shamrock in Texas, Grace's father pulled into an unusual art deco gas station and café, called the U-Drop Inn. Following war rationing, roadside restaurants were starting to pick up momentum and, as had become their habit, Grace and her father were enjoying the unfamiliar freedom of choice on their revitalised menus.

Rejuvenated by giant hamburgers, Randolph and Grace drove back onto the highway, and continued their discussion on the seventeenth-century's bubonic plague pandemic, but more specifically on its aftermath.

'By the 1640s,' Randolph began, 'just as Nicola Amati had started to recover the loss of momentum caused by the plague, he was suddenly faced with an overwhelming demand for instruments. Desperately in need of help for his rapidly expanding business, and having as yet no children of his own, Nicola had little choice but to break with tradition and employ non-family members as violin makers. Consequently, as a direct result of the plague pandemic, an entirely new group of violin makers was trained by Nicola Amati in Cremona.'

Randolph was about to continue when Grace proudly added, 'According to the research of W. E. Hill and Sons of London, this new group included Giovanni Baptista Rogeri, Giacomo Gennaro and the inventor of the Piano Forte, Bartolomeo Cristofori and eventually of course, Nicola's own son, Hieronymus Amati II. But, without doubt, the most important addition to this group was Andrea Guarneri – the founder of the Guarneri family of makers.'

'That is exactly right, Grace,' Randolph replied, once again proud to see his daughter's keen interest in the history of the violin. 'Although documentary evidence is minimal, all other indications suggest that Francesco Ruggeri, Jacobus Stainer and possibly Antonio Stradivari were also among Nicola Amati's many apprentices.'

At the mention of Francesco Ruggeri's name, Grace winced, and when her father pretended not to notice, she felt even worse.

'Eventually,' her father continued, 'either directly or indirectly, it was Nicola's rigorous instruction that laid the foundations for further development of the violin, especially at the hands of Antonio Stradivari and Joseph Guarneri del Gesù. In turn, all of these great Cremonese makers went on to inspire the world. Even though much has been lost, including their famous varnish recipes, the world is a richer place thanks to these celebrated Cremonese violin makers and their legacy.'

'Yes,' Grace agreed, 'that's undoubtedly true, and I appreciate that being able to understand the relationship between these important Cremonese makers will eventually help me to identify the methods and styles of other schools, and ultimately the individual makers working in those schools.'

'That's right, Grace. For the purpose of instrument recognition, the importance of these influential Cremonese makers cannot be overestimated. The designs created and brought to perfection by the Cremonese school are the stuff from which virtually all subsequent violin makers derived their inspiration. The only notable exceptions being early Venetian cellos and Brescian violas, but we'll get around to that.

'Theoretically, although the influence of Cremona may be many times removed from its original source, even in the most primitive of instruments, its presence cannot be denied. Consequently, as banal as the idea might seem, anyone who can identify the works of these few important Cremonese makers is already well on the way towards a better understanding of *all* violin related instruments.'

Again, Grace agreed. 'But while I understand the truth of your argument, after months on the road, I'm still having difficulty remembering who taught or influenced who. I just can't keep it all in my head. For example, I still don't understand the relationship between Nicola Amati, Francesco Ruggieri and Giovanni Baptista Rogeri, and several other violin makers with the same or similar Ruggieri/Rugerius names, all of whom were directly or indirectly associated with Cremona. And, quite apart from Cremona's extended families, I have already spent endless hours trying to make sense of the Neapolitan Gagliano family of which there are more than a dozen. Then there is the complex relationship between the Testore and Grancino families in Milan, and the illusive and highly mobile Guadagnini family of which there was also a baker's dozen. And apparently, these are relatively easy to classify when compared to contemporary makers, both known and unknown, in cities like Brescia and Rome. And that is just Italy, what about the rest of Europe. Sometimes it's just so overwhelming. I'll never get it.'

Randolph was about to explain that at the time of the classical Italian violin makers, not only were family trees notoriously complicated, but names were often misspelled in the official registers of births, marriages and deaths, and that this problem was aggravated by regular outbreaks of disease and war. But before he could begin, Grace emitted a loud groan.

'I admit it's all a little complex, Grace,' Randolph finally said, giving her an encouraging pat on the shoulder, 'but trust me, you *will* eventually get there.'

20

Not unsurprisingly, as the return journey along Route 66 became increasingly arduous, the merry banter between father and daughter gradually ceased. While Randolph had been sitting in the driving seat for almost five days, Grace had shared the Studebaker's remaining space with nine violin cases, their personal luggage and the large Gio Paolo Maggini cello. With only occasional truck-stop breaks and hard motel beds to break the uncomfortable monotony, Grace was no longer in the mood for learning. In fact, she had spent much of their return journey along Route 66 uncomfortably asleep between several angular wooden instrument cases and the cello.

Only as they approached the windy city did Grace rouse herself. With the huge cello hanging over her shoulder, she reached forward and struggled to tune the Motorola to a local Chicago station. As the radio competed with the whine of the Studebaker's tyres on the road, she heard the first few bars of a new song. Catching the exact wavelength immediately increased the volume, causing the old cello to vibrate sympathetically with a sprightly jazz piano. Within seconds the unmistakably smooth baritone voice of Nat King Cole slipped into the captivating rhythm of one of the greatest road songs of all time: *(Get your kicks on) Route 66.*[2]

Grace had been a fan of Nat King Cole ever since she had first heard his song *Straighten Up and Fly Right* in 1943. Only seven years earlier, her heroine Amelia Earhart had gone missing flying over the Pacific, and initially Grace had believed the song was a tribute to this remarkable woman. When she eventually learned the truth, it had not diminished her enjoyment of Cole or his music. And now, here was something entirely new from the maestro and Grace instantly recognised that it represented one of those rare coincidences; the kind that happen only once or twice in a lifetime. Even her father, an ardent classical music fan, recognised the composition's significance with its references to the various towns and cities they had recently visited on this legendary trans-American highway.

These road trips were not only teaching Grace essential things about the business, they were also cementing her relationship with her father. And now, this unusual song, in an entirely different genre, was about to become the duo's theme tune. From the moment Grace had the idea to replace the town *Winona*, with *Cremona*, every time they heard the song on the radio, she and Randolph would sing,

---

2   Written in 1946 by American songwriter Bobby Troup

'*Cremona*', at the top of their voices, before screaming with laughter.

During his all-too-brief courtship and marriage with Grace's mother, Randolph had spent many happy hours in one or other of Chicago's dance halls and speakeasies, watching his fiancée dance. Mary had been an exceptional dancer and he could still remember how self-conscious he had felt, trying to keep up with her elegant and inventive moves, while much to everyone's amusement, he had grappled with the strange new rhythms of jazz and swing.

Some fifteen years later, Randolph had again been exposed to jazz and swing music at the aircraft factory, but even there, he'd had trouble understanding the attraction. Although the women listened while they worked, the music, if that is what it was, could barely be heard above the cacophony of machine noise. And yet, somehow through the din, these young women followed each tune precisely. Without missing a beat, they mouthed the words and moved their feet in unison. This phenomenon had puzzled Randolph for some considerable time. For him, music required serious commitment and some intellectual and emotional input. He could not imagine listening to the opening bars of Max Bruch's Violin Concerto No. 1 in G Minor without being able to hear the sweetness and purity of the melody, or the carefully choreographed interaction between orchestra and soloist. As for Bach's Sonatas and Partitas for Solo Violin, the merest screech of metal or the hammering of a rivet would almost certainly have destroyed his commitment to the composer's work. In truth, he could barely endure it when people coughed at a performance. But now, travelling with Grace and the Motorola, Randolph eventually learned how to filter out the road noise while listening to great classical works and to reconstruct any lost subtleties in his head. Eventually, he realised that the key was his own familiarity with these works.

Recently, most of the music being broadcast on the radio was of short duration. Previously, radio stations had broadcast music live from concert halls, ballrooms and even studios. Consequently, the length of such broadcasts was theoretically unlimited, but once recordings became readily available, on shellac and vinyl disks, in the world of popular music, things quickly changed. Initially, these recordings were cut on disks that revolved at seventy-eight revolutions per minute, but since only so much music would fit on these disks, songs and instrumental pieces were limited to three or four minutes only. And, because performers wanted to sell recordings, even when playing live, they would often limit the length of their performances to match their recordings.

Randolph quickly realised that the short duration of these works did not necessarily diminish their quality. He was also astute enough to appreciate that artists like Nat King Cole were not charlatans; they were quite clearly highly skilled musicians. It was just that listening to such music was an entirely different experience for him. To become familiar with great classical works requires time and resolve. New classical productions in particular demanded a good deal of concentrated effort, not only from players, but from the audience themselves.

21

Following her first cinema dates with Edward, wherever she and her father travelled across the United States, Grace sent picture postcards to Mr Montague in London. Whenever possible, she wrote and posted them covertly, but fearing that one or more might be intercepted by her father, in order to allay suspicion, she also sent cards to her Grandfather Scott. In addition, she restricted her greetings to a few brief comments about the weather, concerts they had heard, and instruments they had seen. There was certainly nothing in her words that might be misinterpreted. Individually these postcards were completely innocent, but collectively they sent a message that eventually even Edward had understood. The series had begun with a picture of the Washington Monument. This was followed by a hand-coloured photo of a giant redwood tree, a lighthouse in Maine and a selection of phallic skyscrapers, including Nebraska's fifteen-storey state capitol building, colloquially known as *The Penis of the Prairie.*

For almost two years, Grace and her father had continued to travel the length and breadth of the United States like two itinerant missionaries. They may not have been peddling religion, but they were most certainly on a mission. In the meantime, Edward had continued to visit Scott's Fine Violins in Chicago. Shortly after Grace's eighteenth birthday, in the spring of '47, after an unusually long hiatus, he returned to Chicago, carrying yet another batch of fine Italian instruments. Once again, without exception, these instruments were of the highest quality. Fully aware of Randolph's expertise and the fact that he was prepared to pay for the best, Edward was not about to waste a journey carrying junk. With the Montague name behind him he could sell his junk almost anywhere, but in the aftermath of the war, his family needed the mighty dollar which the Scotts appeared to have in spades.

This visit also confirmed Edward's opinion that, in spite of her youth, Grace really was an exceptional expert. As she and her father had unpacked and examined his latest offerings, Grace had not only identified each one, she had also correctly estimated the date of their manufacture and their physical condition, and she had done this with the minimum of fuss. *A genuine female connoisseur*, Edward had said to himself. *It could only happen in America.*

Later that afternoon, alone in the Scott family's walk-in safe, Grace had shown Edward a pristine seventeenth-century viola by Nicola Gagliano of Naples. Having pointed out the salient features of Gagliano's work, in order to prove her worth, Grace had gone on to talk about more than a dozen violin-making members of the Gagliano family and other violin makers who were working in Naples in that same period. Unfortunately, Edward was soon out of his depth and forced to rely on the bluff and bluster he had learned at Eton; but he need not have worried. Grace was now so full of wonder for this tall war hero, with his polished English accent, that if Edward had told her that Stradivari had made his violins in a Hawaiian beach hut, she would have accepted it without question. Nevertheless, from this moment, Grace's favourite English war hero carefully limited himself to asking questions, rather than making statements. But since Grace was used to being interrogated by her father and grandfather, even this ploy did not strike her as unusual. The difference was that while the Scotts knew the answer before asking testing questions, Edward did not.

It had been almost three months since Edward and Grace had seen each other. In Grace's case absence had certainly made her heart grow fonder. By contrast, Edward was entirely dispassionate; he was quietly calculating how best to make use of Grace's obvious infatuation. Having completed business with her father, once again Edward expressed the wish to see a song and dance movie. Billed as Fred Astaire's final movie, *Blue Skies* co-starred the singer Bing Crosby. Protocol required Edward to invite Randolph and his father, but inevitably, only Grace accompanied him to the cinema. This time, rather than Ginger Rogers, in most of the dance sequences, Joan Caulfield partnered Astaire. In the story Crosby gets the girl, but Astaire, accompanied only by a troupe of male dancers dressed in matching top hats and tails, performs a magnificent solo set, to the song 'Puttin' on the Ritz'.

Having weighed the odds, not wanting Grace to think him a penny pincher, Edward invited Grace for coffee at an upmarket hotel close to the cinema, where he had also booked a room. In order to execute his entrapment and seduction strategy, he needed to make the right impression; he could not afford a mistake at this stage. He need not have worried. After one and a half years of clandestine courtship, Grace put up no resistance.

22

In June 1947, at four o'clock in the afternoon, a telegram arrived at Montague's London shop. It was addressed to Edward. All too often associated with bad news, the demure secretary who was carrying the envelope handled it like an unexploded bomb. The war had been over almost two years, but she was well aware that bad news could easily trigger an outburst from her notoriously short-tempered boss.

'Sir, a telegram has arrived from Scott's Fine Violins in Chicago.'

'Yes, yes, I'll take it,' said Edward, signalling to his father Horatio, who was just about to leave the room. 'It's probably from Randolph, although why he should send a telegram…'

Tearing open the envelope, he read the short message several times, before turning to the secretary who was still standing in the doorway.

'Yes?' he enquired pointedly. 'What is it now?'

'The messenger boy is waiting, sir. Will there be a reply?'

'What? No! No! Send him away.'

Relieved, the woman turned and left, closing the door quietly behind her.

Eventually Edward's father looked at his son. He could see from his countenance that something monumental had occurred. Worried that Edward might have made a faux pas with their best customer, he candidly asked, 'Did you do something to annoy Randolph?'

'It's not from Randolph,' Edward replied quietly. 'It's from Grace… Grace,' he repeated slowly, as he handed his father the flimsy paper.

To be sure, the old man also read the short message several times. It said simply, 'Edward I'm pregnant.'

Grace had considered adding, 'I hope you are pleased,' but not wishing to influence his reaction, she had decided to keep the text to a minimum.

There was a long pause while each man waited for the other to speak. Edward was clearly struggling to arrange his thoughts. This may have been what he had planned, but confronted with the reality, he was no longer sure.

Seeing the look on his son's face, the old man smiled. 'It's yours, isn't it?'

'Yes.'

'Are you sure?'

'Yes of course!'

'I'm surprised, Edward,' the old man said. 'I did not think you had it in you… So, what are you going to do? If she were in London, I could… *arrange* things for you, but

I don't know anyone in Chicago.' He was smiling broadly now. 'You will have to marry her, of course. The Scotts are too important, we cannot afford to lose them... What is she like?'

It was a while before Edward answered. 'She has red hair and a beautiful face.'

'But?' said his father.

'But what?'

'From your tone there is clearly a problem.'

'She's fat!' said Edward bluntly, before repeating himself, 'She's fat.'

'So what? I've had fun with some extremely fat women,' his father said. He was openly laughing now and had to wait a while before finishing his sentence. 'Unfortunately, what with all this rationing and austerity, there are not many fat women around these days; it's such a shame.'

'You really are an incurable romantic, Farver,' said Edward, not disguising the bitter irony in his voice.

'An American!' his father exclaimed, still amused. 'Well, Winston Churchill's mother was an American and she became a renowned British socialite. Did she go to a good school?... Grace, I mean, not Winston's mother,' and again he laughed.

'One of the best,' Edward quietly confirmed.

'I presume you mean one of the best in America,' his father quipped.

'You're such a snob, Farver.'

'And what is wrong with being a snob? Do you love her?'

'No! Did you love my mother?'

'I loved her well enough.'

'As well as all the others you mean?'

Again, there was a pause as the two men considered new ways to score points.

'And what other qualities does she have?' his father asked.

'Well,' Edward said, having had enough of his father's jokes, 'she's a damned good dancer,' before thinking to himself that indeed she was. And then he suddenly grew serious. 'She will certainly be an asset to Montague's. In my opinion, she is already a serious connoisseur.'

Horatio looked Edward square in the eye. 'As far as assessing someone's expertise is concerned, Edward, I'm not sure that you would be the best judge.'

Edward could feel the old animosity towards his father welling up inside him. But suddenly, it no longer mattered what his father said; it would soon be his show. And, if he married Grace, he would have a new and possibly even better expert to keep the Montague business going. Since Edward had become a partner, more than fifteen years ago, the company had sustained him in the manner to which he had become accustomed, and he was not about to let it go. Admittedly, the war years had been difficult, but under the leadership of its foreman Walter Drake, the workshop was up and running again. And, like his father before him, Drake would continue to work for a pittance and would probably die at the bench.

Not for the first time Edward wondered why people were so damned loyal. He was thirty-four and he had already seen war, death and destruction. He had seen men place their lives on the line because of loyalty; loyalty to a king, a country, a regiment or just some pompous officer. All around him at Dunkirk, on both sides of the front, thousands of men had been butchered because of loyalty. And yet, like his father, Edward continued to visit his regimental club in the City, even though he no longer believed in any of it. None of it made sense anymore. He had lost the mother of his child in the Blitz, and as he saw it, she too had sacrificed her life out of loyalty to her son. Since Daphne's death, Edward had had almost no contact with the boy. The nanny looked after young James when he was at home; the rest of the time the boy was away at prep school.

And now, although very much as he had planned, Edward was about to marry a young woman he knew very little about. Together they were going to bring another child into the world; a necessary child, but nevertheless one that he neither wanted nor had time for. What was it all about? Edward had no idea, but he had long since made up his mind that he would be loyal to nothing and no one ever again. He would, however, continue to expect loyalty from *his* subordinates, and unfortunately for Grace, this would include her.

Being unaware of the turmoil in Edward's brain, Grace had been relieved when his telegrammed reply had been a marriage proposal. Although this was what she too had planned and expected, she was also aware of the risk she had taken. Girls who *got in trouble* often paid a high price; but now at least she could follow the dream of most American women. She may not be about to have a white wedding, but at least metaphorically, she would walk down the aisle before she turned nineteen. In the end, she had bet everything on Edward's sense of honour and his love for her. She would have been alarmed to know that his reason for proposing had nothing to do with honour, and even less to do with love. Edward was being entirely opportunistic. From the moment he had recognised Grace's ability, he had been contemplating marriage. An unpaid in-house connoisseur would be the perfect solution to his problems. The fact that Grace was about to have his child no doubt complicated matters, but at least she could no longer back out.

23

Grace had seen the posters and read the brochures, all of which reminded travellers that crossing the Atlantic on the *Queen Mary*, even for business, was a glamorous leisure experience. Arriving at Cunard's Pier 90, in New York, merely confirmed this impression. More than five city blocks long, the *Queen Mary*'s gigantic hull was as reassuring as it was impressive. However, as Grace made her way up the embarkation ramp and stepped into the ship's colossal interior, she suddenly felt cold. It was as if she were a dead soul, about to come face to face with Charon the ferryman, who would carry her across the river Acheron and on into the underworld.

'Good morning, Mrs Montague,' said a naval officer in a pristine black suit. The gold rings around the sleeves of his jacket belied his youthful appearance. 'Welcome aboard, ma'am.'

Swinging his arm to indicate a smart older man wearing the uniform of a high-class bell hop, he completed his greeting. 'Hodgkins, your personal steward, will show you to your cabin, where your luggage is already waiting for you, ma'am. He will also help you unpack and stow everything away. I understand that Mr Montague will be joining you shortly.'

Hodgkins' smile was wide, warm and fixed, as he led Grace not into Hades, but into the *Queen Mary*'s elegant interior.

After her wartime service as a troopship and a brief stint shipping some 20,000 British war brides and babies to the United States and Canada, in July 1947, the *Queen* had been refitted for passenger service. Air conditioning had been added along with 711 first-class cabins, 707 tourist-class and 577 third-class births. Grace was shown to a first-class cabin; her father's parting gift. Although Randolph usually travelled tourist class, in lieu of a sumptuous white wedding, he was offering Grace a deluxe honeymoon in the bridal suite of his favourite ship. On seeing the tickets, Grace had been elated, but her father and grandfather were heartbroken.

Heading for a new life, with a new life inside her, Grace visualised all those war brides and babies that the *Queen* had carried to the new world, and she wondered if she was the only pregnant mother travelling in the opposite direction.

Inside, this great liner was a showcase of elegant design, decoration and style, all of which harked back to the great days of the British Empire. Its first-class dining room resembled the inside of an English stately home.

Also the product of an unaltered hierarchical society, Hodgkins, the ship's steward, combined civility, friendliness, and respect in a most extraordinary way. Grace was somewhat nonplussed. Like most Americans her ancestors had crossed this same ocean in steerage. She was finding it difficult now to accept her apparent new role as a member of the nouveau riche. Not so her new husband, Edward. Having completed US customs formalities, he had quickly joined them and was soon commanding Hodgkins, as might befit an ex-officer of the Guards.

The *Queen* was built for speed, indeed during the war this had been her main form of defence. Enemy warships and especially German U-boats simply could not keep up. However, even before the war, the *Queen* had displayed a tendency to roll in heavy seas. In 1942, while operating as a troopship in the north Atlantic, she had been hit broadside by a twenty-eight metre freak wave. For several long minutes she had listed fifty-two degrees and had almost capsized, before slowly righting herself.

Grace and Edward were totally unprepared for the terrific battering the North Atlantic was about to administer. It had been said that first-class passengers on the *Queen* often encountered celebrities on board, but the storm they ran into less than two hours after leaving New York kept all but the hardy and foolhardy in their cabins. So far, Hodgkins had hidden his contempt well, but when Edward hung his head over the toilet bowl and with a loud retort proceeded to lose his breakfast, this old seadog had serious trouble controlling the width of his well-oiled smile. Having briefly enjoyed the moment, Hodgkins made a tactical and timely retreat, just as Edward called for his assistance.

It was not long before Grace herself needed a considerable amount of willpower to control the urge to vomit and to pray. Like her father, Grace had renounced God, but during the storm she had more than once considered prayer; she had also contemplated leaping over the gunwale and she may well have attempted this had she been able to find her way onto the heaving deck. Instead, for hours on end, she had simply pressed her forehead against the cool glass porthole of their cabin and stared at the steel grey Atlantic waves, rising and falling in every direction, as far as the eye could see and beyond.

In the meantime, occasionally whimpering for his long-dead mother, Grace's new husband Edward was lying on the bed, slowly pickling in an atmosphere of cigarette smoke, whiskey, sweat and stale vomit.

By the time the *Queen* sailed into the calmer waters of the Solent more than five days' later, Grace finally understood why Amelia Earhart's tiny aircraft, a smaller speck on an even larger ocean, had never been found. And then, almost as an aside, she reflected, *Charon the ferryman has carried me and my unborn child across the river Acheron, I wonder what awaits us in the underworld.* She did not have long to wait.

It was still dark outside as Grace heard the *Queen*'s mighty horn announcing her imminent arrival. With Hodgkins' help, Grace had already packed and was ready to disembark. Meanwhile Edward was still lying in bed. He was unshaven and looked much older than his thirty-four years. Again, with Hodgkins' help, Grace went on deck to watch the great ship make landfall. The morning was cool and damp, but after the stifling atmosphere of their cabin, the fresh clean air was welcome. They were still some way from the Ocean Terminal, and although the *Queen* was being escorted by two tiny but robust-looking tugboats, she was still travelling under her own steam. In the distance Grace could see the lights of Southampton. They appeared welcoming, like the Christmas lights in downtown Chicago. As they drew ever closer, against the skyline, she could make out the black skeletal outlines of what seemed to be hundreds of huge cranes.

Once again, in case anyone in the town had the temerity to be sleeping still, the ship's powerful horn announced its arrival. Outside now, Grace covered her ears, but she was thinking that even the deaf would be feeling the vibration that was coursing through her body. The horn's blast was followed by a series of bells, whistles and whoops, that appeared to be signals for a number of well-rehearsed manoeuvres to begin. Around the *Queen*, several busy tugs churned the Solent's waters to foam, as they pushed, pulled and persuaded their oversized sister to make landfall. Looking down on the expansive dockside, in the dawn's early light, Grace could see gangs of grey men in flat caps, hauling lines; lines that led to ropes and ropes that led to heavy steel cables, until eventually, from an apparent Gordian knot, a balanced web gradually developed that drew the huge ship into her berth at Southampton's Ocean Terminal.

On shore, a crisscross of rail lines guided shunters and mainline steam trains alongside the *Queen*'s hull, while cranes, telescopic gangways, conveyor belts, escalators and porters with wheelbarrows removed and sorted baggage and even automobiles. *How do they know where each piece is supposed to go?* Grace wondered, as she tried to identify her own packing cases amongst the many thousands emerging from the *Queen*'s hold.

Eventually, Hodgkins their personal steward led them to a disembarkation lounge, where on elegant *Queen Mary* stationary, Grace hurriedly composed a letter to her father and grandfather. With minutes to spare, she handed the envelope to Hodgkins, along with a ten-dollar bill. Fortunately, Edward did not notice the banknote changing hands.

Queen Mary, September 25th, 1947
Dearest Papa and Grandpapa,

I hope that you are both keeping well. You will have noticed that I am using the new fountain pen that Grandpa gave me as I was leaving. It writes beautifully and I love the colour of the ink. I was going to write to you both on the Queen Mary, but the crossing was far too rough. Edward spent most of the voyage in the bathroom or lying on the bed. I'm afraid he suffered terribly. I wasn't physically sick, but I could only manage a little bread with water during the entire five days. I think I lost a few pounds which can only be a good thing. The baby seems to be fine. The ship's surgeon took good care of me. Although not a trained gynaecologist, he told me that he has recently treated hundreds of expectant mothers. They were among the thousands of so-

called war brides that only a few months ago were travelling in the opposite direction. Fortunately, he was not called upon to deliver any babies. He was extremely nice, and he spent a lot of time with me. In fact, I saw him more than I saw Edward. In the end he even made a rather risqué joke about my becoming pregnant so quickly in the bridal suite. I am sure he would never have made such a comment even five years ago. I guess the war and its aftermath have changed attitudes considerably. We talked a lot about his job, which he told me mostly consists of handing out seasick pills to passengers. Apparently, he also has a small surgery, where he is sometimes called upon to fix broken limbs, stitch cuts and treat concussion, but his patients are almost always members of the crew that have had accidents below decks. On two occasions he was obliged to remove a ruptured appendix on the high seas. Otherwise he usually sits at the captain's table, apparently more often than the captain, where he has met several famous film stars, including Clark Gable, Errol Flynn, Bing Crosby and Bob Hope. He even met the British Prime Minister, Mr Churchill, and Jesse Owens, the negro who won four gold medals at the 1936 Olympics and enraged Adolph Hitler almost as much as Mr Churchill eventually did.

It turned out that he also plays the violin (the doctor not Mr Churchill or Jesse Owens), which he has carried with him all around the world. He told me that the glue joints had a tendency to come apart in the tropics. Eventually, he had taken the violin to

> *W. E. Hill and Sons in London, where they cured the problem by 'Tropicalising' it. Do you know what that means? Anyway, I invited him to Montague's the next time he is in London. He tells me that he never gets to Chicago. I wonder how long it will be before I get back there.*
>
> *I must finish now, because the train is almost ready to leave, and the steward has offered to post this letter for me. He says it might even return with the Queen. Edward sends his regards. The poor boy still looks unwell. I love you and I am already missing you both. I will write again when we reach London.*

Neither Randolph nor her grandfather could hold back the tears as they read Grace's letter. It was the final confirmation that she was gone. That same night, they both went to bed early and lying in their separate rooms, they both cried themselves to sleep.

In spite of the apparent disorder on the quay, in less than two hours, Grace and Edward had cleared customs and were sitting in the first-class compartment of a smart boat train, en route to London. As they pulled away Grace could still see passengers looking down from the lower decks. Travelling first class has advantages, she told herself, with only the slightest twinge of conscience.

Eventually, as the train pulled away and the mighty *Queen* slipped from view, Grace took in her surroundings. The sun was coming up now and in the dining car, breakfast was being served. While the coaches rattled over dozens of dockland points and junctions, Edward started to devour a large bacon and egg breakfast as if he had not eaten for a week. Actually, it had been just over five days since either of them had managed to digest anything, other than dried bread and a little tea. Grace was also hungry, but her attention had been diverted. For several minutes the train had rolled through a kind of wilderness of weeds and rubble. It was some time before Grace realised that what she was seeing was the devastation caused by German bombs.

Because of its strategic importance, Southampton had been one of the most heavily bombed towns in Britain. At the outbreak of war, the Supermarine Spitfire had been designed and developed there.

Grace reflected on her father's wartime occupation and was grateful that no long-range bombers, from either Japan or Germany, had been able to reach Chicago. In addition, Southampton's extensive docks had played a vital role in the build-up to D-Day. It was said that in less than one year, more than two million American servicemen and sixty-eight percent of all the Allied forces consigned to the European theatre of war had passed through its port, accompanied by their machines of war.

Undoubtedly, Southampton had been a town with a large target painted on its back. It was a surreal experience to be sitting in a first-class compartment, being served tea and toast by a waiter dressed in an immaculate white military-style mess jacket, while beyond the train's windows, signs of widespread death and destruction were visible everywhere. Although Grace was mesmerised, Edward was clearly immune to such scenes, because he was now attacking a second breakfast with gusto; it was hers.

As the train skirted the South Downs and rolled through the beautiful cathedral city of Winchester, Grace barely registered anything outside their tidy compartment. She had been subdued, initially by the uncomfortable sea passage, and now by the realisation that her new home was a land that had been ravaged by war. Southampton had obviously been hit hard, but what awaited her now in London?

24

Devastation was everywhere. It had been tidied up, boarded up and shored up, but somehow that only made things worse; rather like sweeping dirt under the carpet. One after another, houses and businesses had been sliced open like some ritual medieval disembowelment. The contents were gone, but the jagged outlines of buildings where people had lived, worked and died were still on display for everyone to see. Their living rooms, their toilets, their kitchens and their bedrooms, all revealed, like some open-ended Hollywood film set. Occasionally, whole streets were missing, or one solitary building stood alone and defiant, its walls on either side shored up with makeshift wooden beams and spars. Even London's famous West End had not been spared Nazi bombs, but miraculously the Montague house and its workshop had survived intact.

Walter Drake was waiting when the taxi stopped outside an elegant four-storey late Georgian town house. Although only fifty, Walter was already the oldest of Montague's old retainers. Several of his colleagues had not returned from two world wars. Others had been made redundant during the Great Depression and had never been reinstated. Walter was wearing his usual white flannel shirt with a starched detachable collar and a thin black tie. On top of this he sported a shiny black waistcoat that was buttoned to the top. An immaculate white apron protected this elegant attire.

As the newlyweds' taxi stopped in front of the Montague establishment, Walter's hand automatically touched his forehead in a kind of salute. It would have been quaint had it not been so obviously subservient. Grace offered her white gloved hand, but Walter hesitated, looking first at Edward, as if asking his permission. Edward's condescending nod to the older man surprised Grace. Like his relationship with Hodgkins, the *Queen Mary*'s steward, this incident demonstrated the contempt that Edward clearly had for those he considered beneath him. In America, he had always been polite and courteous; the perfect gentleman. Was this the British class system she had heard so much about? She wondered how Edward might behave with people he considered his superiors, but once again, she would find out sooner than she expected.

As Edward helped Grace out of the black hackney cab, Walter struggled towards the door with two heavy cases. He was about to set them down when the door opened wide. A smaller, older version of Edward stood in the doorway. He was blocking the entrance, but rather than stepping aside, he simply pushed past Walter who somehow managed to jump out of the way without losing his balance. 'Steady, Walter!' the old man announced, but it was a rebuke rather than a friendly warning. Again, Grace caught the tone.

'I'm sorry sir,' Walter had quickly replied. She was half expecting him to drop the cases and touch his forelock, but fortunately the man had already moved forward to take Grace's gloved hand, before lifting it gently to his lips. Although he looked and acted much younger, Grace guessed he was at least sixty years old. While travelling with her father she had met many mean-spirited wealthy men, and within seconds she had established that this one was cut from the same cloth; charming and arrogant. As her grandpa would have said, 'Someone has wiped his butt since ze day he voz born.'

With the slight lisp that only appeared when he addressed his father, Edward said, 'Farver, may I introduce you to my wife, Grace Montague, formerly Grace Scott.' Then, turning towards Grace, he simply said, 'My farver, Horatio Montague.'

'After Admiral Horatio Nelson,' the old man added. 'Both born on the same day, don't-you-know?'

When Grace calmly answered, 'September 29, 1758 I believe? And, if I might say so, you don't look so old,' Edward's father was genuinely shocked.

In the pause that followed, Edward looked at his father and raised his eyebrows, as if to say, 'I didn't tell her.'

'We do study history in America,' Grace added, and she smiled for the first time in several days.

Her new father-in-law immediately took her to his

heart, and Grace's quick retort would pay dividends for years to come.

Horatio Montague wore a stylish double-breasted suit with a matching waistcoat and a white silk shirt. He also sported a distinctive black silk tie with diagonal light blue stripes. Grace would soon learn the importance of such ties to men of a certain standing. They might wear an MCC tie, if they happened to be following cricket, or a tie indicating their old regiment, and of course there were old school ties, like the old Etonian ties that both Horatio and his son were wearing at that very moment. Indeed, it was not long before Grace realised that such ties were a kind of abridged uniform. A uniform that revealed a gentleman's social status and provided him with a sense of belonging. They were worn by men already blessed with every advantage that life can offer. Grace would also learn that these ties somehow endowed the wearer with astonishing self-confidence, and an innate, unshakable feeling of being right, even when they were palpably wrong. It was a trait that Grace would soon find infuriating.

25

The Montague establishment had a marble pillared entrance, leading to a wood, leather and polished brass interior. Rather like the *Queen Mary*'s interior, its style belonged to Britain's colonial past. The first three floors, otherwise known as the violin gallery, were given over to the retail side of the business. The top floor and an extensive attic had been the family's living quarters for much of the war, and on and off, it would be Grace's home for the next two decades.

During the London Blitz, the family had spent most nights in the cellar, along with their stock of instruments. The cellar had been reinforced with several sturdy beams and thick steel plates, but a direct hit would almost certainly have buried them alive. Apparently, Walter Drake, who had served as a wartime fireman, had assured them that such defences would not prevent death; they would merely prolong the process of dying.

Behind the house, a small courtyard led to a long, narrow and rather austere outbuilding, where in a fatherly manner, Walter Drake supervised his fellow craftsmen, a couple of ancillary workers and Harry the cleaner. These workshop employees were obliged to come and go via the workshop's rear entrance; a large fireproof steel door.

Ostensibly to avoid confusion, Montague's employees were required to address Edward and his father by their first names, the caveat being that they should always attach the prefix 'Mister', as in Mr Edward or Mr Horatio. However, in a further bizarre twist, as Mr Edward's wife, Grace was to be addressed as Mrs Edward. Conversely, the Montagues *always* addressed their employees by their surnames *without* the prefix. Grace had immediately seen this for what it was; English class distinction, and she hated it.

Under no circumstances were workshop employees ever to cross the courtyard without permission, and it was made clear that merely entering the gallery would result in their instant dismissal. Even the Montagues' privately educated sales staff were largely confined to the violin gallery. Consequently, other than family members, traffic between these two premises was rare; the only exception being the workshop manager Walter Drake, who acted as a kind of go-between.

In spite of Horatio's bonhomie, Grace had been pleased to hear that she and Edward would be more or less alone in the house. Because of Walter's warning in May 1941, her father-in-law had purchased a large house close to the Epsom racecourse. He had moved out just as the London Blitz came to an end.

As soon as Grace was settled in her new home, she sat down and with her new fountain pen she composed a second letter. She was already in love with the distinctive blue-green ink that her grandfather had provided, and from that moment it became a characteristic feature of her correspondence.

October 1st, 1947

Dearest Papa and Grandpapa,

We have already been in London for five days. Time flies. I would have written sooner, but since our arrival there has been so much to do. Unpacking, meeting Edward's family and generally just settling in. Quite honestly, Edward and I are still exhausted from the journey. How on earth people managed to travel before steam ships, steam trains and automobiles, I cannot begin to imagine.

The Montague house is everything that you said it would be, Papa, especially the violin gallery, as they call it. It immediately reminded me of the Queen Mary's opulent interior, not that I saw very much of that.

The main impression I have of England is how badly it has been damaged. In Southampton, large areas of the docks and much of the town itself have simply been flattened. The people must have suffered badly, but I think that London's pain was probably even greater. I guess that familiarity with the devastation has hardened Edward. He barely seems to notice the enormous bomb sites that are evident even now, five or six years after the Blitz; it is truly shocking. I have not yet begun to explore, but what I have already seen from the train and taxi has filled me with some trepidation. However, I don't want you both to worry, Edward's father appears to have taken a shine to me and I am sure he will attend to my needs. He insists that I get my rest and although he now lives out of town, he is constantly checking on my welfare. I have not yet had time to speak with Edward's son James, who was present when we arrived, but had to return to his school the following morning. As you know, he is attending a private boarding school, somewhere to the south of London, where he is being prepared for Eton College. He wears a very stiff and uncomfortable-looking school uniform with short trousers, apparently even through the harshest winters. In a week's time, he will be back home for a few days and perhaps then we can get to know one another better.

Neither Edward nor his father have had time to show me any instruments, but I will send you a report as soon as they do…

Horatio's house at Epsom was less than an hour by train. On most days, it was enough to ensure that he did not arrive at the shop until eleven o'clock and was gone by four in the afternoon. Unlike Edward, the old man was confident around women and as a consequence, he was an incurable womaniser. Whenever he was in town, he would walk unannounced into Edward and Grace's upstairs flat. It was not long before Grace started to suspect that he was hoping to find her in a state of undress. Nevertheless, she continued to give him the benefit of the doubt, wanting to believe that he was only concerned for her welfare. However, in the final months of her pregnancy, he had managed to surprise her several times. It was all fairly innocuous, but it was beginning to annoy Grace. Her father and grandfather had always been careful to give her as much privacy as she needed, but it seemed that here, she would be afforded none. She mentioned these intrusions to Edward, but he was unwilling to broach the subject with his father. His only comment was, 'My father is like a billy goat, Grace, best you keep out of his way.'

Grace was about to say that keeping out of the old man's way was not so easy, when he kept barging into their flat unannounced, but realising that Edward would be no help, she quickly dropped the subject. Instead, she simply walked into a Soho hardware shop, bought a chain door lock and proudly installed it herself.

In spite of their shared language, the unexpected foreignness of almost everything around her, coupled with her pregnancy's rapid progression, was causing Grace to feel exhausted almost every day and she often felt the need to take a nap in the afternoon.

When Edward's father had lived in the flat, the maid who cleaned and polished the violin gallery had also cleaned the family's apartment. Fortunately, when the old man had moved out of town, this domestic arrangement had continued without a break. In addition, after the death of his first wife, Edward had engaged a live-in nanny for his ten-year-old son James. Although Grace insisted that she would look after the baby herself when it arrived, Edward assured Grace that while continuing to act as a minder for his son, Nanny would also tend to the new baby.

It did not take long for Grace to get to know Edward's son better. James turned out to be more like his grandfather than his father. He was already displaying an attitude of superiority towards anyone he considered inferior, especially the company's employees and any member of the opposite sex. Grace quickly established that he was clever, but that he was also manipulative, lazy, and an insufferable snob. It was the kind of behaviour that Grace had observed many times at her old alma mater.

The expected collection of fine instruments turned out to be a disappointment. Grace soon realised that her father had probably purchased most of the Montagues' high-end stock. In fact, Edward and his father had been systematically asset-stripping the shop's pre-war collection of rare violins and bows for many years.

With little to invite her attention in the shop, Grace spent the final weeks of her pregnancy either preparing for the baby, or simply walking around the city, familiarising herself with local places of interest. There would be time enough to assess the Montagues' violin business later.

26

Bomb damage was evident everywhere. Sometimes it was simply large shards and flakes that had been chipped from stone facades, but often the destruction was almost total. Saint Paul's Cathedral now stood in the middle of a virtual wasteland. From Southwark Bridge to Blackfriars, practically every building had been razed to the ground. Thanks to her father, Grace was an exceptional map reader, but at ground level in such areas, her old central London street map was effectively useless. Without the aid of prominent landmarks, like the cathedral and the river Thames, she would have been lost on numerous occasions.

Although the war had been over for two and a half years, uniforms were everywhere. Soldiers, sailors and airmen, mainly American and British, wandered aimlessly around in small groups. There were tough-looking

Scotsmen with tartan kilts and impenetrable accents, being watched by policemen with strange helmets; domed like St Pauls. There were bus and train drivers, conductors, porters, taxi drivers, cinema usherettes, and children's nannies dressed in neat black costumes with little white caps. There were City gents sporting black bowler hats, each carrying a rolled umbrella, even when the sun was shining. There were working men wearing flat caps and greasy jackets. There were white-capped milkmen and coal-black coalmen, with black leather jackets and black leather hoods. There were groups of children in school uniforms, some of which were costly, while others were practically ragged. There were genteel ladies in pretty dresses, wearing fur coats and stylish hats with matching gloves and shoes, and there were rough-handed working women, wearing head scarves and printed cotton aprons.

And, the strangest thing, Grace mused, *is that the members of each group all dress in identical costumes.*

Indeed, at times it seemed to Grace that everyone in London could be identified by profession and class simply by the clothes they wore. It was as if nothing had changed since Chaucer's times. But at least, as Grace had written to her father;

November 24th, 1947.
I was pleased to see that there are no signs showing non-whites where they can and cannot legally walk, talk, drink, or eat. And there are no segregated restrooms. I have asked many Londoners and they all tell me that they never had the kind of signs I saw in Chicago when I was a girl, or more recently when

you and I were travelling in the southern states. In fact, groups of uniformed black servicemen seem to be welcome in restaurants, pubs and clubs, right across the city and apparently everywhere else in the country. It would seem that the only problems that black American soldiers have, are white American soldiers. This does not mean that the Brits have no prejudices. What the Brits have is class distinction. No working-class man would ever be allowed through the doors of any club that Edward or his father belong to. They would even exclude their adorable workshop manager and go between, Walter Drake. Walter is an intelligent, kind and courteous man, and I have grown very fond of him; he really is the gentlest soul, but he is working class. Even I can see and hear it. I have already learned enough to know that in Britain, a person's clothes and the way they speak automatically define their social status.

At the moment, in spite of their perceived lower status, Walter and Nanny are the best friends I have in London, but I must be careful, if I am too familiar with them, I have no doubt they will suffer.

By the way, thank you for your explanation about 'tropicalising', but Walter had already given me the gist. He tells me that placing extra pins through corners and through fingerboards does appear to hold glued joints together in hot wet climates. However, on the whole he is against such pins, because they cause problems when these instruments return to more temperate climes and need to be repaired.

Walter often reminds me of Grandpa. He is a skilled and knowledgeable craftsman. Unfortunately, it is Montague company policy never to discuss information about instrument identification with any of their employees, including Walter. On several occasions I have been reprimanded for pointing out salient features to the violin repairmen in the Montague workshop. In fact, I believe Edward would prefer it if I never went near the place, but you know me...

Edward's father, Horatio, is a genuine connoisseur. He is a good foil for my own studies, but at times he can be extremely difficult. He is an incurable snob, and he thinks nothing of being outrageously rude, even to his most trusted employees. I am often quite embarrassed for them. In addition, he and Edward are always trying to score points off each other. I'm afraid that Edward usually comes off worst, especially in matters of expertise. Horatio contrives the cruellest ways of putting him down, chiefly in front of others, but the poor boy never seems to learn. Horatio is also a womaniser. I am ashamed to admit it, but I occasionally use my femininity to get concessions from him that Edward would never allow. Write soon, I love and miss you both, Grace.

27

Grace was now in her eighth month and her belly was extended and heavy. Her favourite afternoon walk took her east along Brook Street over towards Soho, and if she still had the energy, on into Charing Cross road, with its plethora of second-hand bookshops. On her first visit to Charing Cross, she had found a fine leather-bound copy of Geoffrey Chaucer's *The Canterbury Tales*. Intent on presenting it to Edward, instead she had spent the next few days reading and attempting to understand this recent scholarly translation of Chaucer's old English prose. It was not easy, but it quickly became clear that the people of Medieval England were a rather promiscuous bunch. Grace was pleased that she had bought it. It had cost more than she had wanted to pay, but it would be a wonderful gift for Edward's upcoming birthday and hopefully it would stimulate him into action. The bookseller had explained that this 700-year-old book was one of the most banned pieces of literature in history. And that this particular unexpurgated version was one of the finest illegal translations available anywhere.

By now, Soho Square and Charing Cross Road were becoming a long walk for Grace, but she could not resist the cafés, street markets and barrow stalls that marked her way. Other than tea and an occasional biscuit, there was precious little on offer. Nevertheless, Grace quickly learned that tea with plenty of sugar (when available) was the British cure-all and indeed, usually it did help rejuvenate her for the return journey.

Being a tall, heavily pregnant American woman, Grace was easily recognised in Soho, and she soon found herself being addressed in familiar terms. Men and women called her m'dear, m'love, and even darling. The natives were not being disrespectful, they were simply being nice. Furthermore, as soon as she walked into a shop, or stepped onto a bus, people would immediately stand up and offer their seat. Here again, she quickly realised that they were not intimidated by her size, it was simply the custom. Children were taught to give up their seats for adults, gentlemen for ladies and everyone gave up their seats for old people, people with disabilities, and pregnant women. Even in Soho Square, she never had problems finding a place to rest.

At first, she'd had difficulty understanding the various accents, especially the genuine cockney dialect, with its picturesque rhyming slang, but there was always someone willing to explain. It took her a while to realise the complete rhyme was not always required. One word was usually enough. Her favourite was, 'Here ya' are, darling, take the weight off yer plates.' Apparently, *plates* was an abbreviated way of saying *plates of meat*, which rhymed with feet. Basically, this was an offer for her to sit down and take the weight off her feet. Another term she was particularly fond of was, 'What about a nice cuppa *Rosie Lee,* m'dear,' which translated as, 'Would you like a cup of tea?'

In spite of their recent and continued sufferings, jokes and laughter seemed to be everywhere. At first, Grace had assumed that this might be relief that the war was finally over, but eventually she realised that this is how these resilient people cope with life's everyday hardships. It had certainly seen them through the darkest days of the Blitz.

Immediately after her baby was born in January 1948, Grace was too absorbed with her day-to-day routine to walk very far, but in the middle of March, an unusually warm and sunny spell caused her to roll her new baby carriage down to Soho Square. Already something of a celebrity, Grace was welcomed back with open arms, while Phillipa, her new daughter, was like a magnet to all her new street friends. Indeed, it was in Soho that Phillipa was first given the name *Pippa*. Edward had immediately disapproved, but gradually, Grace and eventually even Phillipa herself adopted this rather appealing shorter version.

In Soho, advice on baby care was forthcoming on every street corner, and it was in just such a place that Grace was first introduced to the black market. Talking to a little old lady about the difficulty of finding nappies eventually led to a shopping bag being opened. Inside, neatly wrapped in brown paper, there were three brand new cotton nappies; Grace paid in dollars.

Although the war had been over almost three years, wartime rationing was still in force and it was about to get worse. During the war, many essential and non-essential foods had been rationed, along with clothing, furniture, and especially fuel. But in the war's aftermath, shortages had become arguably even more acute. Bread, which had never been rationed during the hostilities, was suddenly restricted. In the United States rationing had stopped in 1946, one year before Grace had left home. However, in Britain, rationing would not end until 1954, a full nine years after the armistice.

Following their wedding, Grace and Edward had filled trunks and suitcases with canned and processed foodstuffs and other items considered essential for the expected baby, but none of these things had lasted very long. Trying to still his hunger after his difficult Atlantic crossing, within days of landing, Edward had already eaten most of the canned meats.

It was comparatively easy to obtain goods on the black market, especially with American dollars. Unfortunately, Grace did not have a limitless supply. The substantial sums of money that her father was transferring to the UK went straight into Edward's bank account and was gone almost as soon as it arrived. When Grace attempted to tackle Edward about her father's endowment fund, initially he had insisted that registering her as a British subject had been extremely expensive. Later however, with growing self-assurance, he had simply told Grace that he was her husband and as such, *he* controlled her financial affairs;

adding that if she needed things for the baby, it would have to come out of Nanny's allowance.

With a sinking heart Grace realised that the money her father was sending was now effectively Edward's. The final straw came when the few dollars that she had managed to save disappeared from the drawer in her bedroom, where she also kept her underwear. Grace said nothing to Edward, because by now she knew exactly how he would react. He would blame the maid, or Pippa's nanny and then he would dismiss one or both of them.

With her dollars gone, Grace was completely reliant on the small and irregular payments Edward gave their nanny; but Nanny was already struggling to make ends meet and had almost nothing left over for Grace. In any case it was an embarrassment having to ask one of the family's employees for money.

Shortly after Phillipa was born, Grace had attempted to open a bank account in her own name, but she had been told by an unsympathetic bank manager that this would not be possible without her husband's written permission. It was some time before Grace understood that in this brave new democracy that millions had died to secure, almost no married women had bank accounts of their own and joint accounts simply did not exist.

And, this was not just custom; English law effectively denied women all forms of financial autonomy.

Gradually Grace started to realise that she was not alone, women from every walk of life were running households and raising children with no power or funds of their own. It did not seem to matter whether their husbands were well-paid civil servants or unemployed labourers, the procedure was the same. Men controlled how, when and where the household budget was spent. As Grace now saw it, British women may have won the right to vote in 1928, but that was pretty much the limit of their emancipation. It was exactly as her grandfather had predicted. In spite of their efforts in the war, the minute peace had been declared, women reverted to being inferior submissive beings. And while it was true that under this system, some women were indeed living happy and fulfilling lives, even these women did so only with their husband's active consent. And the sad reality was that like so many British and American women, Grace herself had aspired, planned and schemed to achieve her aim of becoming a happy housewife, supported by a handsome and benevolent husband. Instead it seemed, she was destined to become a captive woman, with little chance of escape. Edward even held her passport; while Pippa, who had no travel documents whatsoever, held her heart.

As with most women of her generation, in any gender conflict, Grace had a tendency to blame herself. Because her father and grandfather had been afraid that she would never find a suitable husband, they had provided her with the opportunity to become a completely autonomous connoisseur. Although she was extremely grateful for their support, in the back of her mind, Grace had seen this as a somewhat patronising act; an act that had made her all the more determined to prove them wrong. She had set her sights on Edward and his violin business, but in seducing him, she had gone too far. She had wanted the best of both worlds and in effect she had won, but it was clear now that the price had been too high.

Grace was aware that times were hard. Signs of austerity were everywhere, but with a little careful management, her father's dollar allowance should have been more than enough to support both her, and her daughter Pippa. In any case, Grace realised that the Montagues must have money, after all James was still attending one of the world's most expensive private schools. Moreover, unlike travelling with her father in their ancient Studebaker, Edward and his father always travelled first class. In addition, they were both members of several exclusive London clubs. So why had Edward suddenly become so mean with money? Since their arrival in England, he had not once taken her dancing, or to the cinema, not even after Pippa had been born. And, unless it was necessary for business, he had even refused to pay for her beloved concert tickets. In fact, Grace was increasingly convinced that, not only did Edward no longer love her, but that he was actually ashamed of her.

In bed, Edward wore a striped cotton pyjama suit, which he never removed, even during their infrequent and not particularly enjoyable sexual encounters. In the winter months, on top of his pyjama jacket he wore a long-sleeve pullover. On his feet, he wore thick woollen socks. But most off-putting of all, just before he climbed into bed, he would pull a woollen balaclava helmet over his head, so that only his eyes and nose were exposed. These extra items were clearly ex-army. They were a dull greenish-brown colour, known as khaki. Grace knew that khaki was a colour designed to camouflage soldiers in the landscape and she wondered if perhaps Edward was attempting to hide from her. If so, she mused, he was about as invisible as a polar bear in a coalmine.

This extra winter attire did not actually prevent Edward from making love. Every month or so, usually after an evening alone in the town, he would lift Grace's thick cotton nightshirt, exposing her hips and belly. He would then lay on top of her, move her legs apart and insert his already erect penis into her vagina, before proceeding to thrust rhythmically for several minutes, until with several loud grunts his orgasm arrived. During this uninspiring operation, Edward did not remove a single item of clothing. Admittedly English houses were cold, especially in winter, but Grace found this behaviour somewhat extreme. Since he always dressed and undressed alone, she had never seen him totally naked. She even began to suspect that perhaps Edward did not want her to see his war wounds.

Every morning after breakfast, Edward kissed Grace on the cheek, before going downstairs to the violin gallery. Preferring to eat at his club, he rarely returned to their flat until late evening, by which time Pippa was usually sleeping. At this point, he would kiss Grace again on the cheek, before sitting down in front of their small coal fire with his newspaper and a glass of port. These pecks on the cheek marked the extent of Edward's kissing skills. He never kissed Grace on the lips even when they made love. Neither were there any preliminaries to speak of. It was most unlike the cinema, or even the romantic literature she had recently started to acquire, from her friendly second-hand book seller on Charing Cross Road. Finally, at some point, Grace realised that Edward had only ever kissed her passionately once or twice, when they had made love in the Chicago hotel, after an evening watching dance movies. In conjunction with all her other guilt feelings she was beginning to wonder if Edward only saw her as a poor substitute for Ginger Rogers. After all, although Grace had always believed that they both had similar red hair, it transpired that for years Rogers had been dying her hair blond and that previously it had been auburn, rather than ginger. This was something not immediately apparent from her mainly black and white movies. But of far greater importance for Grace was the inescapable fact that her full figure simply could not compare. As Chaucer would have said of Rogers, *As any weasel was her body, graceful and slender.*

It never once crossed Grace's mind that it might not be Ginger Rogers or Scarlett O'Hara or even the rather prim Joan Caulfield that had been turning Edward on.

28

Edward was torn between nature and nurture. By nature, he was a homosexual. He had sensed it from an early age, but as his body and mind had matured, the world in which he found himself would not allow him to admit such a thing; not even to himself. Edward was not simply afraid of the fact; he was terrified. At Dunkirk, he had been surrounded by death, and men with appalling life-changing wounds, but he had never been afraid. He had done what he had been asked to do without question, and given the circumstances, he had fulfilled his duties with considerable bravery. But Edward was aware that there were things far worse than being killed or maimed.

In the 1940s and 50s, the stigma surrounding homosexuality meant that the lives of gay men and women were lived in secrecy and fear. Gay men in particular often went to great lengths to cover their tracks, including getting married and having children.

Homosexual acts between men had always been illegal, but during the war, when men of all persuasions were needed to fight and die, homosexuals in the armed forces were more or less tolerated. Indeed, for a while, many visibly gay men were even celebrated as performers in military comedy reviews. Blackouts and certain recognised meeting places were also reputed to have afforded opportunities for wartime homosexual liaisons. Nevertheless, an undercurrent of homophobic aggression had persisted, and as soon as the war was over, the witch-hunts returned with a vengeance. In 1952, the British newspaper *Sunday Pictorial* asked: 'Is it true that degenerates infest the West End of London and the social centres of many provincial cities?'

In that same year, the recently knighted actor Sir John Gielgud had been arrested in London and charged with a homosexual act. In spite of giving a false name, the press found out and reported the incident, at which point, it was splashed across the nation's newspapers, causing a national furore. Unable to bring themselves to mention the nature of the transgression, the press spoke of *gross indecency*. As a direct consequence of such reporting, young people in particular had no idea what homosexuality was, much less that it was a criminal offence. But having heard lewd talk, both at school and in the army, Edward knew enough to be extremely wary.

Throughout the 1940s and 50s, penalties for homosexuals who were unmasked were draconian. Widely regarded as a mental illness, by the mid 1940s, the alternative to spending most of their lives in either a prison or a mental asylum was chemical castration. By the mid 1950s 'aversion therapy' had become psychiatry's latest fad and it was peddled as a cure for everything, from nail biting and thumb sucking, to paedophilia. It was said to work by conditioning the patient to associate a *bad sensation* with being sexually attracted to a person of the same sex. The *bad sensations* that psychiatrists employed to combat such feelings were generated by vomit-inducing drugs and the application of electric shocks.

These measures alone would have been bad enough, but for Edward, the very idea of being exposed and ostracised by those around him was unthinkable. The regimented and regimental structures that had supported him since early childhood were all he had. Ever fearful of being unmasked, Edward became aggressively homophobic, and like everything else he had learned at school and in the military, Edward had learned his homophobic abuse by rote. *Backs to the wall* jokes and songs were endemic in both institutions. They might be told and retold a thousand times, but they were always followed by raucous barrack-room laughter. At such times, Edward strove not to laugh too little or too loud, and the stress of getting the balance just right often made him sick to the stomach. He learned quickly to think twice about every word he spoke and every gesture he made. Nevertheless, at some point, he was unable to resist the urge to seek release.

Meanwhile, Grace, who had once seen Edward as her salvation, was also wracked with guilt, wondering what on earth she was doing wrong. Having no one she could confide in, Grace again turned to books, but she found no answers, until one day while browsing through her favourite second-hand bookshop on Charing Cross Road, she came across a copy of *Mrs Beeton's Book of Household Management*. There had been at least twenty editions in her school library back in Chicago. Pure nostalgia caused her to open the work. It had clearly been well used and someone had added a number of comments in the margins. There are people who say that writing comments in books is a crime. At her old school, 'defacing literature' in this way was punishable by death or worse, but Grace often found such appendages quite profound and turning the pages slowly, she started to read them. Totally absorbed she eventually reached the end. Placing the book back on the shelf she said quietly but audibly, 'Why didn't Mrs Beeton write about marriage?'

'Do you mean about the intimate side of marriage?' said a voice through the wall of books in front of her. Shocked, Grace fumbled Mrs Beeton, almost dropping her in the process. Gazing between the rows of books she saw the old gentleman who had sold her the illegal translation of *The Canterbury Tales*. He had his face in a book, which is probably why Grace dared now to answer.

'Yes, I suppose so.'

'Well I could point you in the direction of several bookshops in Soho, but I expect you are looking for something more discerning.'

Grace remembered her father-in-law. Either by accident or design Horatio had twice left copies of *dirty* magazines in their flat. In both cases they had been placed inside old covers of a violin journal known as *The Strad*.

These magazines contained black and white pictures of naked women. Seeing these young women had instantly made Grace feel jealous. She was not jealous of their figures. One or two were easily as fat as her, but she had nicer breasts and her face and hair were undoubtedly more beautiful. In this respect these magazines had been something of a revelation, nevertheless she was jealous; she was jealous of their confidence and poise. These women clearly celebrated their appearance. They had no hesitation whatever exposing themselves for the camera, and then she thought, *Why should they feel ashamed?*

'Something more discerning. Yes,' she finally said.

The man turned to look at her. 'I believe you told me that you were from Chicago,' he said.

'Yes, that's right,' she replied, attempting to appear as confident as the girls in Horatio's magazines had obviously been.

The man hesitated before replying, 'I have a book in my personal collection.' He paused again. 'There are no photographs or diagrams. It is a kind of philosophical instruction manual, rather like Mrs Beeton, I expect you'd say. It was written by a German physician, Dr J. Rutgers, but it has since been translated. This particular edition was published in Chicago, in 1940, which is why I asked. Perhaps you know it? ... Yes, well I can see from your face that you don't. Just a moment, I know where I can put my hands on it.' As he turned to go, he whispered, 'It is not a proscribed work. At least not yet.'

The book took all the cash that Grace had left, but she was determined to give it a try. Nevertheless, before taking the money from her hand, the bookseller looked Grace in the eye and said, 'Are you sure, madam? This is a good book and quite possibly the only book of its kind that is available, but in my experience, it will only prove useful if both parties are keen to make it work, if you know what I mean? As we English say, "You can lead a horse to water, but you cannot make it drink".'

The book was indeed informative, but not quite in the way that Grace had imagined. She had been particularly intrigued by several headings in the book's Table of Contents referring to 'Strong Erections'. In spite of her misgivings, Grace read the work several times. The book began with an extensive and often rather dubious philosophical discourse about the relationship between men and women, but from a practical point of view it was of little value. In any case, without Edward's active participation things were unlikely to improve. Not only had he refused point blank to read the book, in a rage he had thrown it into the corner of the bedroom, declaring that he would not have his wife reading such filth. Grace later retrieved the book. Looking at the unassuming beige cover, she again read the title; *How to attain and practice… THE IDEAL SEX LIFE.* But if Edward was simply refusing to read the book, there could be no experimentation and no fulfilment. The bookseller had been right. You can lead a horse to water, but you cannot make it drink.

By now Edward was making love to Grace only rarely and even these sessions were uninspiring. Nevertheless, she continued to blame herself, wracking her brain to find a solution, or at least to understand what she might be doing wrong.

29

Grace was not one to be easily depressed, nevertheless, aside from her relationship with Edward, she was still somewhat disheartened by the present state of London and above all the city's severe air pollution. Fortunately, around this time a letter arrived from Chicago. It was not from her father or her grandfather, it was from the only friend she had ever had at school; Amanda Kowalski. The letter was short and to the point, but it filled Grace's heart with joy.

October 20th, 1950

Dear Grace,

A few days ago, your father came into our delicatessen to buy sausages, apparently for your grandfather's birthday. I found it a rather strange present, but he was convinced that it was exactly the right thing. He told me that his daughter had often spoken about our shop and since I was not busy, we started chatting. I simply could not believe it when I realised that he was your father. We talked for a long time. He seems such a nice man. You are very lucky. He told me that you are married, that you have a little girl and that you live in London, England. I also have a little girl – her name is Maja. She is eighteen months old. I am married to a Polish immigrant. He was a pilot in the Battle of Britain, but he is always saying that he is not a hero, and that he is just grateful to have survived. Before the war he was studying to be an eye surgeon, which is why he was able to come to the United States, but he could not have gone back to Poland anyway, because it is now occupied by the Russians. He is a lot older than me and he is not very handsome, but I love him. He is called Dawid, but everyone here calls him David.

If you have time, please write and tell me about England and your wonderful work in London. I sometimes wonder why I was given such an exceptional education, when all I do now is sell groceries to help pay for Dawid's studies. At least you appear to have benefited from your time at the 'Latin School', but then you always were a high-flyer. Best wishes, Amanda.

That same evening Grace sat down with her trusty fountain pen and on six closely written pages she poured out her soul.

November 1st, 1950

Dearest Amanda,

You cannot possibly imagine how happy I was to receive your letter. I had thought that with the exception of my father and grandfather, everyone in America had forgotten that I exist. Your letter was especially welcome, because of what you said about my father. In August this year my father wrote a long letter, in which he explained that as a result of his time working at the aircraft factory, he had contracted asbestosis. As you can imagine this news left me shocked and despondent. Over the next few days we exchanged numerous telegrams. Each time a telegram delivery boy arrived on his bicycle, I remembered those awful envelopes that families received during the war, informing them that their son, father, or husband was 'missing in action'. And I quickly turned into one of those unfortunate people, whose loved ones were 'missing in action'. Like them, I knew with absolute certainty that the next boy on a bicycle would be a harbinger of death. It took a long exchange of expensive telegrams to calm me down. However, since you did not know any of this, and because my father apparently came to your shop alone, perhaps the treatment he is getting now is helping. I am informed that there is no cure, but I take some comfort from your observation…

…I was also happy to hear that you have a little girl. Maja is a nice name and she will have no problem spelling it when she goes to school. My daughter Phillipa has quite a bit of trouble even

speaking her name. It's a good thing that everyone here calls her Pippa, even though my husband Edward doesn't like it...

...You asked about London. Well, it is difficult to explain how I feel about living here. London is not a very happy place. During the war they suffered badly, and a painful aftermath still persists. Nevertheless, other than Pippa, my greatest comfort are the people, in spite of all they have been through, they are always helpful, polite and friendly...

Even so, there is a greyness about the city and its residents, especially around their eyes. There is almost nothing in the shops and what there is cannot be purchased without government ration coupons or black-market dollars...

As for work, even though we have a nanny, Pippa is only two years old and consequently I am mostly concerned with domestic matters. Finding suitable food and clothing for her is never easy. Rationing slows the pace of food shopping considerably, and most of Pippa's clothes are second hand, but by comparison we are well off...

I mostly try to avoid what most poor Londoners eat and appear to enjoy, except for their fish and chips, which I have developed a taste for. However, I can barely even look at their jellied eels, or their boiled cow's stomach and udder, which I find quite disgusting. They also sell several kinds of sea molluscs, called whelks, cockles and mussels. All of these delights, like the fish and chips, are wrapped in old newspapers and served with salt and vinegar. A large mug of tea usually helps to wash these things down...

Many of London's children are the very definition of street urchins. Their clothes are ragged and like their faces, arms and legs, they are filthy. Their knees are either bloody or scabbed. Even in this climate, many run the streets barefoot. What shoes they have are scuffed and worn. If they wear socks, these are generally gathered around their ankles. When pulled up, they are so full of holes, you wonder why they bothered putting them on in the first place. The boys wear short trousers, while the girls wear thin one-piece cotton dresses. These garments are invariably either too large or too small. In cold weather, both sexes simply pull a woollen vest over the top. For the most part these children are skinny to the point of emaciation. Beneath the dirt, they have incredibly white skin. They have snotty noses and they look timeworn. They break my heart. It's not that I have not seen such children before; I have. While traveling with my father in the United States, I saw many. They were mostly black or American Indian children. I never believed that black, white, or even red and yellow, were appropriate terms for describing racial differences. Whatever the natural colour of their skin, something about these desperately poor children gives them all the same sickly grey countenance.

Quite apart from appearance, there is also an unpleasant smell about poverty. I guess it's caused by poor hygiene and bad diet. It's a kind of musty, mouldy odour, but for some reason, like the sound of a rattlesnake I once heard at a truck stop in New Mexico, once you have experienced it, your brain never lets you forget. I first came across this smell on two blankets my pa purchased at a thrift store on Route 66. That was back in 1946. I can still recall that smell. At the time it caused my throat to constrict. This should not be the aroma a child gives off. All children should smell milky-wonderful, like my Pippa...

...It sounds as if you are as disappointed as I am about our wasted education. I was hoping that women would soon be following a new course. I can remember you and I talking about the fact that women can do virtually any kind of work these days, including flying four-engine transport aircraft, but it would seem that society still expects us to cook, wash, iron and change nappies.

Still, it is not always drudge work. I am constantly adding to my father's files and ledgers about instrument identification. I also check out the auctions every month or so. No one seems to have much idea or interest and I regularly find a couple of wrongly catalogued gems. Apart from being entertaining and productive work, visiting the auction houses gets me out of my own house. Even so, it is humiliating to see how quickly everything has returned to the same old status quo (note my use of Latin there – all is not lost)...

I am sorry if this letter sounds depressing. Please don't let that stop you from writing, I will try to be more positive next time. With kindest regards, also to your family.

30

Six months after Pippa's second birthday, Edward sailed to America with five instruments that Grace had discovered at various auctions. Considering the fact that she was a busy mother it was a fair haul. They were not of the first rank, but they were of sufficient quality to warrant taking them across the Atlantic. Edward's father, Horatio, had also supplied a beautiful Cremonese cello by Joseph Guarneri senior. To distinguish this Joseph Guarneri from his violin-making son, who was also called Josef Guarneri, this first Joseph Guarneri came to be known as Joseph filius Andrea, meaning Joseph son of Andrea; Andrea Guarneri being his father and the founder member of the Guarneri dynasty. The whole thing then became almost farcically complicated, because this father and son each had violin-making brothers called Peter. One Peter eventually moved to Mantua and the other to Venice. As a consequence, they came to be known as Peter Guarneri of Mantua and Peter Guarneri of Venice. Meanwhile the son of Joseph filius Andrea, who became the most famous and most valuable violin maker of the Guarneri family, was given the epithet *Del Gesù*.

While studying her father's journals, such family relationships had almost driven Grace crazy, especially since on the Italian peninsula, there were many more equally complex violin-making dynasties. The difference being that while Grace had made the effort to master these convoluted family trees, Edward had not.

In spite of her experiences on the *Queen*, Grace had been keen to travel to America herself. She had been feeling homesick. She missed her father and grandfather terribly, but most of all she had wanted to show them her beautiful daughter. Unfortunately, Edward had refused to sanction the journey, citing Pippa's health as the main reason. Grace had to admit that Pippa had often been ill. She blamed this on London's polluted air and argued that sea air on the voyage would do the child good, but Edward would not be persuaded. In any case, having no money of her own, Grace had no other option. In addition, Edward was still withholding her passport and he made it quite clear that the authorities would never allow her to leave Britain without his express permission. Pippa had a British father and had been born in Britain, she was therefore a British citizen. Edward had even cited the fact that American GI war brides would not be returning home either. It was a statement that sent a shiver down her spine.

Nevertheless, Grace was not a woman to be easily cowed. Her natural instinct was to manage problems with stealth rather than confrontation. She could have written to her father outlining the situation, but knowing that he was struggling with asbestosis, and being herself fiercely independent, she had no wish to involve him in her matrimonial problems. In any case Edward was still the apple of her father's eye. In spite of their *unplanned* pregnancy, her father had been fooled by Edward's charm offensive, just as she had been. For this reason alone, attempting to undermine his reputation would not be easy.

Grace was equally aware that Edward had already taken and would continue to take every opportunity to consolidate his standing with Randolph. This belief was quickly confirmed when Grace received a letter from her father, the day after Edward returned from his latest sales trip.

How ironic, she mused, that it must have been carried on the same ship that Edward had sailed home on.

7th July, 1951

Darling Grace and little Pippa, I hope that you are both keeping well, and that Pippa is over the breathing difficulties that you mentioned. Your grandpa and I miss you both so much, but we completely understand your decision not to risk the little one's health on the journey, especially after your own experience on the Queen. We had not realised how awful it must have been for you, in particular with you being pregnant at the time. Edward told us how badly you had suffered. It was lucky that he was already an experienced sailor and was able to look after you. Although having the ship's doctor close was probably a comfort, under such circumstances, it is always better to be with a loved one.

The photographs that you sent with your last letter show just how beautiful Pippa is, she clearly takes after you and your mother in that respect. Your grandfather and I have never been anything to look at. We can see from the photographs that she is running around and clearly getting up to mischief. Her nanny looks like a nice lady. Edward says that she helps you out in the nursery and the kitchen and that you also have a cleaner to do all your housework. Even so, your grandpa and I remember how exhausting it was raising you. You were such a little bundle of energy. But our real problems with you came later. Neither of us had any idea about women's issues. We have not really talked about this, but we both want to tell you that we never blamed you for your early pregnancy. We blame ourselves. We are really sorry for not having prepared you well enough. Still it all seems to have worked out fine. Neither are we angry with Edward. I admit that we were both shocked at the time, but being the true gentleman that he is, at least he did the right thing, and from the way that he talks about you and Pippa, we are comforted to know that he clearly loves you both as much as we do.

Edward tells us that having a nanny and a cleaner gives you the time to accompany him to the auctions. He also assures me that you are still studying, that you are still a keen student and that he is proud to be of assistance. He certainly knows

> *his stuff. The Joseph filius Guarneri cello was a magnificent find and what an interesting story. It must be fun mixing with royalty, even if they are only Queen Elizabeth's cousins. Connections of this nature are so important, especially in England. The other instruments he found are also very nice. They may not be top drawer, but they are all of exceptional quality. They certainly demonstrate his wide-ranging knowledge, which will undoubtably help you in the long term...*
>
> *I think Edward enjoyed the 4th July celebrations here, even though he made some unfunny remarks about America being a British colony...*

The letter continued in a similar vein for three more pages, but a final paragraph in her grandfather's hand gave Grace an idea. Her grandfather had written about wanting to start a fund for Pippa's future and he asked if he should send the money to the same bank account that her father used. Her grandfather had always been a touch suspicious of Edward's smooth upper-class rhetoric; perhaps he sensed something. Either way, since travelling to the United States was likely to be out of the question for some time, Grace was suddenly mindful that her most important task now was to somehow regain control of her money. Exposing Edward's frailties would have to wait.

Quickly hiding the letter, she sat down and composed a reply to her grandfather, in which she urged him to wait a few days. Having dispensed with the usual greetings Grace wrote;

> *16th July, 1951*
> *Dear Grandpapa, Under the circumstances I think it would be best to send the money to a lawyer, who can then set up a proper fund for Pippa. That way it will not get mixed up with our everyday expenses where it might prove too much of a temptation should I wish to buy a new dress. We don't need to concern Edward with this, the poor boy has more than enough to do. If you agree I will make the arrangements and let you know.*

Grace was not sure if this ruse would work, but her grandfather's quick response suggested that he was not as naive about Edward as her father clearly was. After a long and rather rambling preamble, about the weather and a repair job that he was working on, Hermann Scott, who was a born sceptic, sent the following paragraph:

> *July, 1951*
> *… I was also happy for your suggestion about keeping work and pleasure separate. We all need a little privacy in our lives. But in spite of feeling well, I am slowly getting old and I have also been thinking about making arrangements with a lawyer for Pippa's future. You never know what might happen. What do you think? Should I do this? You know that I trust your judgment, please let me know. But please Grace, don't mention this to your father, under the circumstances he is keeping well, but you know how he worries.*

The message could not have been clearer. It may not have been written in code, but her grandfather had been careful to avoid writing anything that might interest an unauthorised reader.

After receiving her grandfather's reply, Grace wandered across the courtyard with Pippa, ostensibly to give her daughter a little exercise and catch some of the sunshine that filled the space for a few hours each afternoon.

Grace already had a good working relationship with Walter Drake. Although Walter was ten years younger than her grandfather, they were similar in so many ways. They were both skilful, experienced craftsmen, and, if she had not misjudged Walter, like her grandfather, he too was a born sceptic.

Grace had chosen a time when both Edward and Horatio were out of town. Nevertheless, she spoke guardedly with Walter. Having no wish to cause him grief, she suggested that he might like to join her for lunch at a small worker's café she knew of in Soho. The very nature of this proposed meeting place immediately indicated that their rendezvous would not simply be private; it would be clandestine. Neither Grace's father-in-law nor her husband would have been seen dead in such a place. It was also unlikely that any of the violin gallery's staff would venture so low. As for Walter's colleagues, from eight-thirty in the morning until five-thirty in the evening, they rarely left the Montague workshop.

Grace was sitting at a small linoleum-covered table when Walter arrived. She was alone. They both ordered the meal of the day, and quickly got down to business. 'What's the problem, Grace?' Walter had asked, as they waited for their meals to arrive.

'Walter, I don't want to burden you with my problems, it's just that I don't know who else I can talk to…'

Walter held up his hand and said gently, 'Is this about your financial situation, Grace?'

Grace put down her knife and fork and stared intently at the older man. After a few moments Walter continued, 'Eileen, Pippa's nanny, and I are old friends. We went to school together, just around the corner from here and naturally we talk. She has been worried about you and Pippa for some time. She tells me that you cannot access the money your father sends you and you cannot open a bank account. Is that right? Is that the problem?'

But from the look on Grace's face, he could see that it was.

Two weeks later, with the help of a guarantor, Grace had her own bank account. The guarantor was not Walter. For obvious reasons neither had wanted to use Walter's name. Grace and her guarantor met only briefly at a bank on Oxford Street where the man was clearly well known and respected. Walter had been present, but few words were exchanged and once the transaction had been completed, they each went their separate ways.

For Grace, opening this account was like opening the door of her prison cell.

31

Grace was screaming as she ran down the steps and across the fog-bound courtyard that led to the Montagues' rear workshop. By the time she reached the door everyone inside was on their feet. Walter Drake was already standing in the open doorway, squinting into the fog, trying to see what the fuss was about. Walter was not a man to be fazed by screaming. Having worked as a fireman during the London Blitz, he had heard more than his fair share of screaming. But this time it was different. He still could not see Grace, but he recognised her voice. What worried him most was knowing that Grace was not prone to panic attacks.

As she emerged from the green mist, Walter saw that she was carrying her almost five-year-old daughter Pippa and that the child was hanging limp in her arms. Within seconds Walter recognised the symptoms and the realisation filled him with horror. During the First World War, as a raw recruit in 1915, almost immediately after his arrival at the Western Front, Walter had been gassed. Having been treated with oxygen by medics on the battlefield, he had survived and was shipped back home, where after receiving further oxygen therapy, he had slowly recovered. But that had been the Western Front in 1915; this was the West End of London in 1952.

Walter knew there was no time to lose; the child was still breathing, but her lips were already blue. Walter was fifty-four years old, but snatching the child, he ran back into the workshop and out through its steel-clad rear exit. Grace, Harry the cleaner and one of Walter's younger colleagues followed. They almost lost him in the thickening fog as he ran north and crossed Oxford Street. It was not long before Walter felt his own lungs burning, and his mind raced back to the fear and pain he had felt in the trenches more than thirty-five years earlier.

Although it was mid-afternoon, visibility was less than a car's length. Fortunately, everyone was managing to keep up the pace, otherwise they would simply have been lost. Remarkably Walter was finding his way with comparative ease. During the wartime blackouts, he had learned to move around the area in total darkness. He knew that the distance they had to travel was just over half a mile. He was fit for his age but having covered more than half the distance carrying a heavy child, while breathing choking air, he was beginning to slow down. Soon, everyone was taking turns to carry Pippa, while Walter led the way. Taking several short cuts, they finally reached Harley Street, where Walter hammered on a door until an angry nurse opened it.

Having taken one quick look at the child, her anger rapidly dissipated, and she ushered them all inside. Everyone but the child was coughing and wheezing heavily now. As they laid Pippa down on an examination bed, her body was limp, her skin grey and her lips a deep purple.

The doctor took one look and immediately ordered oxygen. Grace heard the word *Hypoxia*, but she already knew that whatever the medical term was, her daughter's illness had been caused by the blanket of thick green gas that was enveloping the city. Even inside this spotless surgery its evil was present. It was as if some Hammer horror movie had spilled out from the set and shrouded the city.

Grace's distress was not helped when the nurse ushered them out of the treatment room. Believing that her daughter was either dead or dying, when Walter put his arm around her, even though she was much larger than him, she fell on his shoulder and cried like a child herself. A considerable amount of time elapsed before the doctor emerged from the room. Addressing Grace in a solemn manner he said, 'I presume that you are the child's mother?' But without waiting for a reply he simply continued, 'Your daughter is going to be fine. She has already told me that her name is Pippa and she is asking after you. Pippa will need to stay here for a couple of days, by which time hopefully this awful fog will have lifted. Nurse will need to take some details; after which you can go in and see her.'

Grace lifted her eyes and for several seconds she looked intently at the doctor as if he were an apparition. Finally, she reached out and grasping both his hands, she thanked him profusely.

'Yes! Yes!' he managed to answer, before turning to

Walter and saying, 'Another good job, Walter, I don't think I need to tell you that you arrived in the nick of time.'

Grace stared at the two men, the grey-haired doctor in his white coat and Walter still wearing his white apron. Again, the doctor spoke. 'And what about you, Walter? In view of your pre-existing respiratory problems, I think we should give you a little oxygen too. It should help to ease that slight wheezing I can hear.'

'I'll be alright, Professor,' Walter answered, but by now Grace was also noticing his laboured breathing, indeed her own lungs were still burning from the exertion.

'Let me be the judge of that, Walter,' said the professor. 'After all, I'm the one with the letters after my name.'

Even with her own concerns, Grace did not miss the irony in the doctor's words, nor the bonhomie that passed between the two men. As the doctor left the room to attend to his other patients, Grace turned to Walter. 'That was him,' she said. 'It *was* him, wasn't it? My bank guarantor?'

'Yes!' said Walter quietly, while at the same time placing his fingers on his lips, indicating that Grace should say no more.

Walter's two colleagues slowly made their way back to the shop, leaving Walter, Grace and Pippa at the Harley Street clinic. The following day Walter returned to work. Six days later, when the fog finally lifted, Pippa also returned home, at which point, along with Grace and her nanny, she was immediately shipped off to Grandfather Montague's house at Epsom.

In the cleaner air around Epsom, Pippa improved rapidly, but air quality in the city was still bad. It had been bad on and off since the Industrial Revolution. For generations, London had been the most overpopulated and industrialised city in the world, and now, like the whole country, the war had almost reduced it to bankruptcy. In order to boost production, safety and environmental concerns had often been ignored, and cheap coal continued to be burned in power stations and millions of domestic fires.

In 1952, the difference had been the intensity and duration of the smog. Grace had been profoundly shocked, but being used to such conditions, most Londoners had not reacted with panic. It was only later, when the true extent of the horror started to emerge, that action was taken. Although figures varied, it gradually became clear that the smog of December '52, was the worst ever recorded. In less than one week, around 4,000 people had more or less choked to death, while a further 100,000 had been incapacitated. Later estimates indicated that up to 12,000 had perished in the smog's aftermath.

It was somewhat ironic that the newly formed National Health Service, which had helped to bring Pippa into the world, had all but collapsed under the strain. Nevertheless, in the long term the NHS had been foremost in supplying the statistics that had eventually led to Norman Dodds and the British Labour Party forcing Parliament to implement the Clean Air Act in 1956. Although this act introduced measures to reduce air pollution, by the time they were implemented, Pippa was already a teenager. Nevertheless, the smog did have two immediate and lasting consequences; it contributed to Grace becoming a lifelong socialist and it cemented her relationship with Walter Drake.

32

On the evening of their arrival at the Epsom house, having packed Pippa and her nanny off to bed, Horatio Montague ushered his daughter-in-law into his private study. On a low table, in front of a blazing coal fire, stood two crystal glasses and a bottle of vintage port. On either side of the table a pair of wing chairs half faced the fire.

'I wanted to take this opportunity for us to have a quiet chin-wag, Grace,' her father-in-law began. 'We never seem to have much time alone these days.'

Remembering her father-in-law's regular incursions into her flat, Grace was already starting to feel a little uneasy, but this time it seemed the old man's conversation was not to be of a sexually suggestive nature.

'First of all, I want to say how pleased I am that things worked out well for Phillipa, it seems to have been a close-run thing. A good job Drake was there, don't you know? Good man that... chap, always seems to know what to do. Even so...'

Grace sensed that her father-in-law was about to warn her not to allow the workers to take advantage of the incident, and it made her angry. Horatio, Edward and even young James had a way of talking to or about their workforce that was nothing short of demeaning.

'Walter Drake saved Pippa's life,' Grace broke in.

'Yes, yes, damned good show! Damned good show!' said Horatio, slightly taken aback by Grace's tone.

'He knew exactly what to do and where to go,' she reminded him, 'And... the Dr... Professor, seemed to know Walter personally.'

'Yes, apparently they worked together in the Blitz, when Drake was a fireman and the Professor was treating the wounded. Drake lost his wife and children just ten days after Edward lost his wife. They were hard times, hard times, but that's a dozen years ago... water under the bridge now.'

'I don't know, I don't think people forget so easily,' said Grace, thinking not only about Walter's loss, but about Edward's apparent inability to forget *his* beautiful debutante wife. In Grace's mind it was the only possible explanation for Edward's total lack of interest in sex since Pippa's birth. She could have counted the times he had made love to her on the fingers of one hand. Neither Edward nor her father-in-law had ever mentioned the dead wife's name, but a large silver-framed picture of Edward and a slender blonde woman stood on the dressing table in their shared bedroom. It had been taken on their wedding day. It showed Edward wearing the dress uniform of a Coldstream Guards officer, while his new wife was resplendent in a white silk wedding dress, whose seemingly endless train could be seen cascading down the cathedral steps. There was no hiding the fact that she was stunningly beautiful, like a genuine film star, and every day when Grace was faced with this image, it broke her heart.

Ignoring Grace's comment, her father-in-law continued. 'Things have not been easy for quite some time.'

At first, Grace thought that the old man was referring to the death of Edward's first wife, but she soon realised that he was talking about the business.

'Financially the company has been going through a rough patch; what with the depression and the war and now the fact that everyone is watching their pennies… To be quite honest, if it had not been for Montague's relationship with your father, we might well be in the poor house.'

'Oh, I doubt that!' said Grace demonstrably casting her eyes around the old man's study. 'I imagine the antiques in this room alone would keep you going for several years.'

'Yes, well you may be right, my dear.' He laughed. 'But we should not be thinking about selling off the family silver just yet. I will be sixty-nine this next week and the only thing good about sixty-nine, or as the French say *soixante-neuf*, is the sexual position.'

Grace's nonplussed expression caused the old man no little amusement, but his only comment was, 'What in God's name have you two been doing for the last… what is it… how long have you been married now… well, never mind. Where was I… Ah yes, sixty-nine.'

Grace rolled her eyes. The old man was seventy-two, he was pretending, just to introduce this rather pathetic piece of sexual innuendo. She hated it, but hated herself even more for thinking, *Why can't Edward be more like his father, just once in a while?*

Her father-in-law started again. 'Look here, Grace! I want to slow down. I need more leisure time. The problem is that if Edward is left on his own, he will ruin the business. As you already know, he has almost no expertise, although he likes to pretend he has. These days he is only interested in playing toy soldiers at the Guards Club. And to be quite honest, my grandson James will probably be even worse. He is a playboy in the making if ever I saw one.'

Grace meditated for a while as they both sipped their vintage port. The old man was right, it did not bode well for Montague's.

'So, what exactly are you expecting me to do about it?' asked Grace. 'It's too late to teach Edward, even assuming he would listen, and he is not about to hand over power to me. As for James, the little prince of Eton, he will not even give me the time of day. He constantly reminds me that his mother was a debutante, whereas I am just an American mongrel.

'For almost two years, James has been safely ensconced at Eton College, for which I am genuinely grateful. Nevertheless, I understand that the fees are astronomical, but then of course, the air west of London is probably also cleaner. In fact, James is always telling me that Eton is close to the Royal Palace of Windsor, which is probably why your new Queen Elizabeth has chosen it as her clean-air-weekend retreat. But in my opinion, Eton air is turning James into a boastful little monster. Indeed, he is fond of telling his American *'stepmother'* that Windsor Castle is the oldest and largest occupied castle in the world, and that it was built in the eleventh century by a Frenchman; William the Conqueror, the first Norman King of England. And, in the same breath, he tells me that the name Montague is of Norman origin. However, in saying so, he conveniently forgets to mention that although his Montague ancestors were indeed French, they arrived in England in the nineteenth century, some eight hundred years later, and that they came not as conquerors, but as itinerant violin makers.'

'Yes!' her father-in-law cut in. 'I had almost forgotten your penchant for history.'

'At least it is accurate history,' she replied. 'Like his father, James manages to provide just enough detail for any gullible listener to draw their own, usually misguided conclusions.

'In exactly the same way, after the evacuation of Dunkirk, using a silly accident, Edward turned himself into a wounded war hero. And, since that time, by carefully combining the fact that when the Germans were threatening to invade England, Edward's regiment... also your old regiment... the Coldstream Guards, and by implication Edward himself, was selected to be the Royal family's personal bodyguard. Indeed, to hear Edward and James talking, they are practically on first-name terms with the Queen, and both their families are steeped in English history. Sadly, most of this history is an illusion born of delusion, but perhaps I should believe it, because even Queen Elizabeth's ancestors arrived in the nineteenth century. Weren't they German?'

Grace took a deep breath to recover. She could feel her blood boiling as she stared at the old man. Eventually, calling her father-in-law by his first name, she repeated her question. 'So, what do you expect *me* to do, Horatio?'

'I expect you to rescue the firm,' he said calmly.

'And just how do you expect me to do that?'

'I think the question should be, what other choice do you have, Grace? You have a daughter who needs your support. Your father is unwell; your grandfather is seventy and for the foreseeable future, he will probably have his hands full looking after his son. My guess is that they will soon be forced to wind up their business.'

It was true, her father and grandfather had been planning to visit Grace this last summer, but Randolph's asbestosis was clearly taking over their day-to-day existence. After that first awful letter and the frantic exchange of telegrams that had followed, in a further series of letters her father had become quite philosophical.

> *…Asbestosis is not a cancer, it's a chronic progressive lung disease, caused by inhaling asbestos fibres over a long period of time. It was working at the aircraft factory. We used asbestos all the time. We used it both inside and outside engines; for asbestos blankets, brakes, cockpit heating systems and general insulation. It was impossible to avoid. The way I look at it, other men and women lost their lives immediately during the war. At least I had*

many years of joy with you and Grandpa. I must be grateful for that. I look upon it now as part of the price that had to be paid to defeat fascism.

To be honest, the disease was already quite advanced when I found out, but since there was nothing anyone could do, this was all rather immaterial. I am only sorry that I will not get to see Pippa, because travel, either by boat or plane, is out of the question for me right now and I really do not want you to bring her here. This is a sick house; it is no place for a child. Just keep sending Grandpa and me those beautiful photographs…

At some point, Grace had offered to travel to Chicago alone to look after her father, but his reply had been emphatic.

…No, I don't want you to come here, Grace. Your place is in London with Pippa and Edward. Grandpa and I are managing well enough and we have a home help.

Her father had laughed out loud as he concluded with the words;

…We're not destitute just yet. If all else fails, I know a quiet stream not far from here, where you only have to dip your beard in the water…

As she read his words, through her tears, Grace had also laughed, but it had ended abruptly, when for a few agonising seconds she had suddenly felt alone and completely helpless.

Her grandfather had rounded off her father's letter with a quick note in his usual neat mini script.

…We are both just fine and dandy.

Grace was pleased now that she had not told her father and grandfather about the deterioration in her relationship with Edward. They would have more than enough to worry about. Neither had she ever mentioned the fact that her new husband was lazy, tight-fisted and mean, or that his expertise barely passed muster. She had been particularly careful to avoid any reference to financial matters, but as if reading her mind, her grandfather had rounded off by asking;

…How about you, Grace, are you alright for money?
I hear that London can be an expensive place.
Especially with a baby.

So often, Grace had wanted to send a telegram by return, but the nature of telegrams made them extremely expensive, money that she simply did not have. Moreover, if they were arriving in an office environment, not only would it be difficult to keep their arrival confidential, but using the excuse that what they contain may well require an immediate reply, Edward might be tempted to open a telegram.

In this respect, although the exchange of information in letters was much slower it was undoubtedly safer. Even Edward would be unlikely to open a Royal Mail letter.

33

Somewhere, through the train of her thoughts, Grace heard her father-in-law's voice again. 'And, I am guessing that when that happens, any income that you might still have from the company will dry up. I am not trying to be mean here, Grace,' his voice had grown mellow, 'but you will need to make arrangements soon.'

'As you must know,' Grace quickly replied, 'I have no income from our family shop. Edward controls all our money, even that which my father sends from the States.'

'Oh, I am sure that you have something put away somewhere; you're a highly intelligent woman, Grace, even if you did marry Edward,' he said with a quiet chuckle.

'Well, if you manage to find out where it is, please tell me. I could certainly use some of it. Since I arrived in England, Edward has always been tight-fisted, with what he calls *his* money.'

Once again Grace was seriously angry, and her father-in-law could see it. 'Look here, old girl—' he started to say.

'I am not your old girl. I am not one of your floozies.'

'All right, Grace, I'm sorry; let's start again. You asked me what I expect you to do. Well, let me answer by telling you that I do not expect you to do anything alone. I will help you.'

Grace gave a derogatory laugh.

'No, I really will help you, and I want to begin by showing you something.'

With that he drained his glass, stood up and beckoned Grace to follow. She was already wary and now she was weary, nevertheless she followed him.

As they crossed the room he spoke again. 'I am going to show you why I bought this house.' From his watch chain he removed a small key. It was the key to a drop-front desk that stood in one corner of the room. 'Do you know what this is?' he casually asked. 'No? Well, let me tell—' But Grace cut him short. She was already starting to calm down.

'It's not really my field,' she ventured, 'but I'd say it is the work of Thomas Chippendale. Those cabriole legs with their ball and claw feet are exquisitely finished. They are more ornate and yet much lighter than Queen Anne work. I have been looking at it out of the corner of my eye all evening. But surely this is not what you wanted to show me.'

'No indeed,' he said quietly, but Grace could tell he was impressed.

Thank you, Walter! Grace said to herself, as her father-in-law inserted the key and opened the top. On hearing the news that Pippa would be convalescing at Horatio's Epsom house, Walter Drake had whispered, 'Try and see his Chippendale desk. It's stunning. He had me working on it during the war, when there was nothing to do in the shop and Hitler had more or less stopped dropping bombs on us. It has a hidden compartment.'

From a small drawer, behind a secret panel, Horatio removed a larger key. Grace was keen to know where all this was leading, but she was also afraid that this might turn out to be another *MacGregor's Gold* story.

Walking first through the drawing room and then the spacious kitchen, Horatio opened a wainscot panelled oak door that was tucked under the house's rear servants' staircase. It was not locked. 'This is my wine cellar,' he said. 'And, as I told you, it is the reason why I purchased this house.' With her father-in-law leading the way, Grace walked easily down the narrow stone stairway. The ceiling was low, but Grace was still able to stand upright. On either side of a narrow passage, wooden wine racks stretched from floor to ceiling. Although they provided enough space for several hundred bottles, most of the racks were empty. Grace was already thinking that for a man who clearly loved his alcohol, he did not have much of a collection. But then she remembered rationing and considered that perhaps he had emptied most of the bottles during the hostilities. She could almost imagine him, sitting alone in this cellar, tasting his wines while the Luftwaffe droned overhead.

As she was considering these possibilities, her father-in-law walked up to the last shelf, which contained only two bottles of vintage champagne, where fifty or more could easily have been stored. Carefully removing the two bottles, he turned and placed them in a neighbouring rack. He then proceeded to slide the now empty wooden shelf to one side. It moved easily. There was no scraping or scratching. Set in the wall where the shelf had been was a steel door, with a keyhole and a circular combination lock. Using the key from the desk and the combination, Horatio opened the door. He made no attempt to hide the numbers; 16981744. Grace immediately recognised the birth and death dates of Joseph Guarneri Del Gesù. She smiled to herself. The combination of the Montagues' West End safe was 16441737; Stradivari's dates.

The space behind the door was not large, but it was deep. There were twenty-one compartments, sixteen small, four a little larger, and one much bigger space below them all. Each compartment was lined with green velvet, but like the wine racks, they were not all occupied. Grace counted. She could see the ends of eleven violin cases, one slightly larger viola case, and in the lower space two cello cases, standing side by side, on their sides.

'Pick any two,' Horatio said, 'and we will take them up to my study.'

Reaching forward, Grace pulled two cases from their deep recesses and the old man did the same. As they ascended the stone stairway back to the kitchen, the old man said, 'I am wagering everything on you, Grace. You are Montague's last hope. I have been observing you since you arrived five years ago, and I am satisfied that you are what I think you are. No one but you and I know about this room behind my wine cellar. Edward and James have been down here numerous times to collect bottles, but neither of them has ever noticed a thing. But then, how would they, it is all so beautifully well hidden? Through the Guards Club, I found a wonderful firm of shopfitters who normally work for the government. They set the place up... real craftsmen. Needless to say, I could have used my own men, but I didn't want any of them knowing my business. And from now on, since neither Edward nor James know anything about this room, it will be just our little secret.'

Grace had always known that the old man was devious, but this was something she had not expected. Back in the study they set the cases down.

'Pick one!' the old man said. 'I want to see how good you really are.'

Grace opened the nearest case and removed a violin. In the meantime, her father-in-law had cleared the small table and spread a chamois leather across its top.

'If you need a magnifying glass, or anything else, let me know,' he said, as he carried a standard lamp over to the table.

Placing a little more coal on the fire, the old man settled in one of the wing chairs and watched Grace. He was not thinking about what she might be about to say, instead, he was studying her as if he were assessing a thoroughbred racehorse. *She is a heavy woman,* he was thinking, *but she is comely, and the way she deports herself with that violin is a pleasure to behold. Edward might be a fool, but he showed excellent judgment when he chose Grace. By now, that bird-brained debutante he was married to before would have ruined this company.*

While Grace rotated the violin under the lamp, Horatio

continued his observations. As she turned her head this way and that, he was struck by the way the light bounced off her shock of golden red hair, it was a phenomenon he had often noticed. He then spent time studying the line of her shoulders and the profile of her breasts against the fire's flickering flames. Finally, he perused her face. There was no doubting the fact that her face and eyes were genuinely beautiful. Not for the first time, the old man speculated that had he been looking for a woman for himself, he could not have made a better choice.

Eventually he pulled himself together. 'So, what is your verdict?' he said.

'That depends on what you want to hear,' she quickly replied.

'I want to hear it all, Grace.'

'Well, it is a violin that almost every top dealer would describe as the work of Antonio Stradivari, from his Late Golden Period, I would say it was made around 1725. To my mind, that would be better defined as his Early Late Period, if you know what I mean? The work is still very fine, but it is no longer his absolute best.'

'Good,' said her father-in-law, but having sensed some hesitation he continued, 'so, what's your problem with the violin?'

'I don't really have a problem. It is an outstanding instrument and it appears to be in an excellent state of preservation.'

'But?'

Grace could see that her father-in-law wasn't about to let this go, and in a way, she was bursting to tell him what she really thought. It had been five years since she'd had a meaningful conversation about an instrument, with a genuine connoisseur, but as Winston Churchill had said of the Russians in 1939, her father-in-law was *a riddle, wrapped in a mystery, inside an enigma.* From various snippets, she was certain that he knew his stuff, but she was still not persuaded that he would be open to new ideas.

Well, she thought, *there is only one way to find out.*

After briefly gathering her thoughts, she began. 'I am assuming that this violin was made in or around 1725?'

She quickly glanced at her father-in-law for confirmation, and when he nodded his agreement, she continued. 'According to the information in W. E. Hill and Sons' 1902 book, in 1725 Antonio Stradivari would have been eighty-one years old. The question I would ask is, could a man of that age produce such pristine work?'

When no answer came, Grace continued. 'At that time Antonio Stradivari had two sons, Francesco and Omobono, who were fifty-four and forty-six respectively.'

'So, what are you saying, Grace?'

'If I remember correctly, the Hills suggested that Antonio's sons were either not very productive, or not very good, and that they were mainly employed doing rough work. And, that they were only occasionally permitted to complete a cheaper order of instrument, bearing a different label.'

'I presume you are talking about the so-called *soto la disciplina d'Antonio Stradivari* labels,' said Horatio, seeking clarification.

'Possibly,' said Grace, 'but over the centuries, most of those *School of Stradivari* labels have been removed by unscrupulous dealers. Anyway, I don't believe that that was the case here. I have just glanced inside this violin and the label appears to be a genuine unmoved Antonio Stradivari label, dated 1726, so I was a year out.'

'I won't tell anyone this time,' the old man chortled.

Grace continued. 'My father has even started to question the true authorship of Antonio Stradivari's acclaimed Golden Period instruments. He believes that having invested time and effort in their education, Antonio is hardly likely to have condemned his sons to sweeping the floor and making tea. My father says the idea that Antonio Stradivari made the Golden Period instruments unaided is frankly absurd. In particular, he believes that the workmanship of the second decade of the eighteenth century was almost certainly dominated by one or both of his sons. As for Antonio Stradivari's personal Golden Period, he believes that this was more likely to have been when the magnificent instruments of the 1690s were created. Well, that's it!'

'My God, Grace. You don't pull your punches, but those are dangerous ideas and certainly not for public consumption. If it came out that the instruments that you indicated might not be the work of the great master, or that they were a kind of joint effort, it might ruin the market, especially if they hear that your father has been expounding this theory. He is well respected in the business.'

'Yes, well this *is* all theoretical stuff,' said Grace, backtracking slightly. 'What counts is whose genuine and undisturbed label is in the instrument. There are numerous instances of artists and craftsmen having had assistants in their workshops. Chippendale is an excellent example,' she said, glancing sideways at the desk. 'Another is the sculptor Rodin. Rodin was not only inspired by Camille Claudel, who was his model, but being a talented sculptress herself, she is said to have assisted him with his work. And then there is the mysterious Katarina Guarneri—'[3]

'Stop right there, Grace! Let's not even set off down that road. You really are a bit of a minx,' he said, laughing.

For the next few hours they continued talking, until it was really quite late, and by the time they were ready for bed, Grace realised that they had only examined the Stradivari. She had not even opened the other three cases. She also realised that the knowledge that her father-in-law possessed was deep. In the shortest time, her opinion of him had been seriously revised, at least as far as his expertise was concerned. In time she would be forced to address problems concerning other aspects of his behaviour, but that night she slept well, and in spite of Horatio's thinly disguised invitations, she slept alone.

It was the end of January 1953 before Grace finished examining her father-in-law's collection, and after placing the final instrument back in its case, she had wanted to begin again. By this time Horatio was more than ever convinced that on the day that Grace had married his son, Montague's had acquired a genuine treasure. She had taxed his knowledge to the absolute limit. The only problems Horatio could foresee were Edward's nature and

---

[3] For more information see: www.roger-hargrave.de / Seeking Mrs Guarneri. Roger Hargrave reassesses a forgotten woman of Cremona, Katarina, the wife of 'Joseph Guarneri del Gesú'

whether Grace would understand and accept his son's true genius. In a quiet moment Horatio decided to broach the subject.

'I know that you are having difficulties with Edward. He is not an easy man to live with and practically impossible to work with. He is also lazy, and rude to anyone he is not planning to do business with. In fact, the people that Edward does business with are possibly the only friends he ever has, and once that business is done, he quickly loses interest in them, which is why he continues to get on so well with your father.

'Now Grace, you may not wish to hear this, but I am convinced that you and Edward could become a highly successful partnership… I am not talking about your marriage. I can only imagine what that must be like for you. You are a beautiful, highly intelligent young woman and you were probably expecting a great deal more… No, what I am talking about is a business partnership.'

Grace looked at her father-in-law with something approaching incredulity. 'What are you talking about, Horatio? I know he is your son, but to quote Hamlet, he's a *wretched, rash, intruding fool*. He has only the most rudimentary notion of expertise and as for repair work, he couldn't replace a broken E string, let alone tune it.'

'Now that is a little unfair, Grace. Just think about it. What is the one thing that Edward is seriously good at?'

'Lying?'

'Well I suppose it's not unrelated.'

'He's a con man!'

'Well, yes, but I prefer the word salesman. Con man is a rather vulgar American expression. But you are right. In fact, in my more than fifty years in the business, I never saw a better salesman. You have never really seen him in action... or perhaps you have, after all, you did marry him. Edward could sell snow to Eskimos, sand to Arabs, and water to a drowning man. But if you are honest with yourself, Grace, you already knew this, because he sold you *love*. A love that he never intended to deliver.'

'Yes!' said Grace almost philosophically. 'Because he still loves his blond debutante; James's mother.'

'Is that what you think?' her father-in-law asked, before answering the question himself. 'Her name was Daphne, and by the way, Edward hated her. At least he appreciates you, even if he does not always show it.'

Grace was stunned. Daphne was her name and Edward hated her?

'But that can't be true,' she gasped, 'he keeps her picture on *my* dressing table.'

'That is just to keep you on your toes.'

'I don't understand,' said Grace, genuinely perplexed.

The old man thought for a while before quoting from a poem by Lord Alfred Douglas, 'Edward's love, is, *"the love that dare not speak its name"*.'

From the puzzled look on Grace's face, Horatio realised that although his daughter-in-law was extremely well read, like most people, she had clearly been shielded from such niceties, and he decided not to pursue the matter.

34

Homosexuality was rarely, if ever, mentioned in polite society. Nevertheless, vague notions of what homosexuality was, and the fact that terms like *gross indecency* and *lewd behaviour* were frequently employed in the crime and gossip columns of national newspapers, created a kind of paranoia. As a consequence, amongst the general population ignorance was common. In fact, being *too* knowledgeable could easily place a person under suspicion. Paradoxically, it also meant that desperate to establish their heterosexual credentials, homosexual men like Edward often resorted to extreme homophobic behaviour. Accordingly, when Edward appeared to reject Grace, it was hardly surprising that she had drawn the wrong conclusion.

Horatio changed tack. 'Daphne spent money like there was no tomorrow. That was OK before the war when money was still available, but if she had not been killed, Montague's would be bankrupt by now.'

It was a harsh thing to say, but Grace wanted to hear more. 'Why did he marry her?' she eventually asked.

'There were two main reasons. She was an exceptional dancer and being a member of the aristocracy, albeit a rather impoverished branch, she had a name and connections. But of course, that's also why he married you.'

'But I don't have a name *or* connections.'

'I presume that you are pulling my leg, Grace. The Scotts are a well-known name in the violin business and your father bought everything that Edward took to Chicago, and he usually paid through the nose.'

'Yes, but they were all top-quality pieces, I saw them.'

'That's because I selected them. I knew that your father was good and that the best way to keep his business was to send him the best. Edward would have tried to fob him off with junk, but I wasn't having that. And then of course Edward met you. Apparently, you can dance, and when he realised that you were also a genuine connoisseur, he could not believe his luck. You were someone he could replace me with when I finally pop-my-clogs; which can't be far off now,' and he giggled like a schoolboy.

'What you need to understand, Grace, is that for a long time, Edward and I have had a highly successful if occasionally rather difficult business partnership. At first, I was involved with every aspect of the business. For a while, I even worked in the workshop with my father. But I caught the expertise bug and spent most of my time studying and eventually buying and selling instruments. That is when we expanded the small workshop that we already had. Our man Drake has organised it ever since. Initially my father did most of the selling. For some reason I just never had the knack. But then we discovered Edward's talent. Suddenly, all that astonishing self-confidence he had picked up at Eton started to pay dividends. It did not matter that it was all bluff, he managed to convey the impression that he knew what he was talking about, even when he had no idea. I would simply brief him and point him in the customer's direction and that was that.

'On one occasion he was offering a customer the choice between a Ferdinand Gagliano violin and a Thomas Eberle violin. Unfortunately, having expounded their virtues, he forgot which one was which. Well, as you know, although they are both Neapolitan makers from the same period, no genuine expert would make such a mistake. But in the end, it didn't matter, because he sold both instruments to the same customer. That is a good example of what he is like. Edward's thing is making money. He loves money and doesn't really care how he makes it, as long as he can do it with the minimum of physical and mental effort. Edward is not even interested in violins. Edward sells instruments, first and foremost by selling himself, and as you pointed out, he will even use his war wound if he thinks it will help. The thing is, Edward needs a genuine connoisseur to back him up, so far it has always been me, but I'm getting too old. You are now his only hope, but you will need to keep him under control, and that will require standing up to him. Are you capable of that, and do you even want to do it?'

Grace was silent for a long while. 'You have answered a lot of questions. I had honestly assumed that Edward was useless, but when I think about how he sold all those instruments to my father, I can see that you are right. My father is infatuated with Edward. Even if I were to tell him the truth, he would never believe me; I think he would probably even chastise me.'

Again, she paused, before saying, 'OK, Horatio, let's give it a try, but we will need some ground rules before I begin. We don't need another Tes-story story,' she said, deliberately mispronouncing the name, and giving the old man a wink.

Edward's latest faux pas had been to purchase a cello, bearing a label of Carlo Antonio Testore of Milan, dated 1739. On seeing the cello, Horatio had called Grace into his study to ask her opinion. With Edward still present, the old man pointedly asked his son why he believed the instrument to be the work of Carlo Antonio Testore. Full of confidence Edward had answered, 'Because the black and white purfling around the edges is not genuine inlay. Instead two parallel black lines have been painted on, imitating genuine inlay.'

'And?' his father asked.

'And, fake inlay is typical of the Testore family.'

'And?' the old man said again.

'And, it has a Carlo Antonio Testore label and it has also been branded with the word Milan and the makers initials, C.A.T.'

'And?' the old man said again.

'And, the cello has a recent certificate from W. E. Hill and Sons, written in 1927.'

Edward's father had smiled, before turning to Grace and asking if Edward was correct in thinking that fake inlay was typical of the Testore family. Grace looked hard at her father-in-law. He was enjoying the fact that she was feeling uncomfortable. He was also enjoying the fact that his son was about to feel even more uncomfortable.

'Well?' he prompted. 'What is your verdict, Grace? Is Edward correct in asserting that Carlo Antonio Testore used fake inlay?'

Grace picked up the cello and turned it this way and that, as if weighing up the details. In fact, she had immediately seen that the cello was wrong. Nevertheless, for Edward's sake, she took her time. Even so, her father-in-law was aware that she had known the truth in an instant.

Eventually she said, 'Carlo Antonio certainly used fake inlay.'

Edward had a beaming smile on his face, until he recognised the imminent threat of a *but*. When it came he was instantly crestfallen. 'But,' Grace added, 'this cello is not a Testore.'

'And why not?' her father-in-law persisted.

'Because when Carlo Antonio Testore faked purfling, he did not paint parallel black lines, he scratched them into the wood. These lines were painted on. In places, you can see where the paint has rubbed off.'

'What else?' Horatio asked again. He was clearly not going to let this matter go.

'Carlo's brand stamp is a kind of double eagle, which incorporates his initials, C. A. T. Here there is no double eagle and as far as I am aware, Carlo's brand did not include the word Milan.'

'But what about the certificate from W. E. Hill and Sons?' Edward was asking this time.

'I can't be sure,' she lied. 'But I believe the Hills always used high-quality headed notepaper and the ink used to print their name and crest was raised up from the surface, so that you can feel it with your fingertips. This is poor quality paper and the print is thin and flat.'

'By Jove!' said Horatio with a sarcastic flourish. 'And we did not even have to examine the cello's shape, its size, or its varnish. Instrument identification is easy… if you do your homework.' And with this parting remark the old man had walked out of the room, leaving Edward, Grace and the fake Testore to sort themselves out.

The following morning the cello was gone, and it was never mentioned again. But the incident had not rocked Edward's confidence in the slightest, and Grace realised that even with Horatio's help, it would not be easy to control her husband's urge to posture, pose and dominate.

35

Towards the end of February, Horatio called a meeting. He chose a wonderful and rather exclusive fish restaurant near Billingsgate Market. That way, he and Grace figured that should Edward turn nasty, at least he would not get loud. During the meal, Horatio gradually broached the subject of his imminent retirement. 'Fortunately,' he said, looking towards Grace, 'I think we have found a suitable successor. Someone with a level head and the required expertise.'

Edward continued eating as if not a word had been spoken.

His father persisted. 'When you and I started working together things generally ran smoothly. But that was because mostly you did exactly what I asked you to do. In part, this was because I was your father and as such, I was a natural figure of authority. But if Montague's is to remain profitable, very soon, you are going to have to take directives from your wife.'

Horatio stopped talking and he and Grace looked once more at Edward; again, he continued eating.

'This is the only way such an arrangement can work,' Horatio went on. 'From now on, you must leave the identification, the evaluation and valuation work to Grace and myself, and later to Grace alone. You will continue to be the sole signatory on Montague certificates, but you will sign only after Grace or myself have given our explicit approval. You are not to make autonomous judgments or challenge our judgment without due cause and consultation. In return, you will be given all the support you will need to present your instruments in the best possible light. Under the leadership of Drake, the workshop is better than it has ever been. The war caused us to fall back a little, but now we can regroup and win. However, Edward, in order to do this, we need you. You are the best in your field. We both acknowledge that, and we want this partnership to work, because if it does, we will not only be ready when the market kicks off again, we will be rich.'

Again, there was a long pause. Edward picked up a bottle of white wine and without a word he topped up Grace's glass and then his father's, before tending to his own.

He's actually being pleasant, Grace said to herself, before realising that this was how Edward always conducted business.

'Look here, old boy,' Horatio began again, 'I think we should let Grace make a contribution. I know she has a few suggestions.'

Grace continued eating. *Two can play this game*, she thought. Eventually she laid her knife and fork down and brushed her mouth with a white linen table napkin. Only Horatio noticed the impression her cochineal lipstick had left on the soft material.

She began slowly, but her voice was steady and full of confidence. 'We all know that buying at the auctions is not just about identifying instruments of high quality that have been wrongly catalogued or undervalued; instruments known as *sleepers*. Although big money can be made from mistaken attributions, I would also like to start looking for badly damaged instruments, insurance write-offs that can be restored by a skilled craftsman and sold at a profit. Our experience in Chicago showed that this can be just as lucrative as buying sleepers.'

No opposition so far, thought Grace, as she contemplated her next move. 'And I want Walter to check out the auctions too!' she said abruptly.

'Walter! Which Walter?' Edward quickly replied. They were the first words that he had spoken since the conference had begun. This in itself was an indication of his surprise, and when Grace looked over at Horatio, his face was also a picture of disapproval.

'Walter Drake, of course. Just think about it, if we are going to buy damaged instruments, Walter is ideally suited to assess the damage and how much time and effort will be needed to put things right. And we should also remember that one of the biggest dangers is missing invisibly mended damage, not to mention clever alterations, where some cheap German or French instrument has been turned into a fine old Italian. And finally, there is the task of identifying top-quality fakes. A mistake there could cost us more than we can win in a month of Sundays. With Walter's help, we can avoid making costly blunders. You both know it makes sense.'

Thanks to Grandfather Scott, Grace could have assessed damaged instruments and fakes in her sleep, but for years she had been existing in a kind of purdah; occasionally assessing auctions but otherwise locked away in the Epsom house, with only Pippa and Pippa's nanny for company. The old man was mostly away on his jaunts and Edward was just away. After almost six years of marriage, Grace neither knew nor cared where her husband was, or what he was doing, but she needed company.

The second concession Grace obtained was a budget. 'It will be better if Walter and I are not seen assessing instruments together,' she reasoned. 'Auction houses have hundreds of prying eyes. We should meet some place close to each sale room. Somewhere we can quietly sit and discuss our findings. It would also be better if no one, in either the violin gallery or the workshop, knows what we are doing.'

This suggestion went down particularly well with the Montagues, who had always adopted a rather draconian divide and rule policy. Long before the First World War, contact between the so-called violin gallery, the workshop and the family themselves had been kept to a minimum, and over the intervening years, little had changed. However, since Walter Drake was already a kind of go-between for all three factions, the two men reluctantly agreed that he was indeed ideally suited for the job.

It was eventually decided that a quiet café or restaurant would be best. Some place with tables where they could sit and share notes. One of Edward's few comments followed. 'Be sure to get receipts for everything.'

In view of Edward's last remark Grace decided it was time to take a stand.

'There are a couple more things, Edward. I want more money for Nanny to feed and clothe Pippa. What you give her is not nearly enough. Your daughter is wearing second-hand clothes while your son is clothed by an official Eton tailor. And, I also want a reasonable allowance for myself. I am sick of you telling me to ask Nanny for money. She is an employee, for God's sake. And, if the amounts are not substantial, Edward, I shall tell Papa that I have not seen a penny of the money that he and Grandpa have been sending since I set sail, and then we shall see how long the Scott family continue to do business with Montague's.'

'My God, Edward, is this true?'

'Of course it's true, Horatio, take a look at his face, it's as red as a Soho basement window.'

'Yes! Yes!' Edward hissed.

'Yes what?' Horatio demanded.

'Yes, I will increase Nanny's allowance.'

'And Grace?'

'Yes, yes, hers too.'

'And I will see that it's done,' said Horatio. 'I had no idea, Grace, I am so sorry.'

And it was done. Grace could not believe how easy it had been. Why had she not taken a stand years ago?

The old man was as good as his word and the following day four large white five-pound notes were pressed into her hand, with the words, 'There are more where they came from.'

Grace's final demand was unusual to say the least. 'Edward, I want you to take me dancing again. Once a month will do for starters.'

Edward's reply surprised both Grace and his father. 'Very well, old girl, if that's what you want?'

This last request had been entirely spontaneous, but it proved to be an inspired proposal; one that would provide the first real bond between the pair since Chicago. It would never make them lovers, but it almost made them friends and it certainly helped with communication.

Although rather grudgingly, Edward accepted all of Grace's demands, until eventually he started to see her ideas paying handsome dividends. From that moment, whenever there was an auction reachable by Southern Rail, Grace and Walter could spend as much time as they felt necessary in cafés, restaurants and occasionally even pubs. As long as they made money and did not encroach on either Edward or Horatio's freedom, they could go almost anywhere and do almost anything, albeit on a tight budget.

Privately, Grace had been attending the auctions on and off since arriving in England. They were one of the few excuses she had to get out of the house and see people and violins. Edward had tolerated this, because occasionally Grace found a wrongly catalogued instrument, which, because Grace had no funds of her own, Edward always snapped up for himself. Later he had taken five of Grace's discoveries to America, where he professed to have unearthed them at the auctions. It had been a mean trick, but at least it had given Grace an idea. Her father was being charged a premium to buy instruments that his own daughter had discovered; why not cut out the middleman? It might take time to implement, but at least it would help her repay the debt she felt she owed her friend Walter Drake.

Moving into the old man's house with Pippa and Nanny had already eased the tension between Grace and Edward considerably. But she soon missed her walks through Soho, and the bookshops on Charing Cross Road, where by now she was on first-name terms with several proprietors, and with her new allowance, she could occasionally afford to invest. There was something about the musty odour of old books which was almost intoxicating. She had a similar reaction to the bee's wax smell of the violin gallery, which in turn, reminded her of that fateful trip on the old *Queen Mary*; so long ago now. And then there was Walter's workshop, with its complex bouquet of turpentine, alcohol, shellac, wood shavings and tea. Although changing from day to day, depending on the work being carried out, it always took her back to her grandfather's workbench. Good and bad, Grace was always fascinated by the way that smells have the power to conjure and evoke particular memories.

36

Much to Grace's surprise, Edward's promise to take her dancing was fulfilled. For Edward it was a further alibi, while for Grace it was pure pleasure. Neither was under the illusion that it would rejuvenate their relationship, nevertheless it was not long before they were both looking forward to their monthly rendezvous. Occasionally, if a good dance band was in town, they would even fit in an extra session.

For the next four years, the Montague family business continued to flourish, with Grace and Edward sharing the load. Horatio, who had recently celebrated his seventy-fifth birthday, was still refusing to let go of the reins, for which Grace was genuinely grateful.

Chasing women was the old man's primary occupation. He also spent one full day each week at the Guard's Club and at least two afternoons in his all-time favourite club, The Doll's House, watching the strip-tease show. The Doll's House was a dive, but its low stage was closer to the dancers than places like the famous Windmill Theatre, which were best known for their *tasteful* nude *tableaux vivants*. At The Doll's House, the second-hand cinema seats had cigarette burns and stains, but the women moved, and they were normal everyday women, rather than the glamourous models that stood naked and motionless on the Windmill stage. However, although Horatio was undoubtedly an aficionado of every kind of woman, Grace suspected that, for the most part, he loved fine violins more than he had loved any of the women in his life.

Neither man was easy for Grace to deal with, but she had the measure of them both; or at least she felt she did. Around this time however, Edward started to lose interest in the business and he was even making excuses not to go dancing. In itself, this would have been tolerable, except for the fact that he was beginning to live above his means. Even Horatio had noticed the gradual depletion of the company's various accounts. In addition, Edward had become as nervous as a kitten. He was starting to jump at the merest sound. Grace suspected he was suffering after-effects from his Dunkirk experience, and she tried to comfort him, but her efforts went unheeded.

Having allowed the situation to slowly escalate, Horatio finally confronted Edward in the company's walk-in safe. The old man had just caught him red-handed, removing a box with four of the company's finest French violin bows. It was a haul worth at least a thousand pounds.

'Who is it, son?' was his father's initial comment.

Then, looking Edward straight in the eye, he repeated his words. 'Who is it, son? Who is putting the squeeze on you?'

'Nothing, no one, Farver, I just—'

'Edward... Son, ever since you were a child, I have always known that you were different. That you were...' Horatio paused before completing the sentence, 'attracted to men rather than women.' Edward was about to answer, but Horatio held up his hand. His voice was kindly as he continued, 'But you're my flesh and blood, son, and I love you... and God knows that's not always been easy.'

The old man gave a short nervous laugh before going on. 'I know how difficult it must have been for you, but I had no idea how to help you. I was out of my depth; I still am. And then you got married and James was born, and I thought that somehow you had gotten over it. And then Grace came along, and I allowed myself to think you really were... cured? But that was all a big mistake too; wasn't it? You're a homo aren't you, son?'

Again, Horatio held up his hand to prevent an answer. 'I know you cannot help it. I know it's a kind of illness, but it's a dangerous illness, son. Every week men appear in the dock. Being attracted to the wrong person can make you a criminal... You could end up in jail or worse. And now someone knows, don't they? And they are extorting money from you. Does Grace know? She certainly knows about the missing money.'

Up to this point, Edward had maintained what his fellow Guards officers would have called a stiff upper lip, but the mention of Grace's name caused him to falter.

'I... I'm sorry, Farver,' he said slowly. 'Please don't tell Grace, I have already done her enough damage.'

'That will be up to you, Edward. What I want to know now is, who it is, who is blackmailing you? Tell me and I will fix it.'

'Please Farver, please… please don't! That will only make things worse.'

The war years may have been relatively kind to homosexual men, but homosexuality had remained illegal, and following the armistice, prosecutions for 'homosexual crimes' were stepped up. Throughout the 1950s, police tactics had become increasingly draconian, and they generated genuine fear. The law which outlawed what it called *gross indecency* between men was widely regarded as a blackmailer's charter.

Ever since the armistice, Edward had been feeling the need to watch every word he spoke and every gesture he made, but at some point, he had dropped his guard. The resulting changes in his personality had quickly become apparent to all concerned. Even dancing was no longer the pleasure it had been for him; it had become just another of the many alibi tasks he needed to complete in order to cover his tracks. Paradoxically, Grace was still convinced that Edward's only redeeming feature was that he was *not* a philanderer like his father. He never looked at other women even as they danced by. Unfortunately, the truth was that he was fearful of being caught taking a sideways glance at their male partners. He was suffering badly, more than he could ever remember, in a life that had been filled with misery.

What finally triggered Horatio's timely intervention was the fact that Edward was actively endangering the entire Montague operation.

'Who is it, son?' Horatio repeated. 'Who is blackmailing you? We cannot allow this to go on. You need to tell me everything. Were you caught committing an act of gross indecency? Do they have photographs or correspondence?'

'What? No!' said Edward emphatically. 'No, it was not like that; not like that at all,' he repeated.

'Exactly what was it like, son?' His father persisted, as he always did. And, realising that there would be no escape, Edward told his father everything, which in the end did not amount to much.

Years of living in a perpetual state of denial and fear had taken their toll on Edward. As far as satisfying his true sexual orientation, he had remained a celibate. His only mistake had taken place at a recent regimental dinner. At this ceremonial feast, a younger officer, sitting across the table, had spent much of the evening catching Edward's eye and occasionally smiling. Once, Edward imagined that he had even detected a wink. These smiles appeared somewhat contrived and in Edward's alcohol-fuddled brain, they were causing considerable confusion.

Smiles from strangers, especially men, had always put Edward on edge. Since his school days at Eton, he had never trusted smiles, either from boys or masters. There was a duplicity about smiles that Shakespeare knew well. Some of the best advice Edward had ever received had come from the bard's pen. He thought of Gloucester in *King Henry VI*. 'Why, I can smile, and murder whiles I smile.' And Hamlet who speaks the words, 'That one may smile and smile and be a villain.' And Malvolio, Shakespeare's lovesick fool, who in *Twelfth Night* is cruelly tricked into smiling manically, when Maria, posing as Olivia, tells him, 'let it appear in thy smiling.'

Edward had been right to be sceptical. This younger officer was not a homosexual, but he made a substantial living entrapping fellow officers and bowler-hatted civil servants who were.

Mindful of the danger to himself, this trickster was always careful to catch his prey when they were alone and preferably intoxicated. Ironically, Edward had never really liked this man, but alcohol combined with desperation for male companionship caused him to lower both his standards and his guard.

Having worked on a plan of action for several months, with consummate skill, this younger man was giving out all the right signals. He approached Edward in the club's elegant restroom. The hour was late, and the ceremonials were more or less finished. Both men were wearing their mess uniforms. In spite of their age difference, they were both the same rank. The younger man had done his homework well.

'I say, old chap, aren't you Edward Montague, I heard from the adjutant that you caught one at Dunkirk?'

Edward, who had not related his Dunkirk adventure for some time, answered with relish. 'Yes, damned close thing, don't ye know,' he said slapping his wounded leg.

'Yes,' his brother officer answered, 'a lot of your chaps didn't make it back to Blighty. It was the same for us. I was with the 4th Armoured Battalion in '45. We were equipped with Sherman and Churchill tanks. I picked up a bit of shrapnel in the nether regions,' he said, half turning and slapping his backside in a provocative gesture. 'Elliot Nugent-Temple,' he added, clicking his heels.

'In '46, the Battalion was disbanded, and we were shipped off to Palestine, where no one knew what the fuck was happening. It was all rather like speaking Polari where only the initiated know what's going on. Don't you think?'

This was a highly unusual comment to make. Edward was well aware that Polari was a kind of secret language. At a time when authorities were actively seeking to arrest and make horrific examples of homosexuals, Polari provided homosexuals who were looking for companionship or sex a way of communicating with one another. Nevertheless, since the police were well aware of its implications, using Polari was in itself a risky business.

Edward was instantly vigilant, but the man seemed pleasant enough and during the course of their conversation, his speech became more hushed and conspiratorial in nature. As the tenor of their conversation slowly calmed, the two men gradually moved towards each other.

Elliot Nugent-Temple's dress uniform, like Edward's own, was immaculate. Reaching forward with both hands, Nugent-Temple touched the silky black lapels of Edward's mess jacket, until it seemed as if he were about to draw him even closer.

'Bona drag,' he said quietly, while running the backs of his fingers down Edward's long lapels.

Here again he was employing Polari, the secret language of homosexuals. Even Edward knew that *bona drag* meant beautiful clothes. The moment was electric and as Edward looked directly into the man's welcoming eyes, he briefly lost control. Reaching forward himself now, he placed the palms of his hands on the man's hips.

'What the fuck are you doing? Are you a fucking homo?' Nugent-Temple's voice had increased in volume and was now bouncing dramatically off the restroom's marble walls. 'You're a damned homo; I can see it in your eyes. Where do you think you are, *The Merchant Navy club*? This is the Coldstream Guard's officers' club. I never thought I would see the day… I'll have you drummed out, Montague. I'll have you thrown in the Glasshouse.'

'What? No!' cried Edward in alarm. 'Please I'm not a homo. Please I'm begging you. Please don't make a scene.'

'You should have thought about that before you tried to grab me.'

In fact, if Edward had thought about the situation at all, he might easily have turned things around. After all he had not been the one smiling and winking and using Polari, but panic had caught hold of him, and he had already switched to defence mode. Instead of going on the attack as his military appearance should have warranted, Edward apologised. 'Look here, I am sure we can settle this amicably.' He was almost whimpering now, he just wanted to get away.

'Oh yes? What are you suggesting; bribery?'

'No, of course not,' Edward quickly replied, and in a misguided attempt to calm things down, he unfortunately added, 'But as a friendly gesture, why don't you allow me to invite you tonight. This has all been a bit of a misunderstanding, old chap. Why don't you let me pay for your meal and let's start afresh?'

'I'm not so sure. I think I owe it to the members to let them know who you really are.'

'Please, just let us forget all this, it really is a big misunderstanding. Come along,' he said, reaching for his wallet, 'let's go and settle your account right away.'

Both men were booked into members accommodation for the night, and before retiring they spoke to the tired mess sergeant. They explained that because of an early start they would both be settling their mess bills right away.

Once the bills had been prepared, it transpired that Elliot Nugent-Temple owed the club a considerable sum. Not wishing to create another scene, Edward paid both outstanding mess bills, and he was well and truly hooked.

'Is that all he has on you?' said Horatio when Edward had finished.

'Yes.'

'Are you absolutely sure?'

'Yes.'

'You're a damned fool, Edward,' his father said. 'Elliot Nugent-Temple. I'll remember that name.'

Horatio was as good as his word. Whatever it was that he managed to *arrange,* the blackmail abruptly stopped, and for a while at least, things returned to whatever it was that passed for normal at Montague's.

37

Not having been privy to the discussion between Edward and his father, Grace was unaware that anything untoward had occurred, but she was not insensitive; she could certainly see and feel the results. Unexpectedly resuming their monthly dance dates, Edward was once again whirling her around their local ballroom like Fred Astaire himself. Unfortunately, it did not stop him from being a boorish prig with everyone else. Neither did it curb his use of homophobic insults and jokes, especially in the workshop. In spite of Edward's churlish behaviour, after several evenings of dancing, everyone was discernibly more relaxed and Grace decided to approach Horatio, not about his son's behaviour, but about the secret collection in his wine cellar.

Edward and James were both still blissfully unaware of the collection's existence, but crucially they were also unaware that Grace was privy to the old man's secret. Although it had been some time since they had visited the cellar together, Horatio had never tired of sharing this particular pleasure with his daughter-in-law. It had been several years since he had taken her into his confidence, and by now he was assured that she would never betray that trust.

One Saturday morning, while Edward was spending the weekend in London, Nanny and Pippa went off to their local stable to visit Pippa's horse. Pippa was now eleven years old and horses were her passion; for her tenth birthday her father had bought her a beautiful Shetland pony. Horatio had arranged for them to be away all day, so that he and his daughter-in-law could indulge in their guilty secret. With everyone out of the house, he and Grace slowly descended the cellar steps like two arch criminals. Although this had never been a sexual relationship, Grace could not imagine an illicit affair being any more exciting.

Later that same day, as they packed the instruments away, Grace casually said, 'You know that you are going to have to tell Edward sooner or later?'

There was a long pause, followed by an even longer sigh. 'I assumed that after all this time, a smart woman like you would have realised that that will never be possible.'

'What do you mean, Horatio?'

'I put this collection together to secure Montague's long-term future, but if ever Edward or young James were to find out what we have here and what these instruments are worth, they would throw caution to the wind and immediately try to sell them and that would be the end of Montague's as a violin business.'

'I understand that would be the end of your collection, but why would that be the end of Montague's?'

'Look, Grace, I thought that you or your father would have worked this out by now, especially with your grandfather being German.'

'Worked what out, Horatio? What are you saying? Are you trying to tell me that these instruments are stolen?'

'Not exactly, I bought them all.'

'What do you mean by not exactly, Horatio? And what has Grandpa's being German got to do with anything?'

'Look, Grace, I really believed that you knew. Your father must have known. I bought these instruments and many more from the German government. From the time that Hitler came to power in 1933, military units known as the *Kunstschutz* were buying up works of art, including violins and other musical instruments. Because of customs restrictions, until 1936 many of these instruments were carried to Britain by German government officials with diplomatic status. But the process became more difficult when Britain's surveillance of the German embassy became more intense. At this point a young Hungarian virtuoso called Zsolti Gnagy was recruited. No one suspected a thirteen-year-old child protégé travelling to London for violin lessons. He was a smart boy with a remarkably Machiavellian character for one of such tender years.

'I still do business with him from time to time. We sold most of those instruments in the United States; quite a few went to your father.'

Grace was truly horrified. Her mouth had gone dry and she could barely speak. 'Are you telling me that you were buying and selling instruments that the Nazis had looted from Jewish musicians?' She was almost croaking out the words. 'And that you sold them to *my* father?'

'They were all perfectly safe, my dear. Everything Montague's sold to your father was... is totally untraceable, even today. Anyway, it was mostly middle-of-the-road stuff... but good quality,' he added belatedly.

Her father-in-law was speaking now as if these transactions had been entirely legitimate. 'As I recall, at the beginning there were one or two fine Cremonese works amongst them. Before war broke out between Britain and Germany, I remember selling Randolph two Nicola Amati violins, a Peter Guarneri of Venice and a fine Golden Period violin by Antonio Stradivari. He was as pleased as Punch.'

Grace's head was spinning, it was a nightmare, and she was praying to a god that she did not believe in, to wake her up. But there would be no respite; no reprieve, not ever again.

Almost as if a dam had burst, Horatio continued unabated. 'But these instruments in my private collection are all well-known and therefore traceable. Which is why they cannot be sold, at least not for many years, especially not right now when details about Nazi looted art are starting to emerge. But I know my son, he does not have the discipline to wait and James is no better, the temptation to make quick money will simply be too great, and it will eventually bring them and Montague's down.'

Gold fever! Grace gasped, suddenly recalling the MacGregor chest. But then out loud, she cried, 'My God, Horatio! What on earth possessed you to want to own something that people have been slaughtered to acquire; instruments that no one can ever hear or see?'

'You have seen and admired them, Grace.'

'But it's a blood collection, Horatio…'

'We don't know that, Grace.'

'Yes, we do. Just because your name is Horatio does not mean that you can turn a blind eye. How on earth could you do such a thing?'

'How else could I ever hope to put together such a magnificent collection. Collections like those of Baron Knoop, or Henry Ford, cost more than I could ever hope to earn in a lifetime. It's one thing to buy and sell instruments, but it's quite another to buy and keep them. This way I could afford to do that. Anyway, I have no idea how these instruments were acquired,' he concluded, dismissing her previous comment. 'For all I know they were legitimate purchases.'

'Oh, come on, Horatio, you cannot tell me that, even I would have asked questions.'

'But you didn't, did you Grace? You have been looking at these instruments and discussing them with me for years, and you never once asked me about their provenance. For that matter neither did your father.'

'That's right,' she answered. 'But instruments are often sold without papers. I see them all the time at the auctions.'

'Exactly, Grace,' the old man cut in. 'You see them all the time, and you never ask who the previous owners were, or where such instruments came from. You are always happy just to find a wrongly catalogued instrument. Sleepers never have provenance papers, that's the very essence of a sleeper, and asking would only alert the auction house to their mistake.'

'But you sold instruments to my father knowing that they were Nazi loot and that is an entirely different story.'

'Is it?' Horatio persisted.

'Yes, it is, Horatio. My father bought those instruments from Edward in 1938. He bought them in good faith, more than three years before America and Germany officially declared war. Edward told my father that they had been in your family's collection for years and *you* even wrote certificates confirming that.'

'A little poetic licence, Grace,' said the old man with a wave of his hand.

'Did Edward know where those instruments came from?' she finally managed to ask.

'Absolutely not, Grace. *Careless talk costs lives,*' he said, quoting a wartime propaganda poster.

As Horatio missed the irony of his own words, Grace's head was filled with images of emaciated corpses piled on top of one another, of thousands upon thousands of gold teeth, spectacles and other personal items; of dreadful ovens where the bodies of men, women and children had been burned in their millions. It had been mass slaughter, torture and exploitation on an unprecedented scale. And then, quite suddenly, Grace realised that she too was caught up in this, the greatest crime the world has ever seen, or would be ever likely to see. Her mind was racing. Albeit unwittingly, she was an accomplice, and so were her father and grandfather.

In 1933 Hitler had become chancellor of Germany. By the time World War II had started in 1939, the Nazi's propaganda machine had already persuaded most of Germany's adult population that Jews, Gypsies and other minorities were racially inferior degenerates and that they were largely to blame for Germany's woes. As such, it became socially acceptable to discriminate, abuse and dehumanise such people, until eventually they could be systematically murdered, with horrifying cruelty, with hardly anyone lifting a finger in protest.

The first outward manifestation of this had been *Kristallnacht,* otherwise known as *The Night of Broken Glass,* because of the glass shards that had littered the streets following the event. Nine months before World War II, in a carefully coordinated attack on the night of 9 – 10 November 1938, throughout Germany and Austria, Nazi paramilitaries and sympathisers had ransacked and destroyed Jewish homes, businesses, hospitals, schools and synagogues. Up to one hundred people were killed immediately, with many more dying as a result of the night's events. In addition, at least 30,000 Jews and Gypsies were interned in concentration camps.

In the wake of these attacks, Hugh Green, London's *Daily Telegraph* correspondent, had described these horrors in graphic detail. At least from this point on, no informed person in Europe or the United States could claim ignorance.

Mob law ruled in Berlin throughout the afternoon and evening and hordes of hooligans indulged in an orgy of destruction. I have seen several anti-Jewish outbreaks in Germany during the last five years, but never anything as nauseating as this. Racial hatred and hysteria seemed to have taken complete hold of otherwise decent people. I saw fashionably dressed women clapping their hands and screaming with glee, while respectable middle-class mothers held up their babies to see the 'fun'. [4]

In fact, long before *Kristallnacht* marked the start of the Holocaust, the persecution of Jews and other minorities was already being reported in the British press. And, after Germany's defeat and the opening of its concentration camps, even Horatio could hardly have failed to register what had happened. Nevertheless, under the motto *what is done is done,* her father-in-law had chosen to ignore the vivid newsreel films, as well as the many hundreds of press and radio reports.

Like so many Germans had done before him, Horatio had managed to convince himself that buying property expropriated by Germany's Nazi government was a perfectly legitimate business arrangement. But in view of the old man's personal history this was hardly surprising. He had been brought up in the final years of British colonial power and as a young man he had served with the Coldstream Guards in South Africa. Whatever the history books might say about the Boer wars, there can be no doubting the fact that Britain's Lord Kitchener had pursued a scorched earth policy, in which British forces had systematically burned crops, destroyed farms and homesteads, and raped Boer women and even children as young as ten. Indeed, long before the Nazis, Kitchener

---

4   In October 2021, I talked to the *Daily Telegraph*. Having outlined the situation and asked for permission to quote this paragraph, the lady told me that I could use the quote free of charge.

had been responsible for developing the world's first concentration camps. At least forty were constructed for Boer refugees and sixty more for those native Africans who had worked as servants for the Boers. Between 18,000 and 28,000 Boers are said to have died in these camps, eighty percent of them children.

Although the British did not bother to keep records for native Africans housed in such camps, it is believed that their death toll was similar to that of the Boers. Regardless of his involvement in this campaign, Horatio's lack of empathy should have surprised no one.

Conveniently ignoring his own French ancestry, for Horatio, anyone who was not a white English protestant male was inferior. This he calculated on a sliding scale that began with the Scots, the Welsh and the Irish, and finished with any kind of, to use his word, *darky*.

Horatio's revelations instantly killed any relationship Grace had ever had with her father-in-law. Clearly, she could not avoid him at the violin gallery, but she vowed she would leave and never return to his Epsom house. Within the week, Grace had moved back into the flat above the violin gallery. For a while at least, because of school, Pippa and her horse would remain at Epsom with Nanny. Although Grace had often stayed in the flat after working in the city, this new arrangement caused considerable consternation, especially for Edward and James, who both cherished their freedom whenever Grace was out of town. By way of explanation Grace implied that Horatio had made inappropriate sexual advances. It was perhaps significant that neither Edward nor James had problems believing her story.

Grace gradually began to realise that she was being confronted with the kind of dilemma that most of Germany's adult population had faced after Hitler's election in 1933. Whether her father and grandfather had ever been aware of the source of the Montague instruments was almost irrelevant now; if she were to inform the necessary authorities, they and even she herself would be implicated, and their hard-won reputation would be in ruins. In addition, the company would almost certainly be forced to close, putting its workforce, including her old friends Walter, Eileen and Harry the cleaner, out on the street.

It seemed that the only alternative was to remain silent and do nothing, but as history had already taught Grace, silence and inaction are never the best response to injustice.

Grace needed time to think, to gather her thoughts, and her first and most disturbing thought concerned Horatio's assumption that it had been both acceptable and safe to tell *her* his appalling secret. He had addressed the subject as if she were a willing accomplice. Grace could not believe she had been so naive, but the whole scenario had been just too unthinkable to imagine. Clearly, in Horatio's mind, she was an accessory after the fact. Grace had always considered herself a liberal thinker. She assumed that this was the impression that she gave everyone around her, but clearly, her silence and her naturally agreeable nature had by implication given Horatio and God knows who else the wrong impression. In future she would need to be more explicit.

38

As she often did at times of stress, Grace turned to the journals she had compiled while travelling in the United States with her father. As well as containing a wealth of technical information, they also provided comfort. They chronicled her youthful impressions of America, from its bustling high-rise cities to its forests, deserts, rivers and seas. For more than a decade they had provided a lifeline to a land and a life she had once loved with a passion, a love that nostalgia and the passage of time had simply magnified. But now, in the light of recent events, her journals started to take on a new and more sinister significance. Various comments and notes added in the margins made reference to events or topics that she and her father had heard about or discussed on the road.

In the third volume, dated 1946, Grace found what she had been looking for; her first trip along Route 66.

She grimaced briefly as she recalled their uncomfortable thousand-mile return journey from Santa Fe to Chicago. While her father had sat comfortably in the driving seat, she had been forced to share the Studebaker's remaining space with nine violin cases, their personal luggage and a large Gio Paolo Maggini cello.

As they had passed through Tulsa, her father had told Grace the story of the *Greenwood Riots*. Her father had not witnessed the events himself, but seven years later he'd had occasion to visit Tulsa while on honeymoon with his new wife Mary, the daughter of Pay Dirt Bill MacGregor, and of course Grace's mother. Already knowing something about the riots, the newlyweds had tentatively asked about the rebuilding work that was clearly going on in the town. The response from Greenwood's black population had been muted, but most of the white folk they had spoken to saw nothing negative about the events of 1921.

As Grace usually did whenever a story interested her, after hearing and noting her father's explanation, she had researched the subject at her local library. Not without some difficulty, Grace discovered that Greenwood had been a kind of black enclave within the city of Tulsa.

Following the civil war, for many ex-slaves and their families, escaping the brutality of apartheid in the southern states became a priority, but around the turn of the twentieth century a real alternative started to emerge. Out of necessity, groups of freed slaves and Native Americans settled in so-called *Indian Territory*, in what would eventually become the State of Oklahoma. Rather than face segregation in white communities, activists created the Greenwood Community in Tulsa. In effect, at a time when segregation kept whites and blacks apart, this group chose to segregate themselves, by creating an all-black economy in Greenwood. It became a kind of barrier against any extension of the Jim Crow laws that were still in force almost everywhere in the United States, but especially in the south. In this respect Greenwood represented the hope of change. Sensing the opportunity to start afresh, thousands more travelled by every possible means to Oklahoma and eventually to Tulsa's Greenwood enclave.

During the early twentieth century Greenwood became a prominent symbol of black success. Booker T. Washington, whose works Grace had read during her research, referred to it as *Negro Wall Street,* others called it *Black Wall Street* and the name stuck. Either way, in the early twentieth century Greenwood became a place of black entrepreneurship and wealth. Along with banks, libraries, hairdressers, grocery stores, and many more successful businesses, Greenwood Avenue boasted one of the largest and best non-white hotels in North America.

The Jim Crow laws had been designed to prevent America's black population from achieving independence and upward mobility, but in Greenwood, racial segregation actually helped the black community to succeed. They succeeded because Black Wall Street was one of the few neighbourhoods where blacks were allowed both to gain and spend their money. They succeeded because of segregation, not in spite of segregation.

Tragically, this success created friction and in 1921, the Tulsa race riots began. In many respects, this event was comparable to Germany's *Kristallnacht* riots in 1938.

It was certainly driven by the same mentality. Beginning on May 30th, by June 1st, Black Wall Street had been looted, burned and razed to the ground. At least twenty-six black residents were massacred and hundreds more injured. The national guard are said to have indiscriminately shot into black residential buildings from the air. Meanwhile, the police, who had largely supported the white rioters, took many of Greenwood's black residents into custody, while most of the remainder fled the city. This violent three-day action, some of the worst in US history, effectively destroyed Greenwood's once thriving black community.

It was not that Grace had not heard of such events; since the beginning of slavery they had occurred on a regular basis all across the United States. Many had been of monumental proportions. She was equally aware that following the civil war and the freeing of slaves, things had not improved much either for black people, or Native American Indians. Laws that had kept blacks and whites apart before the civil war had hardly changed. The physical separation of racial groups simply continued. Across America, signs were still being used to indicate where non-whites could legally walk, talk, eat, drink and even which toilet facilities they could use. While travelling with her father, Grace had seen such signs herself.

Particularly in the southern states, severe penalties, both official and unofficial, were applied to enforce these so-called Jim Crow laws. These penalties included lynchings, shootings, torture, rapings and beatings. In particular, following World War I, returning black veterans were targeted. In 1918, the Ku Klux Klan lynched sixty-four black men and a further eighty-three in 1919. In the face of such violence thousands of black Americans fled north. Many found their way to Chicago, Grace's hometown, which, before 1915, had a good reputation for its treatment of Black Americans.

Regrettably, even in comparatively liberal Chicago, mass migration from the south put enormous pressure on the city's logistics. Overcrowding led to the formation of ghettos, where racial segregation and tension flared up on a regular basis. Eventually, in 1919, a major race riot occurred in the city. Here again, unrest had been fuelled by the increased militancy of black veterans returning from World War I. Having fought for their country, black Americans were no longer prepared to accept the status quo. Unfortunately, white Americans proved unwilling to make concessions, and in Chicago they attacked black Americans, starting an eight-day battle that resulted in thirty-eight deaths, and over 500 serious injuries.

In 1946, while Grace had been travelling with her father in the Midwest, a further series of racially motivated riots had taken place back in the city. Chicago's housing authority had attempted to provide temporary housing for black veterans, this time returning from World War II. And, as if this were not enough, in '47, around the time that she and Edward were courting, yet another terrible race riot had taken place in the city. Here again, black veterans were involved. Several veterans and their families had been moved into a housing project that was intended to integrate blacks into white communities. This strategy resulted in three days of violent mob action, in which white gangs attacked black people in street cars and automobiles. By the time things had calmed down at least thirty-five black people had been seriously injured.

Grace had seen the kind of hardship and poverty that created such unrest, but until she had arrived in London it had always been from a distance. Although she rarely mentioned it in her journals, some of the images she had described were jolting her memory now. On one particular occasion, she had referred to the kind of dusty run-down settlements in the middle of nowhere that they had often driven through.

The days of one-horse towns may be over, she had written, but the days of single-track towns are most definitely not. Railways may have opened up America and provided increased prosperity at their major terminals, but other than smoke, disruption and a lonesome whistle, the mile-long freight trains that travel along these lines provide little for the run-down communities they pass through.

At the time, Grace could remember thinking there was no right or wrong side of these tracks. Low dilapidated shanties flanked these rusting rails like flotsam on a beach. After the prosperity of her suburban Chicago existence, seeing whole families living in huts hardly bigger than the Studebaker had come as a shock. The poverty and deprivation Grace had fleetingly witnessed in her hometown had all been seen in passing, usually through the window of her father's automobile. Like a series of sepia photographs, at the time these horrifying vignettes had seemed strangely romantic, almost artistic. Grace remembered them now; those ragged little boys and girls with their big eyes, staring at the Studebaker as it floated by on a cloud of dust.

Recalling these images a dozen years on made Grace feel acutely uncomfortable. Via the family's Studebaker and Wurlitzer radios, Grace had heard about and duly recorded the Chicago riots and other similar event in her journals. But recording these events was not the same as understanding them, or being able to empathise with the plight of such persecuted minorities. Looking back now Grace was appalled by her apparent lack of sympathy. Seeking excuses, she concluded that this was a result of her youthful optimism, her sheltered existence and the fact that she had been in love with Edward, and busy planning her future life with him in England.

Paradoxically, it was seeing wide-eyed childhood poverty in England that had triggered her memories of the poverty and deprivation in the United States. The difference being that the poverty she had witnessed in America was not directly related to wartime austerity; it was largely the result of America's laws.

Gradually, Grace started to realise that the persecution of minorities in her homeland was raising the kind of moral questions that cannot be avoided whenever society begins to examine cases of historical evil. For hundreds of years, racial minorities in America had been subjected to slavery, exploitation and even genocide; all of which had been perpetrated by the kind of thinking that had created the Holocaust in Europe. Almost with a start, Grace realised that the United States that she knew, loved and revered was only a hair's breadth from what Nazi Germany had become under Hitler.

Shortly after the first settlers had arrived in North America, the persecution of minorities had begun, until gradually it had almost become second nature. In 1775, King George II of England had issued one of many similar routine proclamations from those in authority. This decree called for; *'subjects to embrace all opportunities of pursuing, captivating, killing and destroying all and every of the aforesaid Indians.'*

At other times, colonists were paid for each Native American they killed; fifty pounds for adult male scalps, twenty-five for adult female scalps, and twenty for the scalps of boys and girls under the age of twelve. There was no doubt, even in Grace's young mind, that this had been systematic genocide.

Between 1830 and 1838, federal officials removed around 100,000 Indians from land sequestered by white cotton growers. They were force marched from their homes in the southern states onto land known as *'Indian Territory'*. This action became part of the events that eventually led to the Greenwood tragedy. On this march some 4,000 Native Americans died of cold and hunger. Little more than a dozen years later, in 1851, Peter Burnett, the governor of California, proclaimed, *'A war of extermination will continue to be waged between the two races until the Indian race becomes extinct.'*

And the horror continued. Although Britain and the United States had officially banned the African slave trade in 1808, in the mid-nineteenth century, African slaves were still being forcibly shipped across the Atlantic. Before slavery was finally stopped, millions had died while being captured or transported. Others died in bondage, from brutality, disease, deprivation or from abnormally high rates of infant mortality.

Grace was beginning to realise that although the times were different, all too often the treatment of minorities in her homeland was entirely consistent with the Nazi's final solution. Nevertheless, in spite of her discoveries, and the accounts were as endless as they were horrific, until Horatio's revelation much of this information had been a kind of history lesson for Grace. It was not unlike hearing the stories about the tribulations of Italy's violin makers. Indeed, as a young woman, until she had witnessed the destruction in London, even the wars of her father's and grandfather's generations had always seemed remote. Empathy is difficult to generate without some form of personal experience, but for Grace now, a picture was gradually beginning to emerge of man's inhumanity to man.

To some extent Grace had always known it; even with her own limited experience, she had witnessed discrimination. It materialised in the subtlest of ways. At her exclusive school, there had been no black or Native American girls. In the violin business, indeed in the whole classical music world, there were no blacks or Native Americans. Even in so-called progressive areas of Chicagoan life, segregation thrived. The huge and exclusive Trianon ballroom, where Grace had first danced with Edward, was an excellent example of how things worked. Accommodating up to 3,000 dancers, with a similar number in its alcoves and upper levels, much of the ballroom's popularity with white middle-class Chicagoans was its racial exclusivity. Although this venue was billed as a *'marvellous tribute to democracy'*, in reality, interracial dancing was not permitted. In fact, blacks had been refused entry from the moment the place had opened, and this rule had continued until long after the Second World War was over. Blacks and American Indians, who had helped the United States to triumph in both world wars, were still second-class citizens when they returned home, and they were kept in their place by violence and threats of violence.

Grace had neither witnessed nor seen the aftermath of the Chicago riots. Indeed, she had been only vaguely aware of the extensive slums that had developed on Chicago's South Side.

Known as the *Black Belt,* this group of neighbourhoods, some thirty blocks long, housed three-quarters of the city's growing black population. Only with hindsight was she able to piece together the tragic story of Chicago's black population, and only later did she extend this to include the general oppression of racial minorities right across the United States of America.

39

Grace spent more than a month thinking about what she should do with the terrible knowledge her father-in-law had revealed. Her immediate instinct had been to call her own father, but she was worried about the affect it would have on his health. The same applied to her grandfather, who was approaching eighty and busy nursing his son. Eventually the question was taken out of her hands. In spite of her grandfather's valiant efforts, before Grace had the opportunity to speak with him, her father succumbed to his illness.

Confused and grief stricken, Grace boarded a BOAC flight to Chicago. Any nervousness she might otherwise have felt on the twenty-hour flight was dissipated by her sorrow and fear of the future. She travelled alone. If Edward had not refused permission for Pippa to leave Britain, she would almost certainly have abandoned everything and remained in Chicago with her daughter. Unfortunately, although Edward was unaware of the treasure in Horatio's secret vault, he was not about to let Montague's best expert leave the country without ensuring her safe return. It was the same mentality that barely two years later would separate families on either side of the Berlin Wall.

Since her father's illness, Grace had often considered the possibility of running the Scott's Chicago shop herself, especially because her grandfather had expressed his wish to continue working, realistically however it was a pipedream. Her grandfather was already too old, and even if she had been allowed to take her daughter to America, Grace was sure that she could never become a successful dealer; she simply did not have the mentality. And now, since Horatio's recent revelations, she was even more convinced that while expertise might occasionally be fun, buying and selling instruments was most certainly not. The sad truth was that in spite of their many personal difficulties, for the past five years, she and Edward had worked well together. Freed from the burden of dealing with the business's commercial side, Grace had largely enjoyed her time identifying and assessing instruments, especially when working together with her friend Walter Drake. Nevertheless, Edward continued to control her life and she longed for freedom and independence.

Grace had been expecting a great deal of work helping her grandfather to organise the funeral and close the business, but having anticipated this event, the two men had already sold both the shop and its contents to a nice young couple. Randolph had first employed this couple in 1949, some twelve months after Grace had left for England. Initially they had been taught the trade by Randolph and Hermann, but once Randolph's health had started to deteriorate, by the mid 1950s, they were more or less running the place alone. The best part of this sales agreement was the fact that Hermann, who in spite of his seventy-six-years was still fit and healthy, could continue working in the shop for as long as he wished, and as he had pointed out to Grace, when Stradivari was ninety-three years old, he was also still working in his Cremonese workshop.

Three weeks after her father's funeral, Grace returned to London. Just before leaving Chicago, she had summoned the courage to raise the question of the Nazi violins. Her grandfather had been genuinely horrified.

'I alvays neffer trusted doz Montagues. Zay are bandits.' His accent was strong, as it always was when he was excited. 'Do you really believe zat your papa vud do such a ting? Zis is not possible. Not possible. 'Ow could you tink such a ting. Your papa alvays taught you neffer to cheat nobody, not ever. You know dat.'

'I know, Grandpa. I am just telling you what Horatio Montague said. And you are right, he is a bandit; I know that now.'

'And that Edvard too. He stole your money. Don't tink I don't know dat.'

'I know that you know it and that you rescued me by sending money to my lawyer.' But as Grace said the word lawyer, she realised that she must now tell the whole truth about her relationship with Edward and his father.

Before Grace finished the story, her grandfather had several more emotional outbursts, but eventually she managed to calm him. She explained that from now on she would be running the Montague business and she reassured him that she would find a solution to the problem of the stolen instruments. She was not sure what that solution might be, but it arrived much sooner than she had anticipated.

Two days after Christmas in the final week of the 1950s, Horatio Montague was found dead. He was sitting in a dirty cinema seat at The Doll's House, surrounded by cheap baubles and tinsel. The exact moment of his passing had gone unnoticed. The ladies and management were used to their older clientele falling asleep, especially in the front row, where they were able to stretch out their legs. Horatio had arrived around lunchtime and by late evening rigor mortis had already set in. Normally, the club's burly bouncers would have quietly picked him up, frogmarched him to the nearest park bench and left him. However, because Horatio was already stiff and therefore difficult to move, they simply searched his pockets, removed his cash and called the police.

Other than the *News of the World*'s scandal columns, a well-known violin dealer dying in a striptease club barely caused a ripple in the newspapers, and certainly not amongst the Soho gossip mongers. Nevertheless, it did cause quite a stir between Edward and Grace.

Initially, Edward had considered moving to his father's Epsom house alone, and to have Pippa join Grace in the flat above the violin gallery. In spite of this, fears that living alone might result in his secret being discovered again quickly caused him to reject such plans. Although he had no desire to sleep with his wife, he was convinced that however distasteful, his present predicament called for just such an arrangement.

Either way Grace had no intention of staying in the city. She could not leave the instruments where they were, because with their penchant for expensive alcohol, there was always the possibility that either Edward or James would discover the old man's hidden safe. Of more immediate concern, however, was the fact that she would not be able to deal with the problem if she were stuck in the West End of London, while Edward was living in the Epsom house alone. Arguing that Pippa still needed fresh air and that the problem of Horatio's inappropriate behaviour no longer applied, Grace moved back into the house that she had vowed never to enter again. When it was eventually decided that Nanny should also remain, Edward was deflated.

Remarkably, Grace was still blissfully unaware of Edward's sexual orientation, and she continued to maintain the forlorn hope that her relationship with him might still blossom, especially in view of her father-in-law's rather romantic sleeping arrangements. Horatio's bedroom was dominated by a huge four-poster bed with a canopy. An ornate dressing table that had belonged to Edward's mother also stood against one wall. Edward had been adamant that both these items should be preserved, but eventually, a compromise was reached when he had allowed Grace to purchase a new mattress and hangings for the canopy.

Finally, it was agreed that Grace's stepson James, who was now a twenty-two-year-old playboy, would move into the flat above the violin gallery and that the following year, eleven-year-old Pippa would attend Roedean, a private boarding school for young ladies on England's south coast.

Shortly after this decision had been taken, Grace received even more bad news, when a telegram arrived, informing her that her beloved Grandfather had died quietly in his sleep at the Scotts family home.

The shock of the old man's passing devastated Grace. He was not just her Grandfather, he was her last remaining parent. On reading the news Grace had fainted and fallen to the workshop floor, hitting her head in the process. Fortunately, on Grace's insistence, all of Montague's employees had recently attended a St. John Ambulance first aid course and everyone quickly gathered round with helpful advice. In the end however, as with violin repair work, Walter quickly took the initiative. Nevertheless, in spite of raising her legs above the level of her heart, it was several long minutes before Grace recovered and she remained woozy until the following day, at which point Walter's Dr. friend diagnosed a mild concussion. The good Dr. kept Grace under observation at his clinic for several days. Even when faced with her protests he remained adamant that she should on no account take a long transatlantic fight. As a result, Grace had been forced to miss her Grandfather's funeral.

Even with the support of Walter, Eileen and Harry, Grace remained inconsolable for several days. Edward, however, was wide awake. Keen to see if he had been named in the will, acting as Grace's spouse, through his own lawyer, he had attempted to deal with the correspondence between Grace and her Grandfather's legal counsel, only to be informed that her Grandfather had arranged things so that Edward could not interfere with any of the arrangements that had already been made or were about to be made.

40

Walter removed a pristine white linen handkerchief from his jacket pocket and handed it to Grace. It had been carefully ironed and folded and it felt unusually stiff against her cheek. Desperate and distraught, Grace had waited weeks for a suitable time and place to disclose the terrible secret that had tormented her day and night since her father-in-law's revelation. In the end she had chosen their favourite little Soho café to tell the sorry tale. She had wanted to remain detached, but the moment they sat down together, she started to cry.

Walter had saved Grace's daughter's life, which was clearly an act that she could never repay. Even before this, with the aid of his Harley Street doctor friend, Walter had helped her to open a personal bank account. At one of the most difficult periods in her life, this account had provided Grace with a welcome modicum of independence. And now she was about to ask Walter to help her resolve the problem of Horatio's chamber of horrors.

Initially Grace had been determined to solve this terrifying predicament herself, but her grandfather's sudden death, only two months after Horatio's ignominious demise, had undermined her usual tenacity. Reluctantly she had come to the conclusion that she could not manage the task alone.

'How many instruments are there?' Walter had asked when Grace had finished her account.

'There are eleven violins, one viola and two cellos, but they are all of the finest quality.'

'And who knows about them?'

'Like I said, Walter, as far as I am aware, I am the only one who even knows about Horatio's wine cellar safe. It is now more than ten months since his death, and no one has mentioned or even hinted that they might know something. Certainly, if either Edward or James had suspected anything, they would not… could not have kept quiet.'

'That's undoubtedly true, but what about lawyers or the family solicitor?'

'Horatio's testament was read by the family solicitor only two days after the funeral. There were only four beneficiaries and they were all present at the reading.

'As might be expected, the bulk of the estate was left to Edward, with James and Pippa each receiving a large monitory bequest. Horatio left me his small but beautiful library of violin books, and the company's archives, most of which were the work of my father and myself anyway. He also left me his gold watch and chain. James had actually raised his eyebrows at this announcement, but no one complained. I suspect they were just happy that he had not left me more.

'Even at the reading, no reference was made, either about the collection or the cellar safe. Neither was there any mention of the key to the Chippendale desk, which was still attached to Horatio's watch chain. At the first opportunity, I opened the desk and its secret compartment and removed the key to the wine cellar safe. So at least that is in my possession. I also checked to see if the instruments were all still there; they were. Although I have not been tempted to look again, I know that they have not been disturbed, because I glued a tiny piece of tape to the sliding shelf and it is still unbroken. However, if they ever find the safe, they will do everything in their power to get inside. Because the combination is so obvious, even Edward would eventually work it out, after which I imagine it would not be too difficult for a skilled locksmith to organise a key. But, knowing Edward and James, rather than waiting for expert help, they would use force, which could well result in damaging the instruments.

'Leaving me his gold watch and chain, with the desk key, was a smart move on the old man's part. While he was still alive, he was able to keep Edward, James and even Pippa in check. After his death, he realised that left uncontrolled, one or all of them might easily run amok. He was also aware that in order to survive, the business would still need me and that I would need some form of power and authority; especially over Edward and James. It might seem that by giving me the archives, I would be entirely free to return to the United States, but Horatio knew that this was virtually impossible. Pippa is still only eleven years old and no English court would allow me to take her to the States without her father's permission. This is the hold that Edward will have over me until Pippa reaches the age of majority. In any case, what would I do in America now? Grandpa Scott's death earlier this year, almost exactly one year after my father's death, upset me even more. At least we knew that Papa was seriously ill. Not only did Grandpa's death come as a shock, I am convinced that he died of a broken heart and believing that has been difficult for me to live with.

'Horatio also knew that divorce was out of the question. Even if I were to petition for divorce, Edward would fight it tooth and nail. Obtaining custody would be almost impossible, but even if I could take Pippa to the US, the Scott's shop has already been sold. With Grandpa gone, I would be on my own with a child, needing to start a new life and a new company, in a male-dominated business. And to be honest, Walter, I was not even capable of arguing with Edward and James about sending Pippa away to that elite boarding school. The very idea had appalled me, but I simply didn't have the energy to oppose them. And now, this stupid immoral collection of Horatio's is just making things worse. While he was alive, I could somehow put it to the back of my mind, but… Oh, Walter, I am so sorry to have dragged you into all this.'

'Grace, we have been close friends for a dozen years, during which time we have been through a lot together. You have no reason to apologise to me.' And with these few words, a fresh flood of tears rapidly softened Walter's stiff linen handkerchief.

Leaning around the small table, Walter held Grace in his arms and allowed her to vent her grief. Her body was soon shaking violently, and he needed all his strength to prevent her from falling from her chair. As she buried her head in his shoulder, the old man could see and feel her beautifully soft red hair against his face, and her tears running down his neck. Since the death of his wife and children, Walter had always known that he could never allow himself the luxury of becoming emotionally attached to anyone ever again. But life has ways of changing everyone's *best laid plans...*

For a long time now, Walter had revered this young woman, she was kind, respectful and unusually strong willed. She had entered a rat's nest and had nevertheless retained her dignity. Indeed, had it not been for her arrival, he may well have renounced the company and even the profession he loved. Like those black and Native American soldiers returning from two world wars, Walter had had his fill of subservience, and so far, only Grace had offered him a real alternative; true friendship.

Slowly Grace calmed down, and as Walter relaxed his hold, she gradually regained her equilibrium. Tea, the British cure-all, was ordered and Walter was thankfully able to swing his legs back under the small linoleum-covered table.

'It's really not the end of the world, Grace,' Walter proffered. 'We just need to work our way through the problem systematically, but perhaps we should wait a few days until you are feeling better.'

'No, if you have any ideas, let's go through them now.

I've had enough of waiting and worrying. The longer I leave this, the greater is the chance that someone will discover the collection. As for it not being the end of the world, I'm not sure that I can agree with you about that, sometimes that is exactly how it feels.'

'Very well,' Walter said, lowering his voice reverently, 'let's work through what we have. As far as we know, only you and I know that there is a safe and only you know what it contains. Do you know who originally sold the boss these instruments and might they start making enquiries?'

'Horatio only told me that he had purchased them from the German government, and that before the war they had been smuggled into Britain, initially by German diplomats, and later by a thirteen-year-old Hungarian child protégé, who frequently travelled to London for violin lessons. Because it was so unusual, I still remember the boy's name, it was Zsolti Gnagy. I don't know if this particular story was true, but it would seem to make sense. Before the war started in 1939, this talented young Hungarian virtuoso was probably crossing international borders with impunity. According to Horatio, the boy always arrived with a double case containing two valuable violins, but he returned home with two worthless factory instruments, supplied by Montague's.'

'I really would not know,' Walter intervened. 'And I think I would have remembered an unusual name like that, but of course we were never privy to that kind of information.'

'Anyway,' Grace continued, 'because Horatio indicated that he was still doing business with this man, I searched the company's records, but I found nothing. Later, I managed to find several pre-war references to a talented young Hungarian player called Zsolti Gnagy, but after 1945 no one seems to know what happened to him. If he is still in Hungary things might be difficult for him. Almost one million Hungarians died in the war. And in spite of the '56 uprising the Soviets are still in charge there. As for the German officials, even if they survived, my guess is that they would rather forget having handled instruments that were confiscated by the Nazis.'

After pausing to consider Grace's words, Walter then asked, 'What about tracing the original owners? Would that even be possible?'

'Horatio told me that the instruments in his collection were too well known to be sold and that it would be many years, perhaps even several generations before they could be placed on the open market. If this is true, it means that he and his accomplices must have known something. I found nothing among Horatio's papers, but he is unlikely to have kept any incriminating evidence. However, although many records were lost or destroyed in the war, a few still exist. Ironically, much of this documentation was created by the Nazis themselves, but working through these ledgers would require a trained archivist with a strong stomach. Nevertheless, it might still be possible to trace original owners, or at least their relatives, should any of them have survived the Nazi death camps. And, whatever we decide to do, this will need to be taken into consideration.

'The problem is that although the instruments in Horatio's cellar are clearly special, they represent only a fraction of the many thousands of musical instruments that were stolen, and even they pale into insignificance when compared to the trainloads of artwork and valuables looted by the Nazis.'

'Yes, but nevertheless,' said Walter quietly, 'I expect that even instruments that were not important enough to have papers will still have cost lives; sometimes the lives of entire families.'

'That's certainly true,' Grace agreed. 'In fact, the greatest obstacle to establishing ownership is that whereas much of the stolen artwork, especially paintings and sculptures, was well documented, most musical instruments were not. Consequently, unless they were exceptional, like those in Horatio's cellar, I imagine it will be almost impossible to match instruments to their owners, especially if those owners and their families were brutally murdered or worked to death in concentration camps.'

'What about photographic records?' Walter suddenly asked. 'Dealers have been photographing instruments for a long time.'

'That's right,' Grace answered. 'My father was already photographing fiddles in the 1920s, but that was unusual, most normal violin dealers never bothered with photography. Papa had a small studio set up in our basement just for that purpose. The pictures he took were developed and printed by the Chicago Camera Company, at 33 West Monroe Street. I can still remember their stamp on the back of each print.'

'Even before the First World War, Montague's had a similar arrangement,' said Walter. 'And since 1952 the firm has been attaching photographs to their certificates of authenticity. Of course, although we suspected a photographic archive, we were never given access to such things. In fact, if you had not tried to teach me and the boys how to identify instruments, we would not have known about those files even today, and I've been working here almost forty years. I can still remember the shock when you showed me the first ones, and then I was both afraid and elated at the same time. It was a dangerous game we were all playing. The old man would have flipped-his-lid if he had ever found out, and Edward and James would do the same today.'

'I've checked Montague's entire archive,' said Grace, 'but significantly, there are no prints or even negatives of the instruments in Horatio's cellar. And that is the nub of the problem. Right across the violin business, photographs have always been carefully guarded *trade secrets*. They were never in the public domain. Even today, each violin dealership has its own jealously guarded collection of prints and they have no wish to show or even discuss them with anyone else. As a result, other than a few pictures of Stradivaris, Guarneris and Amatis that appear in the press from time to time, there is still no easy way to establish an instrument's provenance through photography; at least, not without asking a lot of awkward questions. What's more, even if you can identify an instrument, it may still be impossible to establish who the rightful heirs might be.

'For this reason alone, I am sure that thousands of instruments looted by the Nazis are still in the hands of German and Austrian musicians, or form part of the inventory in German and Austrian music schools and museum collections.

'As for the actual number of musicians that were

slaughtered to obtain these instruments, this is simply too awful to contemplate. Nevertheless, since being confronted with this problem I have thought of little else. Together with Gypsies, communists, religious dissenters, homosexuals, the incurably sick, and in fact anyone they considered troublesome or inferior, in less than a dozen years, the Nazis cold bloodedly murdered the equivalent of London's present population twice over. The problem is that I am starting to think about this whenever I see crowds on Oxford Street, in Trafalgar Square, or queuing for West End theatres. I know that these groups represent the tiniest fraction of the numbers that were killed, and it is driving me crazy. But the worst is when I think of the lost children.'

Too late, Grace remembered that Walter had lost his wife and children in the Blitz. 'Oh, Walter, I'm so sorry,' she suddenly blurted out. 'I wasn't thinking.'

'That's alright, Grace,' he said, nevertheless she had seen the momentary flicker of pain in his eyes. 'But you cannot go on thinking about these things all the time, or they *will* make you crazy. You cannot save the world alone, Grace. You need to choose your battles carefully. Right now, you and I need to concentrate on finding a solution to *this* problem, and the sooner the better. Let me think about it for a while. Give me a week and we will discuss this again.'

41

Exactly one week later the pair met again. Both had researched various possibilities, but Walter spoke first. 'After all their good work finding and returning art works looted by the Nazis, the Monuments, Fine Arts, and Archives program was apparently wound down in 1946. Responsibility for further discoveries and repatriations was moved to the American State Department. When I heard this, for a moment I considered just leaving the instruments outside the US Embassy, after all, it's just a few hundred yards down the road from where we are sitting. The problem is that leaving a lot of bulky boxes with no explanation would cause a great deal of consternation. And then I realised that the same would happen almost everywhere else I thought about leaving them. I even flirted with the idea of sending them anonymously by post, but I believe the risk of them being thrown around and damaged in some sorting office would be too great.'

'I agree,' said Grace, 'and sending them to another country will also be impossible, because customs clearance will be required. Whatever we come up with, it will have to be in the British Isles.'

'That is also true,' agreed Walter. 'We could, of course, just report what we know to the authorities. The question is what would that achieve? The old man is dead, and presumably his heirs cannot be prosecuted. What is more, they would almost certainly put up a protracted legal battle against any claims made against the company. Win or lose, the fallout would surely result in Montague's innocent workers being made redundant and more expenses and stress for the holocaust survivors.'

After a debate that lasted almost three days, Grace and Walter finally decided that the instruments should be presented to a respected Jewish association that had been established in the late 1940s. This was a specialist legal aid service, designed to assist victims of Nazi persecution. Amongst other things, its mission was to provide restitution for artwork looted by the Nazis. Grace and Walter felt that they at least would know what to do. Moreover, the association's head office was in Central London.

Having removed anything and everything from the instruments and cases that might link them to Montague's, the action began. Very early one Sunday morning in the spring of 1960, while Edward was out of town and James was sleeping off another busy Saturday night, in a carefully coordinated operation, Grace and Walter quietly removed the instruments from Horatio's safe and drove them to a stretch of pavement just a few yards from the stage door of the Royal Albert Hall. Other than a few cooing pigeons, the whole area was as quiet as a grave and as they unloaded the cases, the building's old stone facade and walkways echoed their movements.

Leaving Walter with the precious load, Grace parked the car in an almost empty nearby street. Donning a blond wig, she then walked back to the Albert Hall's stage door, arriving only minutes before a black London taxicab. The cab had been ordered under an assumed name the previous day. It had also been paid for, cash in advance. It had been decided that should anyone see them, either loading or unloading a large group of musical instruments, at least this venue would not appear unusual.

A short time later, the pair and their load were transported by taxi to King's Cross station. Under normal circumstances Grace loved the hustle and bustle of large mainline stations. The noise and smell of powerful engines blowing off steam, sparks and smoke had always excited her. Unlike the new diesel locomotives that were being introduced, steam engines were almost living, breathing entities. But today, as one by one the instruments were carried from the black cab and deposited at the left luggage office, none of this mattered anymore.

Having paid the fees, the tickets for each instrument were placed in an envelope with a carefully worded letter. Ever mindful that someone might attempt to trace the depositors of these instruments, Grace and Walter had taken many precautions. The letter and envelope were typed on *Basildon Bond*; a common paper for correspondence and one that could be bought over the counter at any newsagent or stationary shop. Even the typewriter they used was a common model. However, having learned that the print of each typewriter is unique and that police are able to identify exactly which machine was used, they purchased one second-hand at the Portobello Road market. After typing the letter to their satisfaction Walter smashed the machine and distributed the pieces in various litter bins around the city. To an outsider these precautions may have appeared extreme, but Grace was aware that they were dealing with multiple murders and possibly millions of pounds' worth of antique Italian violins. They needed to cover their tracks carefully.

Rather remarkably, the one thing they had not considered was the question of expertise.

Weeks went by with no mention of the instruments either in the press, in the business, or on the streets. And then, almost out of the blue, a request was made for someone to value several instruments at a solicitor's office in Middle Temple Lane, London's exclusive legal district. Realising the significance of this address, Edward was keen for Montague's to do the valuation. The question was who should represent the company. Obviously, Grace was the only one capable of making such an assessment, but the possibility of a profitable deal was already exciting Edward. In the end, it was decided that he and Grace should attend together, as the husband-and-wife team of Montague Fine Violins.

The Montagues were greeted at the door by a secretary and escorted to a plush office on the second floor. The oak-panelled room was large and comfortably furnished with leather armchairs and a highly polished eighteenth-century writing desk. Leather-bound volumes, presumably legal books, lined the walls. A fine Persian carpet covered most of the floor. Three distinguished-looking elderly gentlemen were standing on the carpet in front of several elegant musical instrument cases. The number and quality of the cases had already caused Edward's heart to bump and race. Edward may not have known much about expertise, but at least he knew quality cases when he saw them, and these bespoke silk-lined etuis were not cheap run-of-the-mill factory boxes.

Until this moment Grace had entertained the forlorn hope that the instruments they had been asked to value were not from Horatio's collection. But now, the reality of her predicament was hitting hard. For several minutes she had difficulty focusing her eyes as she fought the floating feeling in her head. It was as if she were in a kind of drug-induced dream. Fortunately, she managed to regain control before the first instrument was placed on the desk in front of her.

Grace had brought along her leather attaché case, containing her notebook, various mirrors, inspection lamps and a chamois leather spread, but she was only going through the motions. She already knew the ins and outs of each instrument as well, if not better, than she knew her own husband. From the start, she had been convinced that these three men, experienced at extracting the truth from hardened criminals, would see right through her charade. For this reason, she took perhaps longer than would normally have been necessary.

Although Edward had fussed and blustered around, trying his best to appear knowledgeable, within minutes the three men had assessed his worth. Eventually, the men settled in three leather armchairs where they continued to observe Grace with considerable interest. Tea and delicate sandwiches were served several times, but no one suggested taking a prolonged break. In the end, Edward confirmed the men's assumptions by settling into the last leather armchair and closing his eyes thoughtfully.

When Grace had finished examining the violins, before turning to the viola, she glanced quickly at a Victorian wall clock. She had been working for four hours without a break. From the corner of her eye she could see Edward; he was fast asleep. Not so the three men, who were still quietly attentive. Grace took a sip of tea and ate a small triangular sandwich. As she did so one of the men addressed her.

'Where do you think these instruments came from, Mrs Montague?'

Without thinking Grace answered, 'Germany and Austria, I presume.'

Too late, she realised what she had done when the man said, 'So you don't think they are from Cremona as the labels state?'

Fortunately, Grace recovered well. 'Oh yes, they are Cremonese all right.'

'Then what made you say Germany and Austria?'

'You asked me where these instruments came from, not where they were made. So far, the instruments I have examined all have German or Austrian fittings and strings. But more obviously, their bridges are all stamped with the names of German or Austrian dealers, in Vienna, Saltsburg, Dresden, Munich and Berlin. As for where they were made, you will receive a written valuation for each instrument, as soon as I have had time to compose them. I would guess two days from now. What I can say is that these instruments are some of the finest I have ever seen, and considering their age, their state of preservation is exceptional. This is a unique and extremely valuable collection.'

'Yes!' replied the man quietly. 'It cost far more than you could possibly imagine.'

Looking over at her sleeping husband, Grace quietly said, 'These instruments really are important examples. If I might make a suggestion, when I have finished my assessment, you should consider getting a second opinion… What about provenance?' she added rather belatedly. 'Do you have any?'

'You *are* our second opinion,' said the man without a trace of humour. 'As for provenance, so far we have none, but we are working hard to establish one for each instrument.'

When the session was over, Grace woke Edward gently and together they took the train back to Epsom. Initially Edward was full of questions, but Grace managed to play the collection down. 'None of the instruments have provenance papers and one of the cellos is badly smashed. If you want my opinion, we should just collect our fee for the valuation and forget we ever saw them.'

42

Since their first exchange of letters in 1952, Grace and Amanda Kowalski had continued their correspondence. Although over time they wrote less frequently, their postings became progressively longer and increasingly intimate. Isolated and bereft of female companionship, these letters were a rare opportunity for both women to unburden their souls. What had begun as a simple exchange of news and views had gradually evolved into a mutual outpouring of their hopes, fears and innermost secrets.

Grace was aware that not everyone is privileged to develop genuine friendships in childhood and adolescence; but that those who do and manage to maintain them into adulthood are truly blessed. Her friendship with Amanda had been forged under duress, but it had also been forged at a time before they had begun to erect the kind of defence mechanisms that protect everyone from the inherent unpleasantness of being human. With luck, the minds of such friends remain as innocent and vulnerable as infants, and it becomes virtually impossible for them to hide behind the barricades that almost everyone develops in later life. Relationships of this nature are rare, because in order to succeed, they require absolute trust. And it was just so with Amanda and Grace; they were free to pour out their hopes and fears without risk of betrayal or retribution. Of course, the fact that they also lived solitary lives 4,000 miles apart did help. It was rather like sitting in a confessional box, knowing who was listening, but somehow sure that what was being said would go no further.

Amanda had been the first to open her heart. She had begun with worries about her father's business, which was apparently having financial difficulties, but she had eventually moved on to the relationship between her husband and her father. At first Amanda's marriage had been happy. They had two beautiful girls and with Amanda's support, her husband David had qualified as an eye surgeon. Unfortunately, his wartime experiences had caused him to drink heavily, until eventually he had lost his job at the hospital. Having managed to curb his drinking, he had started working in the family's delicatessen, but he and Amanda's father were often at loggerheads. They quarrelled noisily in Polish, even in front of their customers, which was the main reason why business had recently declined. Eventually the burden of organising the shop and the family had rested almost entirely on Amanda, and she tackled the men and the business with a strength she had not realised she possessed. The situation was not unlike Grace's own. Had it not been for her children, Amanda would have left the men to their own devices.

For a while, in 1963, political events took centre stage in the correspondence between Amanda and Grace. In particular this eventful year had seen the killing of the civil rights leader Medgar Evers by white activists. This incident had been closely followed by the assassination of President Kennedy, and suddenly the women's letters were filled with the horror of it all.

November 30th, 1963

Dear Amanda, As if mass killings in the Korean War and last year's Cuban Missile Crisis had not been enough to scare everyone half to death, almost every day, in spite of government denials, we read about our involvement in the war in Vietnam. I have the feeling it's going to be another Korea. We have already lost so many young men. I honestly don't understand what the Pentagon is trying to achieve. Wasn't there enough killing in World War Two?

…And this summer we got to hear that white activists shot the civil rights leader Medgar Evers. It seems it wasn't enough that he risked his life fighting for America in the Second World War. And then, after having been shot in the back outside his home, he was taken to hospital in Jackson, Mississippi, where because he was black, they initially refused to treat him. Eventually, when they realised who he was, they admitted him. Apparently, when the

poor man died, less than an hour later, he'd had the dubious distinction of being the first black person in Mississippi to be treated in a whites-only hospital... And then, horror of horrors, this last week, it was the turn of President Kennedy. How can anyone do such terrible things? It never seems to stop. Sometimes I despair. What is happening in our world? What is happening to America? Why can't we just live peacefully with one another? Is it in our blood? Did our Founding Fathers beget a nation of killers?

Dearest Grace, I know it is difficult, but from the tone of your last few letters I am beginning to worry about you. You cannot carry the whole world on your shoulders...

Dear Amanda, you are right, of course. Walter also tells me that I have to stop trying to save the world. It's just that sometimes I would like to be God for a day. The problem is that to put things right, I would almost certainly have to kill a lot of awful people. Perhaps that's what God is trying to do. He is certainly good at the killing part of the equation...

Realising that Britain's grim period of post-war austerity was virtually over, in her next series of letters, Amanda attempted to paint a more positive picture of the world. In particular she was keen to discuss developments in London, which from the mid 1960s had undergone a remarkable metamorphosis. Even in the United States, London's youth-culture revolution was being talked about on television and in gossip columns. Driven by popular music and fashion, Britain was the place where things were supposed to be happening, and ever hungry for excitement, Amanda wanted details. Unfortunately, although she tried her best to describe what she was seeing in and around the city, Grace had little knowledge either of fashion or the pop music scene.

Nevertheless, it was virtually impossible to avoid either genre. By the time Liverpool's Fab Four had appeared on the Ed Sullivan show in 1964, the Beatles were already international stars and 'Beatlemania' was a world-wide phenomenon. During this time, Amanda's correspondence became more frequent and more up-beat. Fired up by what she had been learning about the London scene, a further raft of letters followed. Eventually, barely able to contain herself, Amanda wrote;

March 4th, 1964

Dear Grace, I checked an old London street map. Your shop is only a few hundred yards from Wimpole Street where Paul McCartney lives with his girlfriend Jane Asher. I don't suppose you ever see them? It's incredible, she is only seventeen years old and her parents allow them to live together in their house. Is that what is meant by free love? My father would have had a heart attack if I had as much as suggested such a thing…

…The London fashion scene is so fabulous. I just love Mary Quant. I wish we'd had the miniskirt and hot pants back at the Latin School, can you imagine? These days I'm probably too old to wear such things,

but I might still try. Actually, we are only one year older than Mary Quant and she looks 'outta sight' in hot pants. Maybe then David will look at me again. The mini is just so liberating, what do you think? And what about that bob cut? I swear I'd love to cut all my long locks off. Maybe I should come over and have a bob cut in London. These days, Chicago is so drab. It's a drag. By comparison, London looks so incredibly colourful, groovy and sexy. I hope I don't sound too frustrated, but if I do, that's because I am. I'm fed up of being a good Catholic wife. I want to be a groupie. The Beatles look nice, but if I'm honest, I'd prefer Mick Jagger. His lips are so sensuous…

Having read this letter, Grace sat down and drafted an immediate reply. In her trademark blue-green ink she wrote;

Dear Amanda, I don't know what has come over you. And where did you learn all that 'groovy' new language? Ha! Ha! As for turning David on with a mini skirt, if I thought that would work with Edward, I would wear a wide belt. I haven't been able to interest him for years…

…Yes, I do like the look of Mick Jagger's lips, but I'm not sure about his dance moves. Don't you think they're a bit too explicit?

April 2nd, 1964
…Quite frankly, Grace, the more explicit the better, I'm not looking for love anymore, I have my family

and that's more than enough commitment. But I would once again like to experience the kind of feelings I had when David and I were still making love with real passion…

…There is an older man who comes into the shop once or twice a week. He is probably ten years older than me, but he is just so sexy. He never says very much, but I have noticed that he only comes into the shop when I am alone. I am tempted to ask his name, but it seems so improper. I am also afraid that I might lose control if I do ask. I often think about him, especially at five in the morning, when David goes off to the wholesale market. Last week I was warm in bed, so I removed my night shirt and hugged my pillow. We have a long Polish bolster pillow. I was still half asleep, but when I woke up properly, the pillow was wet. I feel embarrassed telling you this now, but so far, you and I have always been straight with one another and I just needed to tell someone. It was a nice moment, but rather strange, because the bolster had been my mother's and I started wondering if she had ever done something similar. And now I have been sitting here wondering if I should tear this letter up. If you have received it, you will know my decision.

From this moment, it was as if a curtain had been drawn back. For years they had been revealing details about their families and their business problems, but now they had crossed a line. It was almost as if they were challenging one another to reveal their most intimate sexual desires.

April 28th, 1964

Dear Amanda, I am so pleased that you felt able to confide your erotic dream. Your story has given me the confidence to tell you about one of my own recent fantasies…

…From a rear window on the third floor of the Montague building, I can quietly observe the comings and goings in the courtyard that separates the violin gallery from the workshop. This window faces north east, which means that over a twelve-month period, direct sunlight enters this part of the building only once or twice a year, on mid-summer days. Otherwise, this room is dark and rather gloomy, which is how I prefer it. Indeed, darkness was a contributing factor when I selected this space as my private study. Recently, however, with the help of a pair of old opera glasses I have been spending an inordinate amount of time studying the grain structure of the workshop's ancient wooden door.

It has been more than a dozen years since the smog of 1952, and largely due to the Clean Air Act of 1956, the city's pollution problems have improved considerably. This improvement has been especially noticeable in and around the workshop, where on fine days this door and the two large windows on either side are thrown wide open. In fact, during their lunch break, the men often sit in the sunlit courtyard eating their sandwiches in the open air.

My father-in-law had always forbidden this, but since his death, I managed to persuade Edward that fresh air is both healthy and good for morale. In fact, Edward couldn't care less about the men's health. All he wants is their loyalty, their hard work and a quiet life.

Well, Amanda, yesterday the weather was glorious, and all the men were sitting outside. They had carefully arranged their chairs in a shallow arc, so that they were all facing the sun; as usual Walter was sitting in the middle. He never assumes this position; simply because everyone wants to hear what the old man has to say, it happens quite naturally. Today, however, there was a new face in the formation. A large rather muscular looking youth was also turning his face towards the heavens. He certainly looked as if he could use some sunshine. Even from my third-floor window I could see that his skin was pale.

Yesterday, in case anyone should look up, I moved slowly to the corner of the window, but today, having closed the curtains, I stared shamelessly down at the young man through my opera glasses. The magnification was not great, but it was enough for me to see the boy's pastel-blue eyes and his long slightly dishevelled blond hair falling down over his ears. Edward will not like that, I thought, but I most certainly did.

Since her father-in-law's passing and the discrete disposal of his collection, Grace's own morale had improved considerably. She, Edward and Pippa were once again living in Horatio's rambling old Epsom house, along with Pippa's old nanny, who now mainly prepared meals and managed the place while Grace was working in town and Pippa was away at boarding school.

Meanwhile, Grace's wayward stepson James continued to live rent-free above the violin gallery. On most days, Grace had not the slightest notion where Edward was, or what he was doing, except that somehow, he was still managing to sell the instruments that Grace and Walter were still managing to find and restore.

Like his grandfather, James was a philanderer and because he was often out all night, he spent most of his days sleeping. As a consequence, Grace's third-floor office was not only dark, it was exceptionally quiet. It was the perfect place to store and study the company's by now extensive archives, most of which were the life's work of Grace and her father Randolph Scott.

Grace was now thirty-five years old, but this did not prevent her from revisiting her childhood fantasies. She frequently imagined herself as the beautiful and noble Queen Guinevere, looking down from her window in Camelot castle; the sexually frustrated wife of King Arthur, watching and waiting for her lover, Sir Lancelot du Lac, to come and carry her off. Unfortunately, until recently, all she ever saw was her best friend Walter Drake and his colleagues, all of whom were undoubtedly chivalrous, loyal and trustworthy; but hardly paramour material. The boy, however, was something else.

Amanda and Grace continued to exchange letters, but the

tone of their correspondence cooled slightly, until being unable to endure the tension a moment longer, Amanda began a course of action which would eventually cause both women to risk everything.

June 12th, 1964

Dear Grace, Even though he is much older than me, I decided that I was getting too old to wait. Last week he came into the shop again while I was alone. I asked him if he lived close by and if he might be interested in our new Sunday morning home delivery service. Bread rolls, eggs, milk and other breakfast items. I told him that we are still in the planning stages, but that we hope to have it running soon. His answer was that he hardly ever eats a large breakfast, but that if I was making the deliveries, he would start next week. He gave me such a beautiful smile that my knees almost gave way and I had to hold onto the counter. I'm sure he did not notice my momentary weakness, but I was shocked; firstly, by what I had said and secondly by his reaction. He has beautiful teeth…

A few days later a second letter arrived.

…For as long as I can remember, every day but Sunday, David is at the market by six o'clock. On Sunday he stays in bed until lunch time. This last Sunday, I attended early morning mass. As usual I went alone. (David has not been to church since we were married.) It was a beautiful quiet morning

and the sun was already high as I marched smartly along the empty sidewalks. But, instead of going to church, I took a small shopping bag with bread and wine and a few breakfast things and I took communion with Peter. I know that I should not joke about communion, but religion has dominated my life for far too long. You cannot believe how much freer I felt communing with Peter. It was a thousand times more liberating than entering the confessional box has ever been. Peter was so nice. He is really quite shy. His wife died a couple of years ago. He has two boys; both are married and live out of town. He is a bookbinder. He has a wonderful collection of leather-bound books, but they are not just on shelves; in his apartment, books are everywhere. There are even books in his bathroom. In case you are wondering how I know this, we had a bath together afterwards. It was almost mid-day when I eventually arrived back home. David was surprised that I had been away for so long. I told him that I had joined the Catholic Women's Fellowship. He was not really interested, but nevertheless, I explained that our mission was to visit old people and to provide them with breakfast and the 'Word of God'. His answer was that he did not care as long as his dinner arrived on time, which it did, because I had prepared it the night before. Are you shocked?

August 9th, 1964
Dear Amanda, I am jealous rather than shocked. I would like nothing better than to take a lover right

now. I have wasted far too much time and energy trying to interest Edward. Expensive perfumes, new clothes, hairdressers and manicures have all brought nothing; not so much as a sideways glance. I know that these things work, because I see the look on the faces of other men as they pass by. In London there are so many beautiful young men around town. They stand out like peacocks against the older generation of bowler-hatted office workers. I love them all. I'm just afraid to love only one...

43

Three or four weeks elapsed before Grace finally sat down and wrote to Amanda again.

Dear Amanda... I told you about the new boy that recently started in our violin workshop. Well, apparently, he is an exceptional Rugby Union player (don't ask, it's a thug's game, a bit like our football – American football, not soccer). By all accounts the boy is something of a rising star. All Rugby Union players are supposed to be amateurs. Officially they are not allowed to receive payment for playing. Top clubs get around this by offering good players lucrative nominal employment, to keep them in the team. Evidently, someone at the Guards Club asked Edward to give this boy a job and for some reason he did. I really don't understand these British 'old boy' networks. Why would he do that? Apart from horse racing and betting, Edward has never been remotely interested in sport...

...The boy doesn't even look like a violin maker. I call him a boy, but although he is still only sixteen, he is already more than six feet tall. He has arms like a blacksmith and hands like dinner plates. Walter says he has talent, but he looks as if he could crush a violin between his thumb and forefinger. They say he has a strong working-class Welsh accent, but since I have not yet spoken with him, I cannot confirm this. What I can tell you, is that observing him through my opera glasses is an absolute pleasure, especially from behind. Right now, Pippa, who is also sixteen, seems to be interested in him. God help the boy; she is such an incurable snob. If she gets her teeth into him it is going to hurt. He may be big and strong, but he is probably not capable of dealing with her caustic private-school mannerisms...

I expect that James will follow Pippa's example. He will no doubt enjoy showing this unfortunate young man who is in charge. Well, James may be in charge, but he has no talent for the business. All he can do is chase women and spend money. I have to watch him constantly, especially with the company's petty cash...

...Sometimes I just long for the whine of tires on those endless American highways; nothing but wide-open skies with wispy high cirrus clouds and hot desert air blazing through the old Studebaker's windows.

September 10th, 1964

Dear Grace, The time Peter and I spend together is just wonderful. Every day I pray for Sunday to roll around. Sometimes I catch myself daydreaming in the stock room, just thinking about our next 'communion'. Peter is so inventive in bed. Sex with David was nice when it happened, but sex with Peter is always an adventure. Perhaps it is because mundane life does not interfere. We both just live for the sex. If that sounds perverse, I'm sorry, but it's how I feel. Even the fact that our relationship is illicit makes it exciting...

...Of course, I don't wear a miniskirt when I visit Peter, because that would not be appropriate for a church meeting. However, I have started to arrive at his flat wearing only stockings and suspenders under my skirt. By the time I reach his flat I am exhausted with anticipation. I am also wet and ready. Often, we start making love, without removing any of our clothing. He just lifts my skirt and enters me. It is so liberating. I think a little Sunday communion would do you good.

By the way, although I never show your letters to anyone, I know that Peter would agree with you on the subject of the continuing escalation of the war in Vietnam. If they ever introduce conscription, both his sons will be old enough to be included. He worries constantly...

...What about your children, are they interested in learning the violin business from their mother? It would be a great opportunity for them both...

October 25th, 1964

Dearest Amanda, First things first. I am not sure that I will ever be capable of being sexually adventurous. My experience with sex is limited to one or two racy black-market books that I managed to procure in Charing Cross Road, none of which offered much practical help. But at least I will have an open mind should the opportunity arise...

...You asked if I will eventually pass on my violin expertise to my children. Unfortunately, I already know that they are not remotely interested. I don't think I am exaggerating when I say that James hates me. From the beginning he has always regarded me as a usurper. Over the years I have tried my best to communicate with him, but he views any attempts to be nice, or even civil, as weakness. In his eyes I am the classic wicked stepmother.

The fact that James and Pippa were away at boarding school most of the time has certainly restricted my influence over them. As I mentioned before, I did not want Pippa to be sent away, but after the deaths of my father and grandfather, I was emotionally too weak to stand up to Edward's demands and now I fear that it is already too late. Becoming a connoisseur requires considerable effort and commitment and the sad truth is that James is already a playboy and Pippa is going the same way; a playgirl I guess you'd call her...

...Since my arrival in England, I have tried to teach Walter and the men in our workshop my father's system of instrument recognition.

Unfortunately, Walter is getting too old and the other men are either not interested, or do not have the required aptitude. Walter tells me that the new boy would make an excellent student. I am sceptical, but for Walter's sake I will give him a quick test to assess his suitability.

As for Peter's boys, I can understand his anxiety, but I cannot imagine that the American government will allow this war in Vietnam to escalate further. Surely they won't risk a repeat of World War Two.

November 7th, 1964
Dear Amanda, Last night I took some books down to the workshop for Wynn Jones (that's the new boy's name). Next week I will check to see what, if anything, he has learned, or if he has even bothered to read them...

...As you know, I am pretty big myself, especially by London standards, but young Wynn Jones is enormous. It was a shock seeing him up close. He is not handsome in the classic Clark Gable sense, but he is very personable and sweet. He kept calling me Ma'am which made me feel old. His working-class Welsh accent is as strong as his body so obviously is. I had difficulty following our rather short conversation. In the UK they often equate working-class accents with being unsophisticated, even stupid. I hope that is not the case here. I left several books with him, but he seemed at a bit of a loss...

Dear Amanda, I was wrong. The boy may not have

been well educated, but he is highly intelligent and receptive. It just goes to show how easily we can be deceived by preconceived ideas and prejudice...

...Because of Edward's rules about fraternising with our workers, Walter has advised me to continue Wynn's education in complete secrecy. I would hate for the boy to be dismissed because of my desire to pass on my knowledge.

Dear Grace, Are you sure that keeping your relationship with Wynn Jones secret is because of your desire to pass on your knowledge, and not simply because of your desire? It seems to me that a cloak-and-dagger relationship with him might prove handy, should you ever wish to start an affair. He sounds rather a dish...

Really Amanda, How can you suggest such a thing? I am old enough to be the boy's mother and he is barely over the age of consent. He has certainly not reached the age of majority, which in England is twenty-one...

Almost before the ink had dried on this last letter, Grace received a reply.

Come on, Grace, how old were you when you lost your virginity? I had just turned sixteen and like most young women, I lost my virginity to a much older man. What is the difference, are we emancipated, or aren't we?

44

Tired of being a frustrated housewife, Amanda's questions were all that Grace needed to tip her over the edge. Nevertheless, she was afraid; she was not afraid of discovery, at least not for herself. She was afraid of her own inexperience and the possibility that Wynn might already be a practised lover.

In spite of her fears, encouraged by Amanda's comments, Grace became increasingly determined to try. There were nights when the very idea of falling into this young man's arms excited her to the point of trembling, sometimes for minutes on end. She was aware that she was playing a dangerous game; that Wynn might lose his job; that she could lose her reputation and for what it was worth, her marriage, but by now she no longer cared. She had already convinced herself that seduction was simply a question of logistics. After all, her plan to capture Edward had worked well enough, even if the end result had been such an awful disappointment.

Following their last exchange of letters, Grace spent many hours in her office, working on a plan of action. In the meantime, she promised herself that she would make every effort to teach this young man all she could about the identification of classical Italian violins. If he turned out not to be interested in her, at least she would be giving him a lift up the ladder.

True to her promise, while never asking for anything in return, Grace gave young Wynn Jones the benefit of her expertise. In part this was because of her own insecurity, but in the end, it turned out to be the best approach. Gradually, as Grace outlined her father's philosophy on violin identification, they both gained confidence in each other's presence. Grace started by explaining the role of the violin family; how and why these curiously shaped musical instruments had become the most important and valuable instruments of all time, and how they were responsible for some of the greatest music ever written and some of the most skilled musicians ever to have performed.

As she worked with this young man, Grace quickly realised that Wynn was like a clean fresh canvas, and for his benefit, she was determined to paint a masterpiece.

In spite of her best intentions, on numerous occasions while standing over him as he made notes, Grace had longed to reach out and arrange the boy's dishevelled hair. Although she managed to resist the temptation, she did make numerous attempts to improve her own appearance. It was not that she had ever neglected herself.

It was simply a genuine desire to shake off the past, to become a modern London woman. She began by having her beautiful orange hair styled; it was nothing elaborate, she did not want to draw attention to these changes. Visiting West End beauticians, she also had her hands and feet manicured. She had facials that included mud packs and the latest cucumber eye pads, and finally, she was massaged with creams and exotic oils. Like Wynn's lessons, these treatments continued for several weeks. And, like Wynn's lessons, although progress was slow, Grace gradually started to feel more self-assured.

Although they had proved useless on Edward, once again, Grace purchased expensive and exclusive perfumes and make-up. Being well aware that she was no Pattie Boyd or Jean Shrimpton, Grace also had a range of clothes made to measure by the most up-to-date and yet tasteful London designers. These included a stunning black and white Op-art dress that she had ordered simply because it reminded her of the beautiful black and white marble floor of St Paul's Cathedral. Although in her bedroom, Grace had worn these dresses several times, she was not yet ready to wear them in public. As for the genuine silk semi-transparent baby-doll negligee that she had purchased last of all, she was not sure if she would *ever* have occasion or the courage to wear it.

After hours in the empty workshop, whenever Edward and James were out of town, Grace continued unabated with Wynn's education. Again, employing her father's methods to ease the tedium of learning places, names and dates, she devised games with flash cards, but there was really no need to motivate Wynn. He was keen to know everything and anything that Grace was prepared to offer.

Step by step Grace became increasingly reckless. One evening, after everyone had gone home, she invited Wynn to examine a violin made by Antonio Stradivari in 1714. In order to do this, she had taken Wynn into the violin gallery. Normally it was forbidden for any violin maker to enter the gallery. The only exception being Walter Drake. The penalty for such a misdemeanour was instant dismissal. Everyone, including Grace, was aware of this rule and yet after dark they had quietly crossed the courtyard, and together they had entered the gallery. As if this were not enough, Grace opened the door to the Montague's walk-in safe; making no attempt to conceal the combination. '16441737, do you recognise the sequence, Wynn? It's a bit obvious, don't you think?' she said with a sly grin.

'I ought to,' he replied. 'You made me read the book about Antonio Stradivari's life and works, and his birth and death dates are printed on the title page.'

'I did not *make* you read anything, Wynn,' she replied with a grin.

The pair continued talking about the Stradivari violin for several hours, until Grace eventually checked her watch and brought the session to an end.

For some time, Grace had been impressed by Wynn's ability not only to assimilate and recall information, but to verbalise it in a coherent manner. In addition, just as she herself had done, Wynn made copious notes, which he then refined in a well-ordered journal. She was proud of what she had accomplished in a relatively short time. She could also tell that he had been bitten by the bug. The bug that had bitten both her and her father, and unfortunately also her father-in-law.

Thinking about Horatio made Grace determined to introduce some moral lessons into Wynn's education. She did not want her young prodigy to be tainted by the often seedy world of violin dealing. Nevertheless, she was aware that if he was to become a genuine connoisseur, he would need to see many more instruments than Montague's alone could muster. And without being involved in dealing, at least on the periphery, this might prove difficult. In Chicago, this had indeed been a challenge, which is why her father had taken her out on the road, but in London, instruments were comparatively easy to find. With so many orchestras, auction houses and museums in close proximity, variety and quality were not the big issue. The issue was finding time for Wynn to view them. However, even this turned out to be easier than Grace had imagined.

For several years, she and Walter had been assessing the auctions alone. And, being devoted to leisure, Edward and James were perfectly happy with this arrangement. Indeed, they only had contact with auction houses or even musicians when it was absolutely necessary. As for visiting museums, the idea had never crossed their minds.

Slipping Wynn in to view the auctions was easy. All that was required was a little flexibility in the boy's working hours, something that Walter had been more than pleased to arrange. And, since concerts and museums were largely free-time activities, it was a simple matter for Grace to make casual introductions. Occasionally, she was even able to provide him with free concert tickets.

In the meantime, in another extravagant display of trust, Grace decided to show Wynn the Montague's company files. These dossiers had mainly been compiled by Grace and her father, with contributions by Horatio Montague; nevertheless, this was a dangerous move. The files contained photographs. They also included details of the various salient features that help connoisseurs to identify the work of specific makers. For Grace, this was a departure from her previous attempts to educate Wynn's colleagues. Books and general information were one thing, but showing Wynn the contents of the walk-in safe and the company's private archives, well, that was something entirely different.

As if to emphasise the danger, during a second clandestine visit to the safe, while studying a seventeenth-century masterpiece by Nicola Amati, the pair were almost discovered.

Intent on celebrating some girl's birthday in the West End, James had returned home to raid the company's petty cash. Fortunately, Grace had managed to intercept James before he encountered Wynn, giving the boy just enough time to slip away.

Since James was already embarrassed about being caught yet again with his hand in the till, nothing came of the incident, but it was a timely warning. From that moment the pair decided to meet in the British Museum library.

45

During their first rendezvous at this new venue, Grace asked Wynn if she could watch him play a game of rugby. Although the question had sounded casual, it had been anything but. Grace had rehearsed the scenario many times; arranging and rearranging her words, as if she were composing a major symphonic work. Night after night she had talked to her mirror, carefully adjusting the pitch of her voice, the tilt of her head and the roll of her eyes.

Delighted to be given a chance to repay Grace for her kindness, Wynn promised to arrange a place in the director's box to watch an away game against 'The Harlequins' in nearby Twickenham. Because players always travelled to away games in a team coach, Grace had driven to the ground alone. She arrived in a brand-new Mark 2 Jaguar, another of her recent image-changing purchases. Wynn had explained where she could park the car and how to enter the ground. After the game they were to meet in the clubhouse lounge.

It was late evening before the game ended, and by the time Wynn had washed, changed and entered the lounge, Grace was surrounded by a group of boisterous ex-players and officials. They were all clearly vying for the attention of the vivacious American redhead standing in their midst. For Grace this was quite flattering, but it was not what she had wanted. She had been hoping for a quiet table and a few drinks alone with her young man, away from the classroom-like atmosphere of their usual meetings.

Other than her shock of orange hair, Wynn could barely see Grace in the multitude, but she was clearly the central figure. Seeing Wynn enter the room, Grace stepped forward, parting her admirers like Moses parting the Red Sea's waters. As she did so, Wynn saw her as if for the first time. She had been transformed. She was wearing a short Mod-style black and white dress, with a matching leather cap and white knee-length high heeled boots. It was all clearly expensive gear, tailor-made to fit her full figure. Up to this point, Wynn had always seen Grace as an attractive and sophisticated woman, but tonight she looked deliciously sexy.

With barely concealed satisfaction, Grace noted Wynn's reaction to her new look. She felt a warm glow pass through her body as she placed one exquisitely manicured hand on his neck and whispered in his ear. 'Let's go, honey. I've had enough *bons amis* for one night.'

Leading him to the door, as they left the room, she turned and smiled sweetly at her admirers.

As much as her transformed appearance, it was the

other men's obvious interest in Grace that had caused Wynn to see her in a different light. And now, for the first time, she was linking his arm and pulling herself against his shoulder. Even through Wynn's official rugby club blazer, Grace could feel the hardness of his muscles and she tightened her grip to prevent herself from swooning.

'It's these high heels, Wynn, I'm just not used to them,' she said, as Wynn reacted by placing his free hand on her bare arm.

Grace drove them to a quiet restaurant, where they both ordered a light meal, neither of which was finished. When the conversation slowed almost to a stop, Grace offered to drive Wynn home. She was devastated. The evening was not going the way she had intended. Wynn was obviously embarrassed; indeed, *she* was embarrassed herself.

Back in the car, once again Grace attempted to steer the conversation as she had rehearsed it in front of her dressing table mirror. In the restaurant they had been facing one another. In the Jaguar now, they were both looking through the windshield out into the black night. Without direct eye contact Grace became emboldened. Realising that this was her last chance, with carefully choreographed questions about the game she had just witnessed, she eventually said, 'You swivel your hips so elegantly when you run past opponents. Do you do the same when you make love?' The question clearly took Wynn by surprise, but it was Grace herself that received the greatest shock. It had all seemed so easy in front of the mirror, but having uttered the words, she finally recognised the implication of what she had just said. Nevertheless, her preparatory work had not been entirely in vain.

'I'm not sure,' Wynn answered, but although he was clearly uncomfortable, his reaction was not a rebuttal.

Using her best classroom voice, Grace pushed the young man further. 'Are you saying that you cannot remember, or that you have never actually made love to a woman?'

Grace was agitated now. She was perspiring and she could also sense the heat coming from Wynn. His body was emitting pheromones and she was rapidly becoming intoxicated by them.

'N-not exactly,' Wynn stammered, feeling the blood rushing to his cheeks.

Grace slowed the car and turned to face him. 'How old are you, Wynn?'

'Seventeen!' His face was burning now.

'Would you like to make love with me tonight?' she finally asked.

Wynn saw the gold in her eyes glint as he nodded yes.

In the hope that something positive might develop, Grace had booked a hotel in advance. When they arrived, she tried to make everything seem impromptu. Certainly, if Wynn suspected anything, he was not showing it. Nevertheless, Grace was acutely aware that her attempts to seduce Wynn had been planned like a military operation. So far, with her new car, her fashion accessories and beauty treatments, Grace had spent a small fortune. The hotel was just a minor 'added extra', either way, she no longer cared. Over the years, her family had spent much more, and unlike her, they had contributed almost nothing to the company's finances. Even so, she knew that at some point she would feel guilty, especially because by comparison, Montague's employees earned so little. Right now, however, Grace was no longer thinking rationally, she revered this beautiful young man and she sincerely wanted to help him, but her sexual desires and fantasies were putting everything in jeopardy. She was ashamed of her weakness, but she was no longer struggling with her conscience; desire had already triumphed over reason. It was her turn to be happy; her turn to join the sexual revolution; if Amanda Kowalski could do this, she could.

4th May 1965

Dear Amanda, I finally did it. I can hardly believe it myself. I am a fallen woman and it is the most wonderful feeling. I am so unbelievably happy. I don't care if the world ends tomorrow. I have finally understood what all the fuss is about. In the space of twelve sweet hours, seven of which I slept like a well-fed baby, I had three miraculous orgasms. Wynn was so sweet and gentle. I can see why he is capable of doing such delicate work. In spite of this, his power is awesome. You know that I am no light weight, but he lifted and carried me as if I were a delicate wood nymph. Last night in his arms, I felt like all my feminine heroines rolled into one. He was my knight in shining armour, my Sir Lancelot du Lac (who, as you will remember, was known for his courtesy and gallantry). But I am going to need your help, Amanda.

Although it was truly wonderful, we were both relying almost entirely on instinct. Wynn is (was) a virgin, and I had absolutely no idea what to do. It somehow seemed to work, but I don't want to lose him because of my naivety and inexperience. He is expecting so much more. He even asked me to teach him about sex. I guess he thought I could teach him in the same way that I have been teaching him about violins, but quite honestly, I am lost, and I told him so.

Amanda, please, if you don't mind, I would like to book a long-distance phone call so that I can ask your advice. It will be expensive, but the firm owes me, so I don't care. I don't want to be in the situation of not knowing ever again. If my relationship with Wynn is to continue, I want it to be open and honest and I want to be able to talk about sex with Wynn, but before I can do that, I will need some information myself. In fact, by the time this letter arrives, I will almost certainly have spoken to you, but that does not matter, I wanted to write and tell you this anyway. After all, I would never have attempted all this without your support. I cannot thank you enough, Amanda.

46

Grace's first sexual encounter with Wynn had certainly not been a failure. In fact, it had been more successful than either of them could have dared to hope. They had both been as nervous as their inexperience had warranted. Wynn may have been taken aback by Grace's unexpected proposition in the car, nevertheless, as far as she was concerned, he had acquitted himself honourably; chivalrously even, as might befit the suitor of a gracious lady at the court of King Arthur.

Leaving aside the enormous sense of joy and fulfilment she was feeling, Grace was initially relieved and gratified that her carefully laid plans had finally come to fruition. Indeed, only now was she beginning to realise how long and how carefully she had planned her apparently spontaneous seduction of this young man, and in future, she was determined to continue in the same vein.

Above all, Grace was proud of the way that she had managed to change her entire appearance and demeanour, one step at a time. Everything, including her manicures, make-up and perfumes, had been introduced gradually. Even her new wardrobe and the car had been presented in ways that at least initially, would be unlikely to attract attention or raise suspicion. Only on the evening in question, when her final approach was made, had Grace concluded her campaign with a series of unequivocal signals. And, in the end, her well-rehearsed dialogue, her stunning Op-art dress, and her pink baby doll negligée had worked far better than she could ever have wished. Nevertheless, although tactically Wynn's seduction had been a stunning success, Grace was aware that certain procedures would need to be refined. Although she was convinced that eventually love would take care of the details, and it *was* love, she was in no doubt of that fact; she had invested everything in this beautiful young man, and she was not about to lose him through ignorance or fear.

On their first night together in the Twickenham hotel, nervous about how Wynn would react to her full figure, rather than allow him to see and touch her naked body, Grace had decided to perform oral sex on him. The problem was that her only experience with sex of any kind had occurred many years ago in a Chicago hotel. The few remarkably rapid encounters she'd had with Edward since her marriage barely counted.

Setting aside her inexperience, true to form, Grace had attempted to prepare herself by reading as much as she could find about oral sex. The problem was that tuition was not only difficult to find, it was also rather vague. Even Soho's under-the-counter black-and-white photographs were not particularly helpful, since they gave no indication as to how long oral sex should take, or the techniques involved. In this respect, the money she had spent on *The Ideal Sex Life* had also been a wasted investment.

Grace was aware that oral sex had been a regular topic of discussion amongst her Latin School classmates. Although she had never been privy to such conversations, she knew that Amanda had at least been permitted to eavesdrop. She was also aware that previously, Amanda had had a fulfilling sexual relationship with her husband, and that now, she had a lover who she described as being adventurous and inventive. She was sure that with Amanda's help, she could master the technique.

Remembering that Amanda's husband David would be away at the wholesale food market by six o'clock, Grace had booked her call for exactly fifteen minutes past six, Chicago time. Even with the help of the operator, it seemed to take forever, until she finally heard her old friend's voice.

'Hello, Amanda, it's me, Grace. How are you?'

Grace could hear static on the line and the faint echo of her own voice. There was no immediate reply, but she waited, apparently there was often a slight delay on transatlantic calls.

'Oh! Hello, Grace. I'm fine, is that really you? Where are you?'

'I'm in London.'

Amanda was clearly not fully awake, and Grace imagined her rubbing her eyes and staring at her clock. As if to confirm her thoughts Amanda said, 'It's rather early in the morning here, Grace, I hope this is not bad news.'

'No, it's not bad news, in fact it's sort of good news.'

After a pause Grace continued, 'It's so lovely to hear your voice again, Amanda. Isn't it strange that one of the few nice things about growing old is that our voices never seem to change? You sound exactly the same as you always have.'

'Yes!' replied Amanda slowly, before adding, 'And, as far as you're concerned, there's still no sign of a British accent; I would have recognised you in a crowded room anywhere in the world.'

'That's probably true, but I am making an effort to learn a few cockney phrases.'

'Look, Grace, I may still be half asleep, but I'm sure you didn't phone me to talk about cockney phrases.'

'Yes! Yes! Of course, you're right. I have already sent you a letter, Amanda. You should receive it in a couple of days, but I simply couldn't wait a moment longer. I need to ask you some things right away.'

'OK! So, go ahead. You've got my attention now and I'm wide awake.'

The two women talked for several minutes. It would show up on the Montagues' bill, but Grace was in no mood to care. She needed help and she needed it fast. She began tentatively, not even sure of the vocabulary she could allow herself to use. It would have been easier just to write what she was thinking, but at the same time she realised that the telephone was the only answer; always assuming she would be brave enough to use this opportunity.

Grace was speaking quickly now. 'I booked a room in a hotel. Everything went very well, and I think that we both enjoyed the experience. Even so it was a little difficult, especially at the beginning. And that is what I wanted to ask you about. It's just that now that I am faced with the prospect of talking about it, I am not sure where to begin.'

'What about the beginning?' Amanda suggested.

'Well, I was afraid of what Wynn might think if he saw me naked. I'm not so young anymore, I never had my mother's figure and now I'm getting a little roly-poly in places. I mean, he did not seem to mind, but I did.'

'So?'

'So, I decided not to undress myself completely and relieve him orally.'

'You mean, you gave him a blowjob on your first evening together?'

'Fellatio, yes.'

'I'm impressed, Grace, but how did he react? It sounds as if you were not entirely satisfied with the outcome.'

'That's just it, Amanda, there was no outcome.'

'What do you mean?'

'I don't really know, I was certainly doing something wrong. I was expecting him to finish quickly, but after a few minutes I looked up and he was just looking down at me with a puzzled look on his face. Neither of us knew what to do next. I tried blowing harder, but he just didn't react.'

'What do you mean you tried blowing harder? Do you mean that you were literally blowing air onto his cock?'

Amanda was not laughing and neither did she think Grace's story even remotely funny. Choosing her own words carefully now, she said, 'Well, how do you, or did you, perform fellatio on Edward?'

'I didn't.'

'Not ever?'

'No, we only ever had intercourse in what I believe is called the missionary position. Of course, I know that there are more positions, but Edward was never interested. And now, after my experience with Wynn, I not only know that there are more possibilities, I also know that sex can last much longer than the few seconds it took for Edward to finish.'

'OK!' said Amanda, 'let *me* start at the beginning, Grace. It is called a blowjob, but you don't blow; you suck.'

47

A few days later a second letter arrived in Chicago, and much to Amanda's delight it was far more positive than she had been expecting after their telephone call.

July 1st, 1965
My dearest Amanda, It is the morning after the night before; although as I write this in London, in Chicago it is still the night before. I could have called you again on the telephone, but knowing that you would still be sleeping, I simply could not wait. Of course, it is nice to hear your voice, but once we have both said what needs to be said, our words are quickly gone; probably floating around in outer space somewhere, with Sputnik and Telstar. Anyway, our letters are too important to give up, just because we can talk on the telephone these days.

One of my greatest pleasures is seeing one of your distinctive airmail envelopes, with its US postal service stamp among the company's mail. The only time I ever really lost my temper with Edward was when I caught him attempting to open one. I'm sure it was a mistake, but I think I really scared him.

So, what is all this preamble about? Well it's my need to say thank you for all the help that you have given me over the years, and although it may seem frivolous to you, this time you really went 'above and beyond'. The advice you gave me about fellatio demonstrated how close we are, in spite of the enormous physical distance that lies between us. I must admit that in such cases the phone is an excellent device, since it allows for questions to be answered that might otherwise take weeks by mail. And your answers were so perfect and matter of fact. Although this is how it should be, I cannot imagine that such exchanges occur often, even between close friends.

As you know, as well as my trusty fountain pen, I received a complete set of violin-making tools from my grandpa on the day I sailed to England. I rarely use them these days, but they were extremely useful when I followed your advice and fashioned a practice penis from a large carrot. I am sure that I could have found something 'ready-made' in Soho, but I am well known in the area and I would never have dared to ask; even if I had thought about it, which I hadn't. I must tell you that even the largest carrot I could find at the barrow market was no match for Wynn's 'willy'. That's what they call them over here; 'willies', cute isn't it? It was also good that you explained that although it is called a blowjob, you don't actually blow. As you suggested I also used my tongue and lips to stimulate him. Although he didn't really need much stimulation, he certainly seemed to enjoy it...

10th August 1965
Dear Grace, Your relationship with Wynn seems to be getting off to a good start. The wonderful thing about my affair with Peter is that we also have no taboos. I have tried several new things with him that I would never have dreamed of attempting with David. It's a shame really. Why are we all so anxious about sex? It should be the easiest thing in the world. I'm sure that having been brought up a Catholic had a lot to do with my inhibitions. What's your excuse? Ha! ha!

...By the way, have you heard the Rolling Stones' new single, 'I Can't Get No Satisfaction'? It is so outrageously suggestive...

Dear Amanda, We've all heard about 'Satisfaction', but it is banned on British radio. Apparently, we can only hear it on a pirate radio station called Radio Caroline, but I'm not sure how to tune in. I'm simply dying to hear it. If it has been banned it must be good. Just like D. H. Lawrence's 'Lady Chatterley's Lover', which was first published in Italy in 1928 and was only published in Britain five years ago. Last week

I sat down and read it again. Since meeting Wynn, it has taken on a whole new meaning. Sometimes when I am standing next to him, even without ever touching him I can feel his sexual energy. In fact, simply looking into his pastel-blue eyes, with their beautiful long blond lashes and the love and desire I can see within them, is often enough to give me a series of mini orgasms. Can you believe it? I would never have thought it possible...

...Did you ever see that Walt Disney documentary, 'Secrets of Life', with its time-lapse images of flowers gradually opening? Because that is how I react when he actually touches me. And I swear, the tips of his fingers are enough to set this process in motion. It is not simply that I blossom, which I do, it is that feeling of opening to receive him, to give him unrestricted access to my heart, my mind and my body; indeed, every part of my being. Is this love?

Dear Grace, If it is not love, it sounds as if it will do until love comes along. I am so pleased for you...

48

Although socially, Grace and Wynn were worlds apart, intellectually and emotionally they were more than compatible. Nevertheless, in the final analysis, it was the physical nature of their relationship that bound this cultured middle-class woman to this young working-class man. The intensity of feeling in Grace's every nerve ending whenever Wynn touched her, entered her and ejaculated inside her, was like nothing she had ever experienced. When they climaxed together in this way, the extent of their passion literally took her breath away, leaving her gasping like a fish out of water. So fierce and all-consuming were these moments that initially Grace genuinely believed that she might be having a heart attack. The incredible thing was that she simply did not care. She would have been happy to die in this man's powerful arms.

It soon became clear, even to Grace herself, that she

was balanced on a knife edge. Madness and irrationality were close to taking over her life, and she felt powerless to prevent it. Often, she would regress into the kind of fantasy that had defined her teenage years. She was actually starting to see herself as a Lady Chatterley-type character, with Edward as her wounded soldier husband and Wynn as her Oliver Mellors. It was a dangerous cocktail and she was as addicted as any hardened junky. No matter how intense Grace's weekly meetings with Wynn were, they were never enough to satisfy her cravings entirely. Day and night her insides physically ached with desire for him. Often during the day, she would lay on the sofa in her private office and relieve herself, but the respite was only ever temporary. Grace had heard of people being driven crazy by love. She had read about it in numerous romantic novels, but until this moment she had never truly believed it.

Grace had never used contraception. While seducing Edward she had been actively trying to become pregnant, and since Phillipa's birth Edward's lack of interest in sex had rendered the question of contraception irrelevant. Now, however, there was the distinct possibility that she might become pregnant, but she simply did not care. For the moment, weighed against the pleasure of making love to Wynn, even consequences of this magnitude were irrelevant. Indeed, somewhere in the back of her mind she recognised that she would actually welcome a second child with this man.

In this fevered state, organising Wynn's education while continuing their torrid affair was proving far more difficult than either of them could ever have imagined. They were both aware that Wynn should not neglect his studies but disciplining themselves was becoming increasingly difficult. Only by seeing sex as a kind of reward for having completed their weekly assignments was it possible to remain focused on the bigger picture. They had tried having sex first and studying later, but that had always left them exhausted, so that all they wanted to do was sleep; after which all they wanted was more sex.

Regardless of these difficulties, Grace was deliriously happy, and it often took a supreme act of willpower to stop herself from laughing out loud and screaming it into the courtyard from her study window. However, she could do nothing about the smiles that kept invading her face at the most inopportune moments. They arrived so unexpectedly, as if she had just remembered a funny joke. They lit up her face, and above all else they caused the gold in her eyes to flicker and twinkle like it had not done for many years. Even Edward had occasion to ask her what was so funny, but that just made it funnier. Nevertheless, in her obvious state of delirium, Grace was aware that discovery of her liaison with Wynn would be a disaster for them both, and for Wynn in particular. And she was also discovering that secret happiness was almost as difficult to live with as the morbid depression she had been keeping at bay for years.

Notwithstanding her overwhelming joy, and Amanda's wholehearted encouragement, Grace could not entirely shake off recurring feelings of guilt. Almost from the beginning of their affair, she had started to reproach herself, especially with regard to their age difference and the calculated way in which she had planned Wynn's seduction. Recently she had even started thinking that she might somehow be stealing his youth. Such thoughts made her all the more determined to justify their clandestine meetings, by providing a well-planned edifying experience, to offset the uninhibited sexual lust with which their encounters always concluded. After all, she kept telling herself, learning the principals of expertise was the reason why they were meeting in the first place.

The problem was that just like Grace, once Wynn had tasted forbidden fruit, he was unwavering in his determination to have sex as often as possible. Sex being one of life's primary rewards; reacting like Pavlov's dog, the very idea of violin identification was enough to arouse Wynn sexually, and once he was aroused, Grace herself quickly succumbed.

Slowly but surely secrecy and intrigue surrounded every move the pair made. Sandwiched between equal measures of danger and elation. Grace was beginning to feel as if she was finally living life. Over the years, she had often reflected on why she had married Edward in the first place. Like so many young middle-class women of her generation, Grace had simply wanted a man to provide security, romantic love, and in her case, to support her enthusiasm for the violin.

Getting herself pregnant had been a calculated risk, and over the years, she had come to realise that Edward had also seen her pregnancy as the means to a similar end. Grace had always loved her daughter unconditionally, but Pippa had proved to be the chain with which Edward had bound her. She was bound to her daughter, bound to Montague's and bound to a life devoid of passion and pleasure. At the same time, it was clear that Edward was caught in the same trap. He had power and money, but he seemed incapable of enjoying either. Moreover, it was not long before Grace came to realise that Edward was also leading a life of secrecy and intrigue.

The first indication of this arrived one morning in the violin gallery. An American musician arrived with a pretty seventeenth-century Dutch violin. He asked Grace if she could write an up-to-date insurance valuation. Having examined the instrument, Grace had replied, 'That will be no problem, sir, this is a rare, and if I might say so, a wonderful example of Hendrik Jacobs' work. Jacobs was working in Amsterdam around 1700. He made exceptional copies of Nicola Amati's work.'

'Well, young lady,' the American confidently replied, 'you are right about it looking like a Nicola Amati, but that is because it *is* a Nicola Amati and not… what was it you said, a Henrik Jacobs?'

'I'm sorry to contradict you, sir, but there is no doubt in my mind that this is the work of Hendrik Jacobs. There is a legend that Jacobs was one of Nicola Amati's apprentices, but this has never been verified. The wood, the model and the varnish closely resemble Amati's work, but the easiest way to tell them apart is by looking at the inlay; the purfling.'

The man bent over and looked carefully at the black and white inlay that ran around the violin's outer edges.

'What's wrong with the inlay?' he finally asked.

'It's just that the black strips are extremely black, which

is what you would expect to see on an Amati violin, but if you look at them carefully, they are also extremely shiny, almost like polished jet, and they have no wood-grain structure, of the kind that you should see on Amati's work. These black strips of inlay are made of whalebone, which was used extensively in the Netherlands, a whaling nation, but whalebone was not used in Cremona, which lies in central Italy and therefore far away from any whales.'

'Well that is all very interesting, young lady, but your boss, who *is* a renowned expert, has already certified this violin. All I need is an updated insurance valuation. The violin is already insured through a London broker; one that was initially recommended by your boss. But I am returning to America soon and I will need to use an American insurance company.'

Grace was perturbed. 'Do you have the certificate with you?' she politely asked.

But the American was losing his patience. He spoke slowly and deliberately. 'Yes, I do, and I also have the bill of sale from two years ago, when your boss sold me this violin.'

Grace's heart was racing. 'I am so sorry, but would you mind if I took a quick look at those papers?'

Clearly exasperated but wishing to be helpful to this beautiful if ill-informed young woman, he removed the papers from a pouch in his violin case and handed them to Grace.

Two days later, after a rather heated family discussion that had involved both Edward and James, the American violinist returned to the United States with a Guarneri violin that was worth considerably more than a genuine Nicola Amati would have been.

Grace was devastated, Edward had violated the only solemn vow that they had so far continued to share; but worse was to come. Following a second protracted argument, it transpired that the Jacobs' affair was not the only unauthorised certificate that Edward had signed. His excuse was that having checked the company's archives, he had made these decisions in consultation with James, his son.

'The blind leading the blind,' had been Grace's final comment as she stormed out of the room.

For several days, tension in the violin gallery was palpable. Unable to face her family, Grace was spending more time in the workshop. However, she was not there to visit Wynn, she was there to consult her old mentor, Walter.

49

One morning, Harry, the cleaner and general odd job man for the workshop, was standing in the courtyard as Grace walked by. Ostensibly he was keeping the place tidy, but as usual he was leaning on his brush smoking an untipped Players Navy Cut cigarette. The large amount of ash hanging from the butt was a good indication as to how little he had moved for some considerable time. As Grace drew close, Harry spoke as he always spoke, from the corner of his mouth. 'Mr Edward is a poof.'

'A what?'

'A homo.'

'What?'

'A homosexual, Grace. No one wants to tell you, Grace, but I think it's time you knew. Walter says it's none of my business, but you have always been kind to me, and it's my opinion that you should know.'

Apart from Walter, Harry was the only workshop employee who addressed her as Grace. Stuck with the most menial job in the company, Harry clearly felt he had nothing to lose. Officially he was only a part-time employee, but having nothing better to do, he was in the workshop eight hours a day, five days a week and occasionally even Saturday morning. He was almost ten years younger than Walter, but he looked considerably older.

From the mid 1960s, even Grace knew what homosexuality was; at least theoretically. Throughout the 1950s, a number of high-profile cases, especially amongst writers, actors and artists, had brought homosexual behaviour to the fore. In 1957, a report compiled by Lord Wolfenden had advised the British government that homosexuality should be made legal.

Around this same time, various groups working towards the decriminalising of homosexuality were formed. Articles in leading newspapers and journals had also caught Grace's attention, and her natural curiosity had led her to make enquiries. Nevertheless, perhaps because of his military bearing, and his powerful homophobic rhetoric, Grace had never considered the possibility that Edward might himself be a homosexual. In fact, their relationship was such that Grace no longer cared who or what he was. As her dead father-in-law had suggested, they were business partners and nothing more. After years of living in a boring loveless marriage, what Edward did or did not do in his own time was no longer of any consequence. She had a lover to satisfy her needs and two close friends in whom she could confide. Consequently, although Harry's matter-of-fact pronouncement had caught her off guard, Grace had reacted calmly, as she always did when faced with any problem. Nevertheless, as the little man's words finally sunk in, everything suddenly came into sharp focus.

Homosexual. This one word explained everything; every question that she had been asking herself since Edward had married her in 1947. It explained his fascination with Fred Astaire films, his hatred of his beautiful debutante wife, his lack of interest in any kind of sexual contact, let alone the kind of sexual adventures that Amanda had so often spoken of. Edward had clearly used both his marriages as an alibi. Even his constant homophobic rhetoric fitted the bill. It was clearly true. Grace was both angry and relieved. Angry that she had been used, but relieved that their unsuccessful relationship was not the result of *her* shortcomings.

'I'm sorry, Grace, but you needed to know,' said Harry. 'Walter has always denied it, but in this respect, he is as naive as you. I love Walter like a brother, but he really knows nothing about such things. I was eleven years in the Merchant Navy and there was nothing that was not talked about below decks. Most homos keep it to themselves. But keeping such a secret is difficult and often dangerous. I know because my older brother was a homo. He tried to hide it and he even got married, but when it all came out, it was a disaster for his wife and for our entire family. It's one of the reasons I ran off to sea… Well, that's it!' and as if to punctuate the end of his revelation, the ash fell from his cigarette.

Harry's pronouncement had been short, but its effect

was momentous. Later that day, Grace asked Walter if what Harry had told her was true, but the look on Walter's face told her all she needed to know.

Grace was devastated, the entire Montague family's existence was founded on lies and deceit, and to her dismay she realised that she was once again part of a Montague horror story; one in which she faced yet another brutal dilemma. She could certainly use Edward's homosexuality to obtain an uncontested divorce. She had wanted freedom for so long and now she was being offered the chance to start a new life.

In spite of her initial anger, Grace quickly developed an overwhelming feeling of sympathy for Edward. Around the world, the 1960s was an age of revolution and change in politics, music and society. Even she had gradually become aware of the terrible persecution of homosexuals in both the United Kingdom and the United States; of McCarthy-style investigations; of life imprisonment in mental asylums; of chemical castration and of brutal aversion therapies. Ever magnanimous, Grace concluded that Edward's behaviour had been understandable, and she decided to bide her time.

Her affair with Wynn certainly offered excitement, emotional escape, and the kind of sexual intensity that she had never previously experienced, but where was it all about to take her? The more Grace considered this, the more she realised that although her relationship with Wynn might well be the finest thing that would ever happen in her life, like her marriage to Edward it was also based on dishonesty and subterfuge. In the long term it would be doomed to failure. She was simply too old for him. She was too old to marry him and too old to have his babies.

50

Walter collected the cups and plates from the linoleum-covered tabletop and placed them on the small washing-up trolley in their favourite Soho café. In the meantime, Grace gathered together the notes they had compiled for the next auction. Although their meeting had been very business-like, they were both in a sombre mood. It had been a number of weeks since Harry had told Grace about Edward's sexual orientation. Although this news had made little practical difference to her relationship with Edward, psychologically its effect had been considerable. After consulting Walter, Grace had chosen not to confront Edward with her newfound knowledge. Realising that she would never want to capitalise on what she knew, there was little point in making a fuss over something that would only create even more complications.

Having paid the bill, Walter had been about to leave

when Grace called him back to the table. 'I just can't stand it any longer, Walter.' Grace almost spat out her next words. 'As if Horatio's bullshit had not been enough, now I have James, not only stealing from the petty cash, but in cahoots with his father to write fake, back-dated certificates, and I am the one that is supposed to have confirmed their authenticity. Everyone in the business knows that Edward and James are incapable of certifying instruments. All they do is sign them after my approval. God only knows how many certificates they have signed without my authorisation. We had an agreement, that nothing, absolutely nothing, should leave this place without my personal validation. Montague's expertise has always been based upon the opinion of either Horatio or myself. Horatio turned out to be a bastard of the worst kind, but at least he knew what-was-what.'

Grace put her face in her hands and sighed. 'I'm sorry, Walter, these days I'm just sick of everything, it seems like the whole world is going crazy and no one is doing anything about it. And I'm no different. Maybe I can't be blamed for James's behaviour, but Pippa is down to me. I brought her into this world, and I failed her. Oh yes! I managed to scream and cry when Medgar Evers, Kennedy and Malcolm X were shot. I protest against the war in Vietnam and I wring my hands at poverty, racism and the oppression of women across the world, and yet what am I doing about it? I am helping to shore up the very system that creates these problems. I am contributing to the rich getting richer and the poor getting poorer. And greed is at the bottom of it all. I'm not trying to be a moralist, I know I haven't earned that right, but why can't we just be fair with each other?'

Grace gently swept her hair back with her fingers, sat up straight and looked intently at her friend.

'My marriage is a sham and has been from the start. I really do feel sorry for Edward, it must have been awful for him, living in fear all that time, but it wasn't easy for me either. I felt such a failure. Well, I have accepted all that now, but it is time for me to move on. I guess what I am trying to say, Walter, is that I am thinking of giving up this elitist business altogether and going back to the States.'

Walter was shocked and disturbed by this sudden pronouncement, but the determination in Grace's voice was clear and he waited respectfully before replying.

'Listen, Grace,' he finally said, 'I have been around for a long time and I have seen some terrible things, but I have also seen incredible acts of kindness and self-sacrifice. I'm not talking about bravery. Bravery is something young men admire, dodging bullets, and as Shakespeare says, "Seeking the bubble reputation even in the cannon's mouth". No, I'm talking about compassion and kind-hearted benevolence.'

'Not in this business,' Grace cut in.

'Even in this business, Grace, or don't you remember that young woman with the beautiful Venetian cello?'

Grace remembered; she had received a phone call from an irate father complaining about his stupid daughter. Apparently, she had spent all the money that her family had donated for her twenty-first birthday on a lopsided cello with crinkly varnish. Grace had had a difficult time calming the man. In the end she had managed to tell him that she could say nothing about the instrument's value until she had seen it.

The following day, the man, his daughter and the cello had arrived at the shop. The young lady's uncle also turned up. Grace rightly suspected that he was accompanying them simply to keep the peace.

As Grace removed the cello from its protective wooden case, she could hear the father's continuous tirade, but she was not registering a single word. Her mind was focused on the beautiful cello that she was slowly turning in a narrow beam of sunlight. Like a wartime searchlight, the beam slipped between the curtains of the reception area, illuminating the instrument's rich, red varnish.

Eventually Grace came to her senses. Turning to the father, who was still blowing hard and whose face was almost as red as the cello, Grace asked, 'How much did your daughter pay for this instrument?'

Her question provoked another tirade.

'Everything; one thousand pounds,' said the father. 'Can you believe it?'

'Look here,' Grace replied, 'I can see that you are upset. Let me give you twice that amount right now. What do you think?'

The father was suddenly quiet. The uncle had a broad smile on his face and the young woman just seemed puzzled.

'What is it?' the girl's father had eventually asked, but in a slower and more conciliatory tone.

'*It*, is a Dominicus Montagnana cello. *It*, was made in Venice; I would guess sometime around 1730. Montagnana made two sizes of cello, a big one and a small one. This is one of the smaller models. These smaller models are highly prized by professional cellists. On the whole, I would say that they are even more popular than Stradivari cellos.'

Grace was enjoying the moment. She had seen and heard enough of this overbearing male, even before he had asked, 'Are you sure, young lady? Don't you think we should ask Mr Montague first?'

'You can certainly ask my husband or my stepson if you wish, but I am offering the money now. They will almost certainly offer much less, but even if you were to accept my offer, you will still be cheating yourself, or in this case your daughter. This cello is worth many times what your daughter paid for it.'

The father's face suddenly lit up. It appeared to be shining as bright as the beam of sunlight that was still streaming through the gap in the curtains.

'Yes,' said Grace looking pointedly at the young woman. 'Sometimes even ladies can be clever.'

Instead of smiling at Grace's last remark, the young woman simply said, 'I have to take it back.'

'What? What are you talking about, Jane?' Her father was back to his boorish self again. 'We're not taking anything back.'

'No, Father, *we* are not, but it was my money and *I* will take it back. I bought it from my cello teacher. She is eighty years old, and she probably needs the money.'

'There you are, Grace. I don't need to tell you what happened. The old lady knew exactly what she had. She sold the cello to that young woman because she was worthy of it; totally in love with it and was prepared to give everything she had to play on it. And, since the old lady had no family to leave it to, that is what she had chosen to do. That was altruism, Grace, and the young woman showed her own generosity of spirit when she attempted to return the cello. I know that such things don't happen often enough, but they do happen.'

'It's no use, Walter, I've made up my mind. I am going back to the States.' Although her voice was gentle, Grace was speaking her words like an automaton. 'I will try to find work in Washington D.C., Chicago has too many difficult memories. I know that Amanda, my friend in Chicago, would help me settle in there if I asked her, but she has her own life and I want to make this move alone. Washington is a place where things are happening, especially for women, and I want to be a part of that.

'The Civil Rights Movement in the States is fuelling the feminist movement as well. Women are demanding equal rights, on the basis that equality for all should include women of all races, not just *men* of all races. An influential group of women have just started a new organisation called NOW. It stands for National Organisation for Women. For the moment it is based in Washington, because that is the seat of government, but I have the feeling that it will grow and spread. No one can be sure, of course, but for the time being, this is where I will be concentrating *my* efforts. When we were dealing with Horatio's horror collection, I remember you saying, "You cannot save the world alone, Grace. You need to choose your battles carefully." Well now I am choosing, and I am choosing to fight for women's rights.'

'Are you really sure that you want to give up the business completely, Grace? With your education I am sure that you will find work in Washington, but I suspect that just like London, the kind of jobs that are available, especially women's jobs, will not be very rewarding. You already have a career; one built upon years of commitment and experience. I hate to say this, Grace, but you are approaching forty, isn't it a little late to be chasing a new vocation? What's more, I can imagine that Washington will be an expensive place to live.'

'Walter, if you are worried about how I will survive; please don't be. I have managed to save enough to get me through the first phase. In any case, I don't really care; I simply can't go on with this any longer. I can change nothing here, as much as I love England, this is not my country and unless I am very mistaken nothing will ever change at Montague's. And, if it becomes necessary, I can still work the US auction circuit from time to time. Two years ago, Sotheby's bought Parke-Bernet, America's leading fine art auction house. This whole sector is expanding in North America. I'm sure that I will be able to find a sleeper from time to time in the States. Otherwise, I might work as a part-time consultant, I could even write certificates. I am still well known in the trade; even in the good old US of A.

'As far as Pippa is concerned, she is heading for America. She will be studying at Harvard University in Massachusetts. Perhaps she will eventually decide to stay there; who knows? She does not consult me. She is not interested in her mother's opinions. From her two grandfathers and her great grandfather, she has already inherited more than enough to set her up for life. As for Edward and James, they will go on doing whatever they like.'

'But that's not the whole story, is it Grace?'

'What do you mean?'

'What about the boy, Grace? What about Wynn?'

'I have already taught him everything he needs to become an exceptional connoisseur, and you have given him the rest. He will be fine.'

'That is not what I mean, Grace, and I think you know it.'

'Know what?'

'Oh, come on, Grace, we have known each other too long to play games. He is besotted with you. Are you going to take him with you?'

There was a long silence.

'How long have you known, Walter?'

'It doesn't matter, I could see how happy you were, and there has never been any doubt in my mind that you deserve some happiness, Grace. In life happiness is often in short supply and, as long as you are doing no harm, you need to grab it whenever you can.'

'So, you think my affair with Wynn could be harming him?'

'What? No! I did not mean that.'

'Whether you did or not, Wynn is certainly one of the reasons why I am planning to leave Britain. And no, I won't be taking him with me. I love Wynn and I always will, but it is not right for me to exploit his youth. In any case, he may find me attractive now, but in ten years I will just be a wrinkled old woman and I could not bear to lose him in that way. If I break it off now, it will no doubt hurt us both, but he will get over it and find someone closer to his own age. And, in the long-term, Walter, you know that I am right.'

Acknowledgements

I am indebted to many friends who have supported my efforts to write *Lovely Dirty Business* and its accompanying works. Particular thanks must be addressed to Louise Gauthier my Canadian editor and incidental English language teacher. Also Canadian, my reader and technical editor Chris Ruffo. From across the world, several old friends, both inside and outside the business have read my initial attempts and chivvied me along with useful advice and helpful criticism.

Bibliography

Giovanni Battista Guadagnini by Duane Rosengard. Pub. Carteggiomedia, Haddonfield NJ USA 2000.

... *And They Made Violins In Cremona* Pub. Consorzio Liutai and Archettai A. Stradivari, Cremona.

I Percorsi di Giovanni Battista Guadagnini (The travels of J. B. Guadagnini) Pub. Ente Triennale Internazionale Degli Strumenti Ad Arco Consorzio Liutai-Archettai Antonio Stradivari, Cremona. 1999.

VSA Journal Vol. XII, number 1. *The Stati D'Anime of S. Faustino in Cremona: Tracing the Amati Family 1641 to 1686*, by Philip Kass.

VSA Journal Vol. XV, number 2. *Nicola Amati His Life and Times*, by Philip Kass.

il DNA degli Amati pub. Cremona 2006.

The Stradivari Legacy, Carlo Chiesa – Duane Rosengard 1998.

Antonio Stradivari, His Life & Work, (1644–1737) by W. Henry Hill, Arthur F. Hill & Alfred E. Hill. Pub. 1902 by W. E. Hill & Sons, London.

The Violin Makers of the Guarneri Family, by W. Henry Hill, Arthur F. Hill & Alfred E. Hill. Pub. 1931 by W. E. Hill and Sons. London.

Giuseppe Guarneri Del Gesù. Published by Peter Biddulph, London 1998.

The Violin Forms of Antonio Stradivari, by Stuart Pollens. Pub. Peter Biddulph, London 1992.

A Genealogy of the Amati Family of Violin Makers 1500–1740. Ed. Daniel Draley, Pub. by The Maecenas Press 1989. A translation by Gertrud Graubart Champe, of La Genealogia degli Amati Liutai e Il Primato della Scuola Liutistica Cremonese, by Carlo Bonetti, Pub, Cremona 1938.

Jacob Stainer, Kayserlicher diener und geigenmacher zu Absom KHM Kunsthistorisches Museum, Wien 2003.

Jacob Stainer, by Walter Senn and Karl Roy, Verlag E. Bochinsky, 1986.

The Brompton's Book of Violin and Bow Makers, John Dilworth, 2012.

Carlo Bergonzi, Ex catalogue, Editor Christopher Reuning. Cremona 2010.

The New Grove Dictionary of Musical Instruments. Pub. Macmillan Press Ltd. London 1984. Ed. Stanley Sadie.

The Secrets of Stradivari by Simone F. Sacconi, pub. Libreria del Convegno, Cremona 1979.

The Stradivari Legacy by Carlo Chiesa and Duane Rosengard, pub. Peter Biddulph, London.

The Late Cremonese Violin Makers by Dmitry Gindin, pub. Edizioni Novecento Cremona 2002.

Pre-publication comments

I have just finished *Angel Eyes* and found a lot that I like. You must have had a world-class English teacher who, in turn, recognized an appreciative pupil. The story held my attention unfailingly. Your feel for times and places I too experienced approaches genius. You've also stuffed a remarkable amount of unchallengeable inside dope into a relatively tight space.

Professor David Schoenbaum
Author of several well-received history books, including an acclaimed biography, *The Lives of Isaac Stern*, and *The Violin; A social history of the world's most versatile instrument.*

Roger Hargrave brings to his novel *Angel Eyes* expertise as a world-class violin maker, restorer, and connoisseur. Now as wordsmith, he weaves a provocative tale on the rich landscape of the international violin trade.

Carla Shapreau
Senior Fellow in the Institute of European Studies, University of California, Berkeley. Attorney and Co-Author, *Violin Fraud: Deception, Forgery, Theft, and Lawsuits in England and America*

I read *Angel Eyes* on my flight back from London on Sunday. It was totally engaging. Your writing is excellent – nice combination of teaching, the story and lust. I loved the character of Grace and want to follow her life a bit further.
(Author's note – more on Grace in volumes 2, 3 & 4.)

Claire Givens
Minneapolis, USA. Accredited violin dealer and connoisseur.

Roger Hargrave is a skilled craftsman and connoisseur, whose intimate knowledge of the violin business gives credence to his often lurid accounts of the trade in antique instruments.

Carlo Chiesa
Milanese violin maker, author and expert on classical Italian violin makers.

I have now completed *Angel Eyes*, good show! As might be expected, your profound violin expertise shines out in the book. Everything you said about fiddles and the trade is spot-on and as you move into relating Grace's relationship with Edward and her move to (1946) London, I found it quite gripping, a bit of a page turner. Also, the tale of the Nazi-looted instruments was fascinating. (There are altogether too many of those, eh?) And the treatment of British women… probably women everywhere… in Grace's era that you related so tellingly was both enlightening and appalling. I also enjoyed the wealth of accurate historical detail you've included.

David Fulton
USA Violin collector and published author.

The *Angel Eyes* story intrigue is great – the 'monuments men' storyline for example about Nazi appropriation of Jewish violins 'imported' through the black market into the UK is brilliant (and frightening). Packaged up the right way I think the historical underbelly of the violin world could have an even wider appeal though a Hollywood lens – especially with a female lead and 1950-80s backdrop.

Chris Ruffo
Canadian – International IT & AI expert and skilled amateur violin maker.

This book is printed on paper from sustainable sources managed under the Forest Stewardship Council (FSC) scheme.

It has been printed in the UK to reduce transportation miles and their impact upon the environment.

For every new title that Troubador publishes, we plant a tree to offset CO_2, partnering with the More Trees scheme.

For more about how Troubador offsets its environmental impact, see www.troubador.co.uk/sustainability-and-community